THE CASE OF THE
BEGUILING
BROOCH

BOOKS BY TERRY AMBROSE

Beachtown Detective Agency

The Case of the Amorous Assailant

The Case of the Beguiling Brooch

Seaside Cove Bed & Breakfast Mysteries

A Treasure to Die For

Clues in the Sand

The Killer Christmas Sweater Club

Secrets of the Treasure King

Treasure Most Deadly

Lies, Spies, and the Baker's Surprise

Dead Men Need No Reservations

The Secret Ingredient to Murder

McKenna Mysteries

Photo Finish

Kauai Temptations

Big Island Blues

Mystery of the Lei Palaoa

Honolulu Hottie

North Shore Nanny

A Damsel for Santa

Maui Magic

The Scent of Waikiki

Mystery of the Eight Islands

License to Lie Series

License to Lie

Con Game

The Scent of Waikiki

Anthologies with Stories

Paradise, Passion, Murder: 10 Tales of Mystery from Hawai'i
Happy Homicides 3: Summertime Crimes
Happy Homicides 4: Fall into Crime
Happy Homicides 5: The Purr-fect Crime

THE CASE OF THE
BEGUILING
BROOCH

BEACHTOWN DETECTIVE AGENCY
BOOK 2

Terry Ambrose

COPYRIGHT

ABOUT THE AUTHOR

Once upon a time, in a life he'd rather forget, Terry Ambrose tracked down deadbeats for a living. He also hired big guys with tow trucks to steal cars—but only when negotiations failed. Those years of chasing deadbeats taught him many valuable life lessons such as—always keep your car in the garage.

Terry has written more than two dozen books, several of which have been award finalists. In 2014, his thriller, "Con Game," won the San Diego Book Awards for Best Action-Thriller. His other series include the Trouble in Paradise McKenna Mysteries, the Seaside Cove Bed & Breakfast Mysteries, and the License to Lie thriller series.

You can learn more about Terry and his writing at terryambrose.com.

Chapter 1

"LADIES AND GENTLEMEN, WE GATHER here today to celebrate the life of a remarkable individual, a pillar of our community, a devoted art dealer, and a dear friend to many of us. We are here to remember and honor the legacy of Benjamin Thompson. Most of us knew him as Benji, a man whose life revolved around beauty, creativity, and unity. He brought color and inspiration to every corner of our lives."

A good friend was dead. He'd died tragically after taking a fall at his art gallery, Timeless Treasures. And though our mayor, Amy Kensington, had plenty of nice things to say about him, the world around me seemed to have shrunk down to a pinpoint in time. I, Jade Cavendish, would miss Benji terribly. Somehow, that felt selfish. Maybe even greedy. As though I were the only one standing here under the warm California sun mourning the loss of a friend.

"Benji was not your typical art dealer. He was a visionary, a mentor, and a community leader. He had an uncanny ability to see the potential in every brush stroke, in every sculpture, in every photograph." Amy paused, her blue eyes glistening with unshed tears. "In every artist."

Clara Thompson, Benji's wife, stood to Amy's left. She wore a conservative dark suit and veil. It was very old-school, but somehow seemed the perfect choice for her. Normally, even though she was only five-foot-six, Clara stood erect and tall from years of yoga and meditation. Today, her shoulders slumped, and she seemed like a lost soul in a sea of darkly clad figures.

Mayor Amy's voice droned on, her words floating on the breeze as though they might drift away into eternity. "Benji was a man who truly understood the value of community. He was always there, lending a hand, offering a word of encouragement, or simply providing a listening ear."

The anger roiled inside me. Why had this happened? Mayor Amy was right. Benji was a good man. He hadn't deserved to die. As a private investigator, I could think of plenty of others who deserved what he'd gotten. But Benji, he'd been special. I bit my lower lip at the sound of a choked-back sob next to me.

Gina Rose, my first client and now a friend, gripped her arms to her sides. Grief painted her face. Gina, a woman of not-so-subtle beauty, had seen her own share of bad fortune. Her very brief marriage had ended with the death of her charismatic husband—who'd been siphoning off her family fortune. The losses and bad press had nearly bankrupted her both financially and emotionally, but they'd brought us together. Now, her star was rising again. She'd been rebuilding her family's trust and had even begun a new art program for kids. Benji had been working with Gina on the program, and Gina had called his death a tragic setback for Carlsbad kids.

I reached out, put my arm around Gina's waist, and whispered, "Are you okay?"

She nodded. A shaky gesture. One filled with uncertainty. She pressed a monogrammed handkerchief to her eyes and dabbed. I recognized the initials on the hanky. They belonged to her deceased husband. I forced down a wry laugh. Gina hated Bert for what he'd done, but she still loved him. Wasn't that just the way of the world? Love and hate always found a way to twist themselves together in a bizarre tapestry that painted our lives.

Mayor Amy closed her eulogy by thanking us for coming and inviting us to the reception. I squeezed Gina's waist again and then stepped away to give her some space. She nodded, still as shaky as before. The mourners began to file by the casket, dropping flowers and offering their condolences to Clara and final farewells to Benji. I breathed deeply and joined the line.

With each step closer to the casket, I waded deeper into the waves of loss washing over me. Benji had been more than just a friend; he'd become somewhat of a confidante and a mentor. And now, he was gone. A deep voice jarred me from my thoughts.

"Jade, how are you holding up?"

I didn't recognize the voice and turned to see who it belonged to. The man who stood there once had a commanding presence. Now, age had taken its toll, turning his once muscular frame into something soft and squishy. His face, though stern, seemed somehow familiar.

"Leo Baxter. I'm a friend of your dad's. Last time I saw you, you were this tall." He held his hand down near his knee.

Seriously? I probably wasn't that short when I came out of the womb. The name clicked, though. Leo was our former Chief of Police. He'd retired several years before my dad. He had been to the house a few times many years ago. I'd probably been about ten or twelve the last time I'd seen him—and I most definitely hadn't been knee-high. I gave him a sad smile. "Sure. I remember you, Leo. Long time, no see."

We hugged. It was one of those tender, tear-filled-moment types of hugs where everybody hangs on longer than they should.

In my ear, he whispered, "Did you see Martini?"

"Yes," I said as I pulled away.

As a matter of fact, Detective Des Martini's was one of the few faces I recognized. She'd been the homicide detective who had investigated Gina's husband's death. Murder wasn't a great way to start a friendship, but Gina and I had been finding our way. Where I tended to go all weepy and clam up at these kinds of things, Gina was more outgoing. Maybe that was part of being a fashion icon or one of San Diego's movers and shakers. On the other hand, she hadn't done much moving or shaking after the press had spent months ravaging her reputation.

"They don't do police work like we used to," Leo grumbled.

"I don't know, Leo. Detective Des is a good cop. I wonder why she's here? Do you think she knew Benji?"

Leo eyed the detective. As usual, she wore a perfectly tailored, dark pantsuit with a white blouse and black, patent leather pumps. She looked like she'd just walked out of the display window at Saks. I knew from experience that Detective Des would look the same at the end of a twelve-hour day as she did at the beginning.

"Cops never dressed that way in my day. We were too busy pounding the streets."

"She is annoying," I whispered. "If I wore something like that, my suit would be wrinkled beyond belief by noon. And those 'sensible' pumps? Forget it. I couldn't spend all day in those."

"That's right. I read about how you chased down that killer a few months ago. You couldn't do that in those girly shoes." Leo winked at me. "Good work on that, by the way."

I felt the warmth start in my chest and rise into my cheeks. Why couldn't I just accept a compliment without getting all embarrassed?

And now, apparently, Leo had noticed. He was staring closely at my face.

"I see you inherited your mother's blushing tendency." The lines of age on his face crinkled into a smile.

Oh, gawd. Thanks, Mom. Rather than endure another compliment about how pretty I looked when I blushed, I shot back a quick, "Thanks, Leo. I stick to wash-and-wear exactly because I'm out there in the trenches. There's no problem fabric softener and a dry cycle can't solve."

Leo looked past me and raised his chin. "You're next."

I steadied myself, turned, and approached the grave. After dropping my flowers, I looked around for Detective Des. It suddenly made sense why she was here. She didn't think Benji had died accidentally. Maybe I should talk to her? Find out what she suspected. Who was I kidding? That would be like walking into Fort Knox and asking for the combination to the vault.

"She suspects it was a homicide," Leo said.

I'd been so focused on Detective Des that I hadn't even noticed Leo standing next to me. "I was just thinking that. The story I heard was that Benji's death was an accident. He fell off a ladder while he was changing a lightbulb in the ceiling."

"You believe that?" Leo snorted.

His jaw tightened as he watched me with piercing brown eyes. Despite Leo having gone soft in the middle years ago, that intense stare of his would have sent a shiver down my spine if I'd been a criminal. Leo was, in a word, intense. Exactly how I remembered him. And right now, I felt like I was back in school being grilled by one of my law professors. "Until this minute, I did."

Leo's tongue-clucking told me I'd failed the exam. Disappointed the teacher. Again. For some stupid reason, I gave in to my insecurities and made the excuse my instincts told me wasn't necessary. "When I saw Detective Des, I started to wonder. I thought maybe she knew Benji."

It didn't work. Leo's skepticism came through loud and clear. Raised eyebrows. Pursed lips. Ouch. Talk about feeling like a rube. Rather than rambling on and reciting the official version of the facts as they'd been published in the newspaper, I decided to go on the offensive. Leo knew something. Or, at least, he thought he did.

I gave him the same steely-eyed gaze he'd been giving me. "What have you heard?"

Before Leo could answer, Gina grabbed my arm. "Jade, come on. You're holding up the line. And there's someone you have to meet."

I held my ground as Gina tried to pull me away. "We're having a conversation here, Gina."

She took one look at Leo, seemed to dismiss him as unworthy of her attention, and said, "You don't mind, do you?"

"It's okay," Leo said. His eyebrows arched, silently signaling a warning of some sort. "Be careful, Jade. Benji hung out with some unsavory characters."

Gina's smile fell. She glared at Leo. "Hey, that's my friend you're talking about. Benji was a good man."

"I heard the eulogy. Don't worry, Ms. Rose, I'm not talking about you."

With that, Gina's jaw dropped. She planted her hands on her hips. It looked like she was about ready to tie into Leo. The last thing I wanted was for one of my friends to create a scene with one of my dad's. The best thing I could do was separate these two before the sparks flew.

"I'll see you at the reception, Leo?"

"Remember what I said, Jade." Leo pressed his finger to his lips, turned, and left.

I gripped Gina's arm and led her in the opposite direction.

"Who was that nasty man, anyway?" she demanded.

"Leo Baxter. Our former police chief. And he probably feels the same about you. Gina, that was rude of you to interrupt."

Gina rolled her eyes and waved away my comment. "He'll get over it."

I kept the rest of my conversation with Leo to myself. If he was right and Benji had been murdered, Detective Des would want the investigation kept quiet. And since Gina would flutter around the reception like a butterfly and dish secrets at every stop she made, I wasn't about to be the one responsible for the leak.

It was hard to believe. Could Benji have actually been murdered? Then again, maybe it wasn't strange at all. People committed murder for all kinds of reasons.

Chapter 2

I HID BEHIND THE DARK lenses of my sunglasses on the drive to the reception. Gina rode shotgun and prattled on during the entire trip about Ethan Harper. She kept calling him "E." My first reaction was that Gina had fallen for another pretentious conman. The irony of a man using a single initial as his name didn't escape me. I'd done basically the same thing. Actually, my friends had. By fifth grade, I tried telling everyone I was J. D. Cavendish, but my friends thought that was pretentious—not that they knew what the word meant. As a result, they started calling me Jade.

These days, the only people who knew I was Juliet Delores Cavendish were my parents and the government. Everyone else knew me as Jade, the girl who had a knack for solving mysteries and ran the family's detective agency.

In addition to being an art dealer, Benji had been a history buff, loved the outdoors, and had been an avid surfer. As a result, his wife Clara had insisted on holding the reception at a park with outdoor gardens, historical significance, and hosting facilities. Magee Park fit the bill perfectly. It had a nationally recognized rose garden, wasn't far from the beach where Benji frequently surfed, and was the site of Heritage Hall, the city's first police station.

Along with everyone else, we parked on the street. But unlike most of the others, I felt like an outsider. I knew so few people here. Benji's wife, Clara, of course. Leo Baxter and Gina. To my surprise, Detective Des was also present. Once again, she stood off to the side with her perfectly tailored suit and stern expression while she watched the proceedings.

"She's here, too? She's going to ruin the party." Gina hissed when she saw Detective Des.

"Gina, it's not a frat party."

She rolled her eyes before she grabbed my arm. "Come on. I want you to meet E."

Talk about feeling like a little kid being dragged to meet the dentist. At least I'd brushed and flossed this morning.

"Jade, this is Ethan 'E' Harper," Gina said with a wide smile as she did the introductions.

Ethan extended his hand. He had a warm yet firm grip, an easy smile, and piercing blue eyes that seemed to look right through me. I couldn't help but feel a little shaky in the knees.

"Hey," he said, his voice smooth as Black Velvet on a hot night.

Oh. My. Gawd. No wonder Gina was gaga over this guy. He was gorgeous.

"Uh...hey," I stuttered. And then the blush started. Low and hot and coming up fast. And when his smile curled the slightest bit more, I thought I might just melt into a puddle on the grass.

Ethan looked sideways at a woman standing next to him. "Gina, Jade, this is Nora O'Sullivan. We call her 'Night Owl' because she always works the night shift."

Nora cut a glance toward Ethan and shook her head. "He's the only one who calls me that. I only work part-time on the night shift. I also have a few private patients."

"Was Benji one of them?" I asked.

Gina slipped from my side and glommed onto Ethan. He seemed unfazed by the attention and turned back to Nora. "You saw him every week or two. Right?" Ethan said.

Nora reached up and wrapped her auburn ponytail around her finger. She had the striking features of a Danish goddess and the athletic build of a long-distance runner. "You know I can't talk about my patients, Ethan."

"Oh, come on, Night Owl," Ethan said playfully. "Benji was very open about his illness."

What? Benji had been sick? I'd seen him several times recently and had no idea.

"You know I hate that nickname. Please, don't," Nora shot back.

It didn't escape me that this woman could so easily let you know when you'd overstepped. Which she obviously thought Ethan had. I couldn't help but feel a little intimidated by her. She seemed confident and in control. Maybe that was because she knew so many of the people who were here. I, on the other hand, was still trying to find my footing in this group of mourners.

If Ethan was bothered by Nora's reprimand, he didn't let on. Instead, he wrinkled his nose and shot back a playful "It's better than some. Besides, I'm not asking you for specifics."

"Let's go get a drink, E," Gina said with a gentle tug on Ethan's arm. "I'm dying of thirst."

To my surprise, Ethan looked embarrassed as he let Gina lead him away. What didn't surprise me was my reaction. My stomach did little envy somersaults as Gina pulled Ethan in close and used her words like a spider wrapping its prey in silk.

I turned back to Nora. "Sorry about Gina. She can be a bit much sometimes."

"Don't worry about it." Nora watched Gina and Ethan leave with obvious disdain for what had just happened. "So, how did you meet Benji?"

I took a breath and tried to push down the feelings of loss. Digging deep, I reached past the emptiness into the pool of feelings I'd been pushing down all morning. "For years, I only knew him as the guy who ran the jewelry store down the street. But a few months ago, we connected because we both love to surf. We kind of developed this rapport. His store was—still is—only a few doors down from our detective agency."

"Wait! You're Jade Cavendish? The private detective?"

A movement on the opposite side of the garden caught my attention. Detective Des was leaving. Apparently, she'd seen what she'd come to see. I wondered who she'd been here to watch.

Nora's gaze followed mine. "Who's she?"

"Detective Des Martini."

"The police were here? I saw her at the funeral, too. Wait—does this mean the cops think someone murdered Benji?"

Feeling a little uneasy, I hedged my reply, "I don't know what to think."

Nora's brows knitted together ever so slightly. At first, I thought she might be counting blades of grass, but then she leaned closer. "Jade, I'm going to tell you something. But you have to keep this quiet. I could get into some deep trouble if anyone found out I talked to you. Benji was not a well man. I was Benji's nurse and met with him weekly to assess and manage his pain. The thing is, he was in a good place right now. He'd come to peace with his past."

What the heck did all of that mean? I wasn't even sure where to start. Until Ethan had said something, I'd never even known Benji had been sick. And, better yet, what did that last part mean? "I don't understand, Nora. Were there things from his past he wanted to fix?"

"I don't know anything for sure. But the last time I saw him was about two weeks ago. He seemed different. Lighter somehow. He told me he'd finally gotten everything set up so he could let go of all the guilt and pain from his past. For months, he'd been talking about making amends. I don't know what it was exactly, but something had been weighing on him for a long time."

Nora's bombshell completely stopped me. I was unsure how to process this new tidbit. I'd never thought about Benji's past. I'd just accepted that he knew my dad, never questioning how or why. To me, he'd been the cool, surfing art dealer with smiling brown eyes and a friendly morning greeting when we'd meet on the beach or as I was walking by his shop. We'd even had some deep discussions about one of my cases. He'd been easy to talk to, but he'd never talked about his past.

Before I could respond, Nora's eyes widened, then she gasped. "Oh, goodness. I just realized how late it is. I have a patient coming to see me this morning." She looked to my right, and her smile returned. "Luna, how are you doing?"

"Quite well, thank you, Nora."

I recognized the name as well as the prim and proper response without even looking. Luna Martinez had been my second client. She was a friend of Gina's, which had gotten me the case when her home had been burglarized several times while she'd been away. The burglaries had stopped shortly after Luna hired me, so she'd been happy with the outcome and generous with a bonus for quickly resolving the problem.

If I hadn't been so desperate for money, I might have turned down the bonus because I'd done nothing except stake out the house when Luna was away. I hadn't even seen a stray cat on the stakeout, but my client was satisfied and my bank account got a boost. In my opinion, my final report had barely been worth the fee, let alone a bonus. Then again, who was I to argue with a satisfied client?

"How nice to see you, Jade," Luna said with a curt nod. Her pinstripe suit was a subdued gray, accented with a brightly colored scarf. A former art dealer herself, she was the picture of subdued elegance.

"You, too, Luna. I didn't realize you knew Benji until I saw you at the funeral."

"Most of the art community knew him. We saw each other at auctions and shows. That sort of thing." Her voice quivered, which made me wonder if she was going to miss him more than she let on. She sighed, then continued, "He had such a great eye for talent. It's a shame he couldn't see it in himself."

"Benji was an artist?" I asked. Something else I hadn't known about him.

"He was quite good," Nora said.

Luna nodded, then smiled wryly. "His work will probably increase in value ten-fold now. You know how it goes with artists. No one appreciates them until they're dead."

Nora and I both let out a morbid laugh. I didn't know that much about the art world, but Luna did. She was probably right.

As the conversation continued, I couldn't help but wonder about Benji and his connection to the art world. In the brief time I'd known him, he'd always been so friendly and encouraging. Yet, at the same time, he was the kind of person who'd exuded an aura of hidden depths, a puzzle wrapped in mystery, suggesting a tapestry of secrets woven just beneath the surface.

Nora's comments about Benji wanting to make amends implied he'd been dishonest before turning his life around. Or was it something else entirely? Drugs? Alcohol? I made a mental note to ask my dad if he knew.

Across the garden, Ethan disengaged himself from Gina and hurried in our direction. He dodged a waiter carrying a tray filled with dirty glasses and plates, then greeted Luna with a tender hug. "How are you holding up, Luna?"

Luna's jaw tightened. "Losing a friend is always difficult. As I was just telling Jade and Nora, there are many people here who will greatly miss Benji. I count myself among them."

So there was more to her relationship with Benji than just a casual business acquaintance? Realizing how little I knew about the people in the local art scene made me feel even more out of place.

"If you'll excuse me," Luna said. "I must take my leave. I must be heading home."

Luna gave us each a polite nod. Before she left, she looked at Ethan, then me. She smiled for the first time since I'd met her. "You two would make a lovely couple."

Ethan and I exchanged a glance, and then we each avoided looking at the other. Okay, the guy was hot. No doubt. But the girlfriend code said he was off limits. I might have gotten away without another blushing session, but Nora suddenly agreed with Luna's assessment.

"She's right, you know."

I turned my attention back in the direction Luna walked, but she'd already disappeared into the crowd. With no place else to hide, I decided a change of subject was in order.

"I didn't know she was so close to Benji," I said to Nora.

Nora waved away my comment. "She and Benji went back a long time. I always suspected they had a friendly rivalry going on."

"Do you mind if I steal Jade away, Nora? My grandmother told me she wants to meet her."

"No problem. I'll just mingle a little."

"Don't you have a patient you have to see?" I asked.

After giving herself a light tap on the forehead, Nora said, "My mistake. That's tomorrow. It was nice to meet you, Jade. I'd love to talk to you again."

"Sure. I'd like that, too," I said politely. While Mom felt she'd failed in much of my upbringing, she was at least proud of my ability to be courteous.

Ethan grabbed my elbow and led me through the crowd. "My grandmother has something she wants to tell you," he whispered as we walked.

Oh, good God. I hoped she wasn't going to jump on the cute-couple carousel. I stopped in my tracks. "Please tell me she's not playing matchmaker, too."

Ethan shook his head. "No. This is much more serious."

Chapter 3

ETHAN GUIDED ME WITH ONE hand on my elbow, his grip tender yet insistent. The sounds of our footsteps, cushioned by the lush green grass underfoot, were lost in the gentle undercurrent of hushed voices.

A tiny woman with silver hair pulled back into a tasteful twist stood under the spreading branches of an old oak tree. In the deep shade, her dark grey herringbone suit almost disappeared. She'd softened the tailored lines of the suit with a pastel silk blouse. A single strand of pearls added a touch of timeless elegance. She stood next to Val Torres, a local investigative reporter who'd interviewed me after I'd solved my first case. Though Val was only about my height, the woman with her looked even smaller in comparison.

I swallowed hard when the woman's deep blue eyes zeroed in on Ethan and me. With her chin held high, she reminded me of a dignified aristocrat from an old movie. "That's your grandmother?" I said to Ethan.

Ignoring my question, his voice softened as he introduced us. "Oma, this is Jade. Jade, meet my oma, my grandmother, Hilda Bauer."

The woman held out a delicate hand. I wasn't sure whether I should kiss it or shake it. I went with the latter. "Mrs. Bauer, it's lovely to meet you."

"My dear, call me Hilda. Or, if you wish, Oma."

Her voice, like her entire demeanor, oozed royalty, and I was once again struck by how out of place I felt in this world of wealth and privilege. Val stepped forward, greeted me with a tender hug, and whispered, "This could be big. Call me." She pulled away and smiled at Ethan. "Thank you for your time. Is it okay if I follow up at some point?"

"Sure, but I don't know how much help I can be."

Val seemed to resign herself to the realization that she wasn't getting more information from this conversation. She again mouthed, "Call me," before turning away. She left, presumably in search of another source. When Val was out of hearing range, Ethan's grandmother said, "Jade, my grandson has told me much about you."

I looked at Ethan with a questioning eyebrow. We'd just met. How could he have told her much of anything?

A small grin played across Ethan's lips. "Oma, I merely said that she was a private detective."

Returning his smile, the old woman tapped her temple with one finger. "Sometimes, words are unnecessary to say what one means."

"I agree with you, Mrs. Bauer." I stopped, caught myself, and said, "Hilda." A second later, I continued, "Ethan said you had something you wanted to talk about?" I shot a confused gaze in Val's direction, wondering if this was why she insisted I call her.

"Yes, my dear. I have a story to tell you. And, depending upon your reaction, a question to ask."

Good grief. Now I had to take a test? At a funeral? Whatever it was, I got the sense she hadn't wanted to talk about it in front of Val. "Do you need a private detective?"

With a wave of a small hand, she brushed away my question. Apparently, Hilda Bauer was used to doing things her way. "How long have you known Benjamin?"

"My father knew him for many years. He couldn't make it to the funeral." Not exactly true. It was more like, Dad had said it would be too awkward for him to go. The strange thing was he refused to explain what that meant.

"Your father is Thomas Cavendish?"

"Yes, ma'am."

Hilda didn't seem to mind the ma'am reference. "I can understand his reason for not coming."

What the heck was going on? I felt like I was in a game of secrets where everyone knew the answer, and I had to guess what it was. "Why do you say that?" I asked, trying to sound insistent but not whiny.

"It is unimportant. What you should know is that I was born in Vienna, Austria, into a family of musicians. I was just three years old when my family attempted to flee due to the impending annexation of Austria by Nazi Germany. I was fortunate in that my parents, who were wealthy, were able to secure my passage to the United States. I grew up amidst the cultural melting pot of New York City."

While I wasn't totally versed in World War II history, I realized from her phrasing that her parents must not have made it out. What incredible courage it would have taken to make that terrible decision. I started to tell her that, but she raised her hand.

"Please, allow me to continue."

Talk about feeling like a scolded child. "Sorry," I whispered.

Again, the hand waved away my apology. "My father liquidated much of my family's private art collection so we would have enough money to start a new life. One of my mother's most valuable pieces was kept in a safe deposit box in a local bank. When my father realized they had but hours in which to make a decision, they sent me away with a dear friend. They hoped to retrieve the jewelry and join me in the United States. Unfortunately, when the Germans came in, they classified my parents as aliens and seized the assets that remained in the country."

"What happened to your parents?" I asked, my throat dry with anticipation.

Hilda's jaw tensed, and then the regal lines of her face cracked. Briefly, I thought she might break down and cry, but she straightened her posture before she replied. "I never saw them again."

"I'm sorry," I covered my mouth with my hand as a cold chill coursed down my spine.

Hilda nodded as though she were acknowledging my condolences, then continued. "Some tried to use their life savings as a bribe to save themselves, but the tactic failed most of the time. The Nazis never saw a need to make a deal when they could simply take what they wanted."

She sighed, then continued, her voice steady but haunting. "Over the past few years, I worked with Benjamin to recover my mother's jewelry collection. The items had been cataloged and redistributed or sold, often to private collections. Some pieces were sold to buyers through neutral countries like Switzerland. Benjamin found a few smaller items, but the one I wanted most always eluded him until recently."

Hilda's eyes misted over, and she touched Ethan's arm. She looked up at him. He smiled sympathetically and said, "The piece Oma wants most is a brooch. It's called A Mermaid's Allure. It has two black opals and is quite valuable."

A brief flash of mild irritation flitted over Hilda's face. "Ethan has never seen the brooch. He does not appreciate its value. Conservatively, it is worth approximately two hundred thousand."

"Dollars?" I gasped.

Ethan put his finger to his lips and made a shushing noise. "We must keep this quiet."

"This is a lot to unpack," I said.

"Yes, my dear, dollars." Hilda smiled in the way rich people do when they're trying not to appear condescending. It made me wonder what role I played in this story. Why had she chosen to share this with me, a stranger? And how much did Val know?

"I'm sorry, but I still don't understand what this has to do with me," I said hesitantly.

Hilda's expression turned somber. "Because, my dear, we need your help. The reason I want to retrieve the brooch is not because of its monetary value. It is because it was my mother's favorite." She paused, looking at each of us in turn before continuing. "Ethan?"

Without hesitation, Ethan jumped in. "The week before he died, Benji came into the bar where I work. It was getting close to midnight, and he seemed nervous." Ethan stopped, shook his head, and said, "No, afraid."

"Did he say what he was afraid of?"

"No, but I'm sure it involved the brooch."

My spirits and my hopes rose a little. "Are you saying he'd found it?"

"He said he had, but he had to keep it hidden."

Wait. What? "I'm confused. I've got so many questions going through my head right now. The biggest one is, again, what do I have to do with any of this?"

"We need you to solve the puzzle."

Puzzle? What kind? Jigsaw? Word search? Sudoku? How many others were there? That was it. I'd had enough of the spy games. "Look, all this veiled talk is not giving me any idea of what you want me to do. Maybe you should come to my office. We can talk privately, and you can fill me in on all the details."

I realized Ethan was still doing double duty as both his grandmother's companion and her bodyguard. The thought made me take a look around. There were plenty of people here, but knowing this wasn't a social discussion had me feeling like chum tossed into the ocean to attract the sharks. How many of those around us were picking up the scent of blood? Leo, apparently—he was loitering nearby and trying to look unconcerned. Val, definitely. She was nursing a drink while she pretended to schmooze with an older couple.

Upsetting either one was the last thing I wanted. Leo was an old friend of my dad's, and Val was a reporter who could sink my business with one story. Dad had always told me to stay on the good side of the reporters, so I felt obligated to play nice. I started to repeat my suggestion about doing this elsewhere, but Hilda quieted me with a raised finger.

"Benjamin had a vast network of contacts, yet even he had trouble finding my mother's brooch. I'd all but given up hope until Ethan told me what Benjamin had given him."

She nodded to Ethan, who reached into his jacket pocket and pulled out an envelope. He opened the envelope, pulled out a small piece of paper, and handed it to me. My eyes scanned the meaningless array of letters. It was jibberish. "What is this?"

"As near as we can tell, it's a cryptogram," Ethan said.

My eyes lit up. I had always had a distant interest in codes. I remembered reading how they'd been used over the ages to secure information. "What's it say?" I asked.

"We believe it contains the location of the brooch," Ethan said.

Whoa. I hadn't seen that coming. "Okay, so where is it?"

"That's what we need you to figure out, my dear," Hilda said.

My jaw dropped, and my breath caught as surprise washed over me. She was a nice enough old lady, but she was off her rocker if she thought I could break a secret code. That was a job for an expert. Someone with some actual experience. I hated to let them down, but taking money for this job would border on malpractice. "I'm not a codebreaker. I can't help you."

"That's where you're wrong," Ethan said.

"Excuse me? What makes you so sure?"

"Because when Benji handed that to me, he told me that if anything happened to him, I was to give it to you."

I nearly fell over when Hilda handed me a check in the amount of $10,000. She'd already made the check payable to me and had signed it.

"Is that sufficient for a retainer? If so, we can settle your bill when you decipher the cryptogram."

Chapter 4

THE THOUGHT OF ME BEING the only person in the world who could break a code was intriguing. But really? Benji must have been on drugs when he told Ethan I could do it. Across the grass, I saw Gina. She was laughing it up with two friends. I'd come here with her for that very reason—she knew so many of these people. I was beginning to feel like I didn't even know the guest of honor. How had Benji been so wrong about me? How had I known so little about him?

"I don't see how that's possible." After a last look at the cryptogram, I refolded it along its creases and tried to hand it and the check to Ethan.

Ethan kept his hands in his pockets and said, "Please, put it away while we talk about this."

Realizing that if I didn't do as he asked, I'd wind up causing some sort of spectacle, I complied.

Hilda's face was a mask of confusion. "You are refusing to help? Do you need a larger retainer?"

I spotted Leo Baxter standing about ten feet away. When he realized I was watching him, he moved on. "It has nothing to do with the money, Mrs. Bauer. Think about it. If I really were the only person who could break a code, how would anyone have ever figured that out? It's not like I've advertised this skill to the world. In fact, I don't even have that kind of skill. There have to be plenty of talented codebreakers out there."

Hilda nodded slowly. It was almost as if a dark cloud were hovering over her face. "Ethan? Could you have misunderstood Benjamin?"

"No, Oma. He was very clear."

"You said it was late at night. Had he been drinking?" I asked.

"He never drank. At least, he hasn't since I've known him. Not a drop."

"Look, it doesn't matter how Benji came to this conclusion. The fact is, I can't help you." No sooner were the words out of my mouth than I realized Hilda could be correct. Maybe Ethan had misunderstood Benji's message. "What exactly did Benji say to you, Ethan?"

"I told you. He said that if something happened to him, I should give that cryptogram to you."

"Did he say anything else?"

Ethan's eyes narrowed, and he spoke with deliberate caution. "No, not really. All he basically said was that you'd know what to do."

I'd seen Benji several times the week before he died. He could have easily given me the cryptogram himself. Which meant maybe we were looking at this all wrong. Tentatively, I said, "So he wasn't necessarily telling you I could break the code. He might have been saying something else entirely."

"Well…I guess it's possible."

If that was the case, I now understood why Detective Des had been here. "What if I can't solve that cryptogram? Do you still want to hire me?"

Hilda looked at me, her eyes flickering in recognition and then with a hint of concern. She grabbed Ethan's forearm, and her knuckles whitened. "Ethan, I must be going. I'm feeling very tired all of a sudden."

"Sorry to hear that, Mrs. Bauer," Leo Baxter said as he sidled up next to me.

"Mr. Baxter," Hilda said curtly. Her blue eyes sparked with a hint of irritation. "I see that you are still as assertive as always."

Leo seemed unbothered by the comment, letting it roll off his back like a duck in the rain. "Just mixing, that's all."

At least I understood why Ethan had become so cautious only seconds before. Leo had been circling us, perhaps even trying to eavesdrop. What was he up to? And why had he warned me about unsavory characters? Did he consider this kindly old woman or Ethan in that category?

"What's up, Leo?" I asked, trying to subtly telegraph my own irritation at how he'd barged into our conversation. I wasn't twelve and didn't need protection, especially in this situation.

"Remember what I told you earlier, Jade." Leo's rich baritone vibrated with a sense of warning.

I raised an eyebrow at him, a silent challenge. I didn't appreciate cryptic comments or being told how to handle myself.

"Ethan, please, I must be going."

I could almost feel the anger in her white-knuckle grip. Ethan looked down, then patted his grandmother's hand.

"Of course, Oma. Excuse us, please." Ethan smiled softly at me, but his eyes shot daggers at Leo as he and his grandmother left.

"I'll be seeing you around," Leo said confidently. He stuffed his hands in the pockets of his slacks.

"What in the world was that all about?" I snapped.

"Just trying to keep you from going someplace you shouldn't go, Jade. That's all. What did she give you?"

"I'm not a child, Leo. Back off." I turned and strode away, hurrying after Ethan and his grandmother. I caught up to them just as Ethan closed the passenger's door of a late-model black Mercedes.

"Wait! Ethan, I'm sorry about that. Leo's an old family friend. I have no idea why he acted that way." I felt bad about the lie, but sometimes the truth just had to be handled like taffy to make others feel better.

Ethan opened the door a crack, leaned down, and said something to his grandmother, then met me at the back of the car. He stood before me and took my hands. The instant his fingers touched mine, a spark inside me burst into flames. Suddenly, I was engulfed in a raging blaze of warmth and light. A powerful urge to be close to this man consumed me. I pulled my hands from his and stepped back, doing what little I could to catch my breath and regain my sense of control.

"You felt it, too," he said, his voice shaking as he ran his hand over his forehead, then back through his hair.

Oh my gawd, he was hot. And so was I. In fact, I felt like I was burning up inside. Honestly, I couldn't say I'd ever felt this way before. Not even with my ex, Jason. Don't get me wrong—there had always been an attraction between Jason and me. He was good-looking, but there was something about Ethan that shook me to my core.

Ethan swallowed hard. His eyes remained focused on mine. It was like we were the only two people in the world. That's when I remembered Gina. The girlfriend code dictated that I should stay away. That she had dibs. I had to get control of this situation. Especially if we would be working together.

"We should probably get going," Ethan said, breaking the intense silence between us.

"Right, of course. Sorry. You need to leave."

"Oma wants me to follow up with you. When can we get together?"

"I'll look at my calendar, and we can set a date." I bit my lip hard and shook my head. "I mean, a time. We'll set a time to get together. To talk. About the puzzle." Crap. Talk about sounding like a blathering idiot. My best hope was to end this before I made a complete fool of myself. I pulled a card from my wallet and handed it to him. "I'll write up a contract for your grandmother's case."

"Great. You can email it to her." He wrote an email address on the back of an Anchor & Ale business card and handed it to me.

After accepting the card, I walked away, listening for the car's engine. The sound of tires rolling on asphalt fell away, at which point I couldn't help but turn and take a last look. "Jade Cavendish, you are so over your head," I muttered.

"What was that, Jade?"

I spun on my heel, a wave of guilt crashing into me at the sight of Gina watching me. I nearly blurted out a guilt-driven confession, but the words froze in my throat before they escaped. I stuttered a quick, "Nothing."

"Why did Ethan leave?" Gina asked, staring intently at the empty space left by the black Mercedes.

"He had to drive his grandmother home."

Gina leaned into me, grabbed my arm, and started walking toward the rose garden, all the while carrying on about Ethan being a gorgeous guy and how she was just sure they were meant to be together. The thought of losing the one man I'd ever truly connected with was like going to the cookie jar and finding only crumbs.

I smiled at Gina and croaked, "I'm happy for you."

"What's wrong with you, Jade? You're not acting like yourself at all."

Gina would never deliberately betray me. Of that, I was sure. But I also knew she was incredibly impetuous. In Gina's case, it was normal behavior for her to talk first and think later. So, as the warnings I'd received earlier played in my head, I considered how to respond. Best practices told me to use one of Dad's old favorites as a guide. He'd solved many cases by taking advantage of the old adage—loose lips sink ships. If I were trying to get information, I'd hope for someone with a penchant for talking. In this case, that meant doing the opposite and keeping my mouth shut.

"I'm fine, Gina. I just got a little choked up thinking about Benji."

Chapter 5

I NEEDED TIME TO THINK, and that wasn't going to happen with Gina hanging on my arm chattering like an excited chipmunk. That wasn't really fair. When we'd first met, Gina was a haughty socialite with a bank account that would be the envy of Rhode Island. It was after she'd almost lost everything that she opened up and showed her true self—someone who was kind, caring, and thoughtful. So now I felt guilty about being selfish. Gina had known Benji, too. She was just grieving in a way that was very different from mine.

"Gina, how many of these people do you know?"

Her perfectly plucked eyebrows rose above the rims of her Wayfarers. She tugged on a strand of blonde hair and surveyed the assembled mourners. "Oh, gosh, Jade. Maybe half. I don't know. Why?"

Did I tell her my suspicions? Lock her out? I'd been told twice already not to trust anyone. What did that mean? "You saw Detective Des here, right?"

"Yes, I did." Gina pulled in a breath. "I tried talking to her, but she brushed me off. Her being here has me wondering if Benji was murdered. What do you think?"

I shook my head, but I knew it was too late. I'd just added fuel to the rumor mill bonfire. In looking at the thorny branches of the nearest rose bush, I realized I'd have better luck jabbing my hand into the branch and not getting stuck than I would in dampening Gina's curiosity. "You can't tell anyone about this, Gina."

She ran her finger over her heart. Somehow, I had little faith in that promise. That was Gina. Good intentions, bad execution.

Her grip tightened on my arm. "What do you know? Spill."

"Nothing yet, but I should mingle. Are all these people involved in the art world?" I asked as we sidestepped a woman with shoulder-length dark hair and a milk-and-honey complexion that made me drool. Her companion was taller, probably around six feet. He had jet black hair, which he'd combed back neatly, and sharp, intelligent hazel eyes. He wore a well-tailored suit and projected an image of professional seriousness.

"Hey, Sam," Gina said.

The woman's lips curled up into a sad smile. "Hey, Gina." Sam had a soft voice, the kind that would be perfect for reading bedtime stories. Her eyes shimmered with a sorrowful depth, a delicate haze revealing her struggle to keep tears at bay.

After Gina and Sam exchanged a hug, Gina slipped her arm behind Sam's back and stood next to her so they were both facing me. "Sam, this is my friend, Jade Cavendish. Sam does art restorations. She worked a lot with Benji."

Sam's companion, who looked like he was miffed over being ignored by Gina, stepped forward and extended his hand. "Isaac Johnson. Friend of Benji's."

I noticed that Sam's eyebrows had risen at the mention of my name. I shook hands with her and Isaac and explained my connection to Benji. When I finished, Sam said, "I'm not really the art restorer.

I'm a tech specialist. Someday, I'd love to be the one to do the restoration, but for now, I'm just an analyst."

"So you handle the research?" I asked.

Instead of answering my questions, Sam turned to Isaac. "Sweetheart, do you mind if we girls talk shop for a few minutes?"

Isaac's jaw tightened almost imperceptibly, but he nodded. "Sure. I've got people I should connect with."

Sam waited until Isaac was gone, then said, "Benji was so passionate about his work, and he always wanted to ensure everything was historically accurate. That's why he hired me to help with that aspect of his projects."

"Wow. And here I'd always just thought of Benji as being this nice guy who had an art gallery down the street from the agency."

"Agency?" Sam frowned, the picture-perfect skin on her nose and cheeks wrinkling ever so slightly.

"Jade owns the Beachtown Detective Agency," Gina said.

Sam nodded knowingly. "Awesome. What kinds of cases do you handle?"

"About anything. I inherited the agency when my dad decided to take early retirement. He was pretty protective at the time. He still is. But he told me I was never to take on a divorce case. So what was my first case?" I paused, laughed, and added, "You guessed it, a philandering husband."

Gina's smile slipped away, leaving me silently berating myself for reopening the wound from her husband's betrayal.

"Oh my God," Sam laughed. "Talk about the universe messing with you."

As far as ethics went, the fact that Gina had been a client was strictly between her and me, and I wasn't about to discuss the specifics of her case with anyone else. Even though I'd kept my explanation vague, I could tell by the genuine interest in Sam's eyes that she was intrigued.

"I'm busy enough now that I have an office assistant. Her name is Zoe, and she's actually turning out to be kind of helpful. My dad always ran the agency as a one-man operation, but Zoe's been good at helping me find new clients. I never thought about it, but I guess Benji had resources, too."

"That's how we knew each other. I was part of Benji's network. He had contacts all over the world." Sam gestured that we should come closer. Once we were in a little huddle, she whispered, "Just between us girls, I'm not sure everything he did was legal, either."

"Like what?" Gina asked, her eyes lighting up.

"Well, I can't divulge details." Sam stopped and looked at me. "I'm like you, Jade. As a private investigator, you can't divulge client details. You know all about confidentiality."

That made two of us in the little circle who understood the concept. "Absolutely."

"But the things I know are private. As in secretive, you know?" Sam said.

I nodded in agreement, and Sam continued. "Let's just say that Benji had a way of finding information and getting things done that most people couldn't. He was like a walking encyclopedia with connections to all sorts of helpful resources."

I raised an eyebrow at her revelation. The thought of Benji having a mysterious, and possibly, dare I even think it, criminal background, intrigued me. If true, it added weight to the conversation with Hilda and Ethan. I nodded understandingly, but a quiet storm brewed in my mind. Had Benji been a criminal? Or was he a master at operating inside the gray areas of the law, someone with contacts on the dark side but who never succumbed to temptation?

"He did help me out with a few cases, though," Sam continued, looking sheepish. "He was kind of my go-to guy when I ran into trouble."

Again, that vague language. What did trouble mean in this context? It was clear to me that Sam had a deep admiration and respect for Benji. She spoke about him with fondness and passion, reminding me how special he was. I couldn't help but wonder what kind of projects they'd worked on together. And what level of detail might have been involved.

Gina was enthralled by this conversation, and that made me want to pursue it less. What Gina didn't know, Gina couldn't blab. "Sounds like he was a great help to you. Do you have a card? If I ever have a need for someone to help me with an art case, I'll keep you in mind."

Sam scrunched up her face. "The company doesn't give me business cards. I'm not supposed to be dealing with customers. My boss likes to keep me in the background."

"That's too bad. I'd really like to put you in my Rolodex."

"Your what?" Sam craned her neck forward and made a face.

"It's like some kind of antique contact list or something," Gina said. "When my dad was grooming me to take over the foundation, he used his a lot. Those things are like a total brick. I got rid of his when I took over."

The three of us laughed, and I thought about the one still sitting on my desk. Gina's laugh was a little forced. She actually looked like she was getting bored with the conversation. I suspected she was ready to flit off and strike up another conversation with someone else, but she was still hanging on, and it would have been rude to suggest she leave.

"My dad had one, too," I said. "I still have it. It's sitting right on my desk, and I can't decide whether to convert it or keep it. It's kind of fun, actually. Sometimes, when there's nobody else around, I spin it around and see whose name comes up. I'll bet Benji's in there. I totally have to check."

A few people drifted by on their way to their cars. It made me realize how long Sam and I had been talking. The truth was, I liked her. I thought we might even become friends if we had some common interests. "What do you like to do in your free time, Sam?"

Her eyes sparkled at the question. "I'm a nerd. I'm totally into computer games, and I love researching historical type stuff. What about you?"

"I like to surf." Sensing an opportunity, I added, "I'm big into puzzles. Especially word games."

"Awesome! I love those. Benji got me hooked on them a few months ago. What's your favorite?"

Uh oh. I'd fudged my answer to gauge whether Sam might be a good resource for me with the cryptogram, not to join a puzzle fan club. But all was not lost. I said, "Word jumbles. I like putting the words together into something comprehensible."

The conversation danced around the subject of word puzzles. Sam, it turned out, had several favorites. By the time she'd finished describing what she liked to do, I was convinced she would be a good resource to help crack the cryptogram. The problem was, how did I approach that without slighting Gina? The solution turned out to be easier than I expected. Gina's boredom got the better of her.

"Jade, I see some people over there I want to catch up with. Why don't you two talk puzzles for a minute while I mingle? We can leave after that."

"Perfect," I said as Gina walked away while I mentally gave silent thanks to the patron saint of PIs—whoever that might be.

No sooner was Gina gone than Sam let out a sigh of relief and reached into her purse. She pulled out an empty keyring. It had two shiny metallic loops, one about half the size of the other. A two-inch-long chain connected the two.

"Thank goodness," Sam said. "I've been trying to figure out how to get you alone. The last time I saw him, Benji asked me to give this to you. He also told me to give you a message—find the stone, the key shall follow."

Irritated by what sounded like another of Benji's little games, I snapped, "What's that mean?"

"I have no idea. But Benji said he had confidence that you'd figure it out. I've been carrying it around ever since he gave it to me." Sam suddenly stopped speaking, her eyes widening as they locked onto some presence over my shoulder. "Hide that keychain. Quick."

Chapter 6

THE FIRST THING I DID when I arrived at the office was write up the contract for Hilda. After emailing it to her, I flipped through the Rolodex. Reading the names of my dad's contacts and his notes about them, I marveled at what a great resource this little deck of cards was. Indeed, Benji was in there. There was a note on his card that read 'Case file: Bauer, Hilda.'

With my curiosity now in overdrive, I went to the files and pulled out a half-inch thick manila folder.

Date: 23 Mar 2021

Client: Hilda Bauer

Subject: Benjamin Thompson

Objective: Determine if subject has connections to an art theft ring known only as The Guild.

23 Mar:

Performed background check on Subject. He has no known ties to Client other than executing a business transaction in which he was hired to recover an antique brooch known as A Mermaid's Allure. Client claims the brooch was owned by her family and stolen after it was left in an Austrian bank safe deposit box.

24 Mar:

08:00 AM - Began surveillance of Subject. He exited his residence. Dressed casually, drove off in a black Mercedes.

8:20 AM - Subject arrived at Timeless Treasures (art gallery). Opened store at 10 AM. Nothing unusual.

01:30 PM - Subject left for lunch. Dined alone at a nearby café.

02:30 PM - Subject returned to gallery.

05:45 PM - Subject closed gallery and drove home.

25 Mar:

08:30 AM - Subject left residence. Same car, different attire, still casual.

8:50 AM - Subject arrived at the gallery. Routine actions and opened store at 10 AM.

03:00 PM - An unidentified woman entered the gallery. Mid-40s, brunette, dressed in scrubs. Photo in file.

03:45 PM - Subject and the unidentified woman appeared to be in a heated argument. Content of argument not audible.

04:15 PM - Unidentified woman left gallery in a hurry. Subject agitated.

05:05 PM - Subject closed gallery and went straight home.

26 Mar:

09:00 AM - Subject left his residence. Appeared to be in a rush.

09:30 AM - Subject arrived at gallery. No sign of the unidentified woman.

Rest of Day - Subject seemed restless, frequently checking his phone.

05:05 PM - Subject closed gallery and went directly home. Spoke with client at 8:15 PM. Reported on results of previous days' surveillance. Client terminated contract, citing lack of results as her reason for early termination.

After reading the report, I couldn't reconcile how Hilda and Ethan had conveniently skipped over these little details. Who did they think they were? Better yet, who did they think I was? Some amateur who would be so grateful for a case that she'd not ask any questions?

There were times in life when I was convinced that the Universe had a perverse sense of humor. This was one of those times because, at that moment, I received an email from Hilda with the signed contract.

All of a sudden, I was irritated at myself for not checking the Rolodex first. Once again, a client had told me what she wanted to and left the rest out. Angry over her lack of transparency, I drummed my fingers on the desktop and let the questions surface. I had so many. The first thing I should do was finish with the old file. Then, I'd grill my dad about this case. See what else might be missing from the case file. He'd known Benji for years, but he'd treated him as a stranger when doing the surveillance. Why?

I went to the file, found the unidentified woman's photo, and immediately recognized the face of Nora O'Sullivan. Making a mental note, I resolved to contact her and ask about the argument with Benji. The next photo was an old 8x10 black-and-white of a piece of jewelry —a brooch, in fact. Could this be what Hilda wanted me to recover? What I couldn't figure out was why my dad had this photo or how he'd gotten it. I thought about calling him, but the front door burst open, and I nearly jumped out of my chair.

I'd been so engrossed in the case file that I hadn't noticed Gina and Zoe approaching. And now, the chattering of the two excited magpies turned my quiet sanctuary into a tight, overcrowded space. It wasn't nice calling my friends names—but, come on, ladies.

"Jade, you're not gonna believe it," Zoe said as she flounced up to my desk. "Gina's met a guy. He's pretty hot, too."

Even though Gina had already told me about Ethan, my spirits still sank. Let's face it: it wasn't every day that you experienced a mysterious spark between two people that said they were right for each other. No—make that perfect.

"Earth to Jade," Zoe said.

I shook my head and tried to focus on her. "Sorry, I was lost in thought for a minute. Gina? Have you seen Ethan since the funeral?"

Gina beamed from ear to ear. "For sure. I went to the Anchor & Ale after the reception. We talked for the longest time. I just can't believe how well he gets me!"

I forced a smile, but my insides had gone cold. I could still see his eyes, warm pools of interest when he'd said, "You felt it, too." Maybe I was wrong. Maybe he was just a player. Did it even matter? "He seems like a nice enough guy."

Saying anything else was impossible because Gina launched into a monologue about how well her time with Ethan had gone. Zoe, on the other hand, was watching me suspiciously—almost like she knew envy was eating at my gut. After what felt like an eternity, Zoe looked up at the ceiling and groaned in agony.

"What's wrong?" Gina asked.

"Zoe, are you okay?"

"Oh, man, I forgot all about our meeting with a new client. Me and Jade need to get going so we don't blow this deal altogether."

Gina's shoulders slumped. "Okay. Well, I guess I'll let you guys go then. I have a meeting with the mayor about the new art program anyway. We have to pick up the pieces after Benji's death."

"You'll figure it out," Zoe said as she hurried Gina to the exit. Just before Zoe locked the door, she added, "I'm totally sorry to rush you off, Gina, but we've got bills to pay. You know?"

"That was abrupt," I said.

Zoe fixed me with a piercing look and marched across the room. "What's up, Jade? You look like someone just stole all your lunch money."

I sighed and leaned forward with my elbows on the desk. "I don't know what you're talking about, Zoe."

"Don't even try to BS me. I know you. Something's up. Do you know this Ethan guy? Oh, wait. Don't tell me you like him. Oh, wow. You do. Don't you? I can see it on your face."

"You're right," I huffed, knowing it was impossible to lie to her. We'd become good friends, and now Zoe knew me too well. I winced, then said, "It's just that I thought Ethan and I had something special. But then Gina comes in all happy and saying how well they clicked. Maybe I was imagining things."

Zoe sat in the chair facing my desk. She reached out and put a comforting hand on mine. "Jade, you don't need to worry about Gina. If you like this guy and he likes you, it's all gonna work out. You know Gina. She's all hot on a new guy every week."

Her words gave me little comfort. "But she says Ethan's different. She thinks he's 'the one.'" I made finger quotes in the air and rolled my eyes. "Like she would know," I said cattily, then silently admonished myself. For all I knew, she'd felt the same connection I had. On top of that, it was possible Ethan had the same effect on all the women he met.

"Jade! Snap out of it. I can totally see you're going down the rabbit hole on this. Gina did the same thing with that stockbroker she met. She was practically looking at wedding dresses until she found out he was married."

I snickered. It was an evil laugh. One that would disappoint my mother. "Yeah. Even then, she thought he'd divorce his wife to be with her."

"For sure. And it wasn't until she found out he had two kids that she came to her senses. You've totally got to trust in your love karma, Jade. You deserve a good guy after what happened to you with Jason."

I pulled in a long breath. Thought about Zoe's assessment, and grinned at her. "Love karma? Seriously?"

"Hey, it got you to smile. Didn't it? Besides, who's to say that there isn't such a thing? It could be, like, out there in the universe, and nobody takes advantage of it because they don't know about it."

While I didn't believe in Zoe's latest life theory for a second, her reassurances made me feel better. "Thanks, Zoe, I needed a pep talk. Besides, it's not like I'll never see Ethan again. I'll be following up with him about the case."

"Case? What case?" She looked down at the file folder on my desk. I'd flipped it closed when she and Gina had come through the door, but now that Zoe had seen the folder and knew I was up to something, I knew she wouldn't give up. If she were ever reincarnated, she'd come back as a little ankle-biter dog that grabs on and won't let go.

So far, I'd kept the entire discussion about the cryptogram quiet. I hadn't even told Mom or Dad. It wasn't that I didn't trust them. I didn't want to put them in danger. Or Zoe. "It's nothing. It's not even really a case."

"You're totally lying, Jade. I can see it on your face."

"What are you? The Dalai Lama of facial cues or something?"

"Don't change the subject. What's this case you're not telling me about? Come on, Jade, I'm your office manager and your friend."

She pointed at the file folder and then tried to grab it. I slammed my hand down to secure it. "You're not going to let this go, are you?"

Zoe shook her head. Her dark-eyed gaze remained firmly on mine.

"Fine," I shot back. "But you have to promise not to say anything about it to anyone."

"Of course." She nodded and grinned enthusiastically.

"No, Zoe. This is serious. If I tell you about this, you're sworn to secrecy. This could literally be a matter of life and death. One man might already be dead because of it."

Zoe's smile fell, and her eyebrows knitted together. "Your friend, Benji?"

"I don't know for sure, but possibly. Yes."

Finally, Zoe seemed to get it. She sat motionless, staring off into space, but then determination flashed in her eyes. "I'm your friend, Jade. Whatever happens, I'll have your back. Now, tell me what's going on."

Quite honestly, I wasn't sure if I was relieved or afraid. Either way, it looked like there was no backing out now.

Chapter 7

It hadn't been my intention to do a tell-all with Zoe, but once I started, it felt natural to keep going. So, I told her about how Ethan and I had met, about the spark, and even about the cryptogram. By the time I finished, Zoe was sitting on the edge of her seat, her eyes wide with excitement.

"That is insane," she exclaimed. "You have to let me help you crack that code."

I wavered, questioning the wisdom of bringing someone else, especially Zoe, into this case. But then again, I couldn't deny that having someone to brainstorm with might be helpful. "Okay. Why not?" I pulled out the cryptogram and put it on the desk. "Come around here and take a look. It's complete jibberish."

xsmfujpwt wskiep

ahvxca, xlfwzxal & pxfrufld oxj

pkyeruhwv

Zoe stood behind me, staring intently at the paper. I watched her face, a smile forming on my lips as I realized I'd probably had the same expression when I first saw it.

"Okay, let's break this down," she said, grabbing the paper from my desk.

"Hey! What are you doing?"

"Making a copy," she said as she crossed the room, laid the paper on the copier glass, and pressed the button. "We can mark up the copies and not worry about messing up your original."

"Good idea."

She returned the original to me and laid three copies on my desk. Then, she grabbed a pencil and drew a line beneath each grouping of characters. I watched her as she counted the letters in each group.

"Looks like there are nine characters in the first word and six in the last word on the first line," she said, tapping her pencil on the paper.

Her conclusion seemed pretty basic, but maybe she was just getting warmed up. I mentally crossed my fingers in hopes that this would be easier than I'd thought. "Okay, so what's next?"

She scrunched up her face and tapped the pencil a few more times. Her eyebrows knitted themselves together. The intensity in her eyes was almost frightening. I'd never seen her so focused.

"I think I know what code this is," she said.

"Really? That would be awesome." No, that was beyond awesome. All I'd seen was gibberish. "How do you know this?"

"I watched a PBS show on codebreaking."

"A TV show?"

"Yeah. It was super informative."

"Zoe, I don't think one TV show is going to help."

"It's a Vigilucci code, Jade." Her head bobbed up and down a few times, and a smile crossed her lips. "That's totally it."

My heart sank. Oh my God. I knew it couldn't be that easy. "Zoe, Vigilucci's is the restaurant down by the beach."

At first, Zoe got a confused look on her face, then she laughed nervously and threw her hands in the air. "Well, it's something like that. It totally starts with a V. But there's a problem."

What? That we didn't even know the name of this stupid code? Or that we had no codebreaking experience at all? "What's the problem?" I sighed.

"We don't have the key. All these codes have a key of some kind. You need that before you can solve it. Unless you've got access to a supercomputer."

I groaned. Was that the kind of key Benji meant when he'd given Sam the keyring? Zoe was going to be far less help than I'd hoped. I was saved from having to tell her all she'd done was muddy the waters by the ringing of my cell. "Let me get this," I said as I answered. "Jade Cavendish, Beachtown Detective Agency."

"Jade, this is Samantha Davis. We met at Benji's funeral."

Thankful for the interruption, I gave Zoe a thumbs-up and focused on the phone call. "Hey, Sam. What's up?"

"I was hoping we could get together for coffee sometime."

"Sure. When?"

"How about now?"

That wasn't what I'd expected. I typically cut off my caffeine by noon, but if Sam wanted coffee, I could always go with a decaf or herbal tea. I jumped at the chance to meet her. Not only did it mean I could delay bursting Zoe's balloon by telling her that her codebreaking skills were terrible, but I'd also get to question Sam about the key Zoe had mentioned.

"Sounds good. Where should I meet you?"

"Would you mind coming to my office? I'm in Encinitas."

"You don't want to meet at a coffee shop?"

"That might be a little too public for me."

Strange. Isn't that what meeting for coffee usually meant? Meet someone in a place where you could forget about the world for a little while—unless this wasn't purely social. Encinitas wasn't that far, so what the heck? "Text me your address. I can be there in about twenty minutes."

By the time I finished the call, Zoe had already moved on to her favorite project, maintaining the company blog. I think Zoe had been as surprised as I'd been when the blog started bringing in new clients. Not only had the investment paid off, but it had given Zoe the chance to do the one thing she seemed to have a real knack for. I snuck out the door, overjoyed that she barely noticed me leaving as she focused on a new post about package-delivery scams.

The drive to Encinitas was uneventful, and I found Sam's office without any problems. She worked on the second floor, and the entrance faced the back of the building. I parked in the lot as she'd instructed, climbed the metal staircase, and entered a space that was a highly organized blend of old and new.

Two work tables, both of which were height adjustable, filled the center of the room. Sam stood at the closest table, her attention focused on a large monitor at one end. Natural light flooded the room from large windows and two skylights. Diffused LED lighting filled in any gaps and created a perfectly balanced perception of standing outdoors at high noon.

We did the usual chitchat about how my drive had gone and if I'd had any trouble finding the place, then Sam led me into a back room. She snickered as she went to a coffee bar that had come straight out of a professional shop. There were pumps with various syrups, glass mugs of different sizes, and more.

Seeing the shock on my face, Sam said, "The owner hates coffee but loves all those fancy drinks you can get in a coffee shop. He spent a fortune on this thing so he wouldn't have to walk down the street three or four times a day. I thought he was crazy when he got it, but now I'm hooked on my Caramel Macchiatos."

I'd heard people ordering those while I stood in line at my favorite coffee shop, Joe's on the Beach. The coffee was good, but the view was spectacular because you could grab a table and watch the ocean waves roll in. Of course, I was usually the cheapskate and got a plain old coffee, but I had wondered why people were so hooked on those specialty drinks.

"Is this why you wanted to meet here?"

"No. Like I told you on the phone, coffee shops are a little too public."

"Do you mean for you personally?"

"I don't like crowds. But there's also a conversation we need to have."

"Why so mysterious?" I asked in my best leading tone.

Bypassing my question, Sam looked wistfully at the coffee machine, only to return to me with a beaming expression. "You want one?"

I threw up my hands. Forget my arbitrary rule about caffeine. This was an opportunity. "Sure. Impress me."

Sam's smile widened as she turned around and added a shot of vanilla syrup to the bottoms of two glass mugs. She followed that up with steamed milk and foam, then poured two shots of expresso over the milk. She topped them off with a drizzle of caramel sauce.

My eyes widened as she handed me a mug. "It's beautiful," I murmured while I did some mental calculations. This concoction could easily keep me up until the witching hour, but the temptation was irresistible. "It's too pretty to drink."

"Oh, you want to drink it," Sam giggled. "You totally want to. Try it."

I savored my first sip, the sweet caramel flavor dancing delightfully on my tongue. "Forget men," I said. "This is way better."

We both laughed. Sam sipped from her mug, rolled her eyes, then said, "I agree. I can never leave this job now. I'd go broke feeding my habit."

"Maybe your boss knew exactly what he was doing when he put this in."

"Hey, I never thought of that. If you ever want another one, come on back. The coffee bar's always open."

"Don't tempt me. I might move my office."

She leaned against the counter and sighed. "As much as I hate to say it, I had an ulterior motive for inviting you out here. Come on. It's back at my desk. This ought to impress you even more than the drink."

I followed, my curiosity in high gear. "Is this going to top the empty keyring?"

"Depends on what the key goes to. But this is totally epic."

I didn't know how Sam could top the mysterious keyring she'd given me at the reception, but I definitely wanted to know more. She'd already hit me with one mystery. It was starting to feel like mystery and Benji went hand-in-hand.

Chapter 8

COFFEES IN HAND, WE RETURNED to Sam's desk. She set down her mug, said she'd be just a minute, then donned a pair of white cotton gloves and went to a locking file cabinet. She opened the top drawer and pulled out a file folder.

"Take a look at this," she said as she pulled out an aging 8x10 glossy photograph. She laid the photo on the desktop and handed me another pair of gloves. "Put those on before you touch it. I hate getting oil on these types of things."

"Uh, Sam, my dad had a copy of that photo in a file for Hilda Bauer's case."

"Your dad worked for Mrs. Bauer?"

"Oddly enough, he was hired to do surveillance on Benji, but she terminated the contract after three days."

"That would make sense," Sam said. "Mrs. Bauer has quite a reputation. Apparently, she hires people, and then she fires them before they can finish the job. Very strange behavior. But I'll bet you another macchiato that the photo you saw was a copy."

I nodded, donned the gloves, and felt the paper. Even through the thin cotton fabric, I could tell that the paper felt old. Judging by the way some of the colors had faded, this photo was probably decades old.

The details were incredibly crisp and clear. Two black gems and brilliant diamonds were separated by the silver setting. I could see why it had gotten its name.

"What am I looking for, Sam?" I asked hesitantly.

"As I guess you know, that's the missing brooch. Mrs. Bauer gave me the photo a few months ago and informed me she intended to bring in the brooch for authentication. I've just been sitting on it ever since."

My dad had drilled one overarching principle into me when I was ten years old and worked in the office as a file clerk. My choice had been that or cleaning, and since I'd always been fascinated by the cool business of getting paid to spy on people, I naturally chose filing. On that very first day, he'd told me, "There's no such thing as coincidence, honey. Remember that, always."

So, as I stood here looking at an 8x10 photo of the very thing Ethan's grandmother had told me about, I started seeing a pattern. Secrets. So many of them. Benji's cryptogram. The envelope he'd given Ethan to deliver to me. And Hilda. She'd hired me to find her family's lost brooch but hadn't told me she had a photograph of the brooch. Why hadn't she mentioned Sam and the photo? Why hadn't Benji told Ethan how to find the key to the cryptogram? My head felt like it was about to explode.

I turned the photo over to see if anything was written on the back. There was nothing. Not even a date. "Do you know how old this is?"

Sam's face lit up like she'd just stepped into bright sunshine. Her voice took on an animated quality, and her words became rushed like a swollen stream in the spring. "At first, Mrs. Bauer tried to give me a copy, but I insisted I needed the original. When she gave it to me, I got curious. It's hard to be exact without damaging the paper, but there were a few things I knew for sure. There was color degradation and the photo had been printed using a silver halide process on fiber-based paper. That meant it was most likely printed before the 1970s. That's when the automated processing machines came into vogue, and labs started putting the processing date and batch on the backs. Since there's nothing printed on this photo, I'm guessing it was processed in a commercial lab over fifty years ago."

"Wow. You really are a nerd, aren't you?" I laughed and looked at Sam with admiration in my eyes. Her excitement reminded me of my own when I first started studying criminal law.

Rather than being offended, she nodded enthusiastically. "I've got a tee shirt that says, 'I speak geek.'"

"You've got me impressed. It sounds to me like Hilda was assembling her own team to find the brooch. She just didn't trust any of them, except maybe for Benji. And she never revealed she was working with him to recover it?"

"Nope. Benji told me to expect what he called 'some movement' about a week before he died. Prior to that, all I knew was that Mrs. Bauer would eventually bring the brooch to me for authentication."

So Hilda had kept everything compartmentalized. The reason was another big mystery. The 'whys' were adding up faster than I could answer them.

"What makes you think this photo was developed in a commercial lab? Couldn't an auction house have done it in-house?"

"In the 1960s, photographic development was largely the domain of specialized labs and photographers, with auction houses concentrating on sales rather than in-house photo processing. The era's complex chemical and darkroom requirements typically exceeded the capabilities and business focus of non-specialized entities."

Okay, that was a lot to unpack. "So you're convinced this didn't come from a private darkroom?"

"Exactly. Back in those days, the technology and expertise required for photo processing would have made it unlikely for non-specialized businesses to handle it internally. Nobody wanted to deal with a complex process that required chemical baths, managing light exposure, and a ton of darkroom equipment. That was way too labor-intensive for most auction houses. They wanted to sell artwork, not develop film."

"My dad did his own photo processing until he switched to digital. He even taught me to process photos when I was in my teens. I got pretty good at it and always enjoyed the methodical nature of the work."

"I know. I've got an old Leica I still love, and I do all my own development using the old methods. I'm pretty traditional that way. I just like the look and feel of the end product. I guess I'm kind of a purist. I want what I want, and I don't really care that it's an expensive way to go. Anyway, the reason I asked you to meet me here and not in public is because I don't want to take the photo out of this office. Now that Benji's dead, I'm afraid of losing it."

Sam's voice trailed off. She bit her lower lip and blinked back tears.

I was at a crossroads. Did I trust Sam? Or not? I needed to decide. Now. So far, she'd been open and honest. She'd shown me a photo of the brooch I was supposed to be trying to recover, which was more than Hilda had done. How confident was I that Sam wasn't one of those unsavory characters Leo had referred to? Still torn, I said, "I want to believe you, Sam. I really do."

"Oh, I get it. You're worried about me stealing the brooch. No worries. Here's the deal. I'm not interested in recovering the brooch for myself. I want to help you get it back to Mrs. Bauer. She was talking your ear off at the reception, so I assume she told you the story about how the contents of her family's safe deposit box were stolen."

I nodded. "She did. But she didn't say anything about this photograph."

"That's because she doesn't trust anyone until they prove themselves to her."

"She trusts you? How did you win her over?"

"I don't think I have. Not totally, anyway. The thing is, I worked with Benji to help recover some of her family's other stolen items. A Mermaid's Allure is the last piece missing."

I observed Sam silently, feeling a mix of confusion and admiration. "Why are you doing all this? How well do you know Mrs. Bauer?"

"Maybe I just have a soft spot for people who have lost something important to them. As far as knowing her, I think the only one who might truly know Mrs. Bauer is Ethan. I suspect she learned to distrust everyone many years ago."

It made sense. After what she'd been through, Hilda Bauer had every right to be distrusting. Which raised the question—why had she trusted me with the cryptogram? The answer was easy. Benji had led her to believe I was the only one who could solve it. "Sam, there's something I should tell you."

Sam's eyebrows rose, and she leaned closer. "Did she give you the cryptogram?"

I didn't respond for a couple of seconds. Between Leo's warnings about secrecy and the way Ethan had acted at the funeral, I was shocked she knew about it. "Who told you?"

"As you PI types like to say, elementary, my dear Jade." She wrinkled her nose and made a face. "Sorry. That didn't come out the way I thought it would. Anyway, Benji told me recently he'd created a cryptogram with information about the brooch's location. He also told me that if something happened to him, the person who showed up with it would need my help to find the key. That's when he gave me the keyring and said that it was an important clue. When I saw Ethan hand you an envelope at the funeral, I was sure you were that person." She flashed me an impish grin and asked, "Was I wrong?"

"You're one hundred percent correct." I scanned the office. This was a professional art-restoration business. Sam was knowledgable, technically savvy, and, most importantly, had been trusted by Benji. If I was going to find Hilda's missing brooch, I needed someone like her. The gravity of this decision weighed heavily on my shoulders. Once I brought Sam in, there would be no turning back. "There's something you should know. If I share the cryptogram with you, it could put you in danger."

"I know." Sam picked up her mug and held it to her lips. She took a small sip, then watched me over the rim of the glass mug. "You asked why I was helping Mrs. Bauer. Well, there's more to it. My mom and dad are both lawyers. But they're not your usual corporate types. My dad is an environmental watchdog, and my mom is a public defender. From the time I was little, they always drilled into me the need to help others. I guess that's just part of who I am. I think you're the same way. There's no decision here. I don't think either of us can walk away."

Sam's words hit me hard. She was right. I couldn't turn away and abandon Mrs. Bauer or the mysterious cryptogram that could hold the key to finding her brooch. And, as much as I hated the idea of dragging anyone else into any kind of danger, that was the nature of the business.

"I know. It's in our DNA." Lifting my mug in the air, I held it out before me. "We're in this together?"

She tapped her mug against mine. "Together."

Oh, yay, someone to help. But I also had a huge problem. For some crazy reason, Benji assumed I'd be able to find the key to the cryptogram. The problem was I had no idea where to look. Or whether I was looking for a physical key or a combination of words and letters. I could only hope Benji's trust in me wasn't misplaced.

Chapter 9

It WAS TIME TO TAKE a leap of faith—faith in myself, in Benji, and Sam. As my best friend in fourth grade and I had agreed when we'd snuck off for ice cream and only had enough lunch money left for one scoop, it was time for sharesies. "This is a copy of the cryptogram," I said, handing it to Sam.

She winced. "A copy? I'll need to see the original."

"What's wrong with a copy?"

Sam met my puzzled look with a level gaze, the kind that hinted at deeper layers of thought. "Because," she began, her voice steady, "just like with the photo, there could be aspects of the original that a copy won't reveal. For instance, the original might have a secret code written in invisible ink. I could examine for that. A peculiar watermark or the age of the paper could provide crucial clues. Those subtleties get lost in replication. We might be missing out on vital evidence without even knowing it."

Her explanation made perfect sense, and I marveled at the depth of her insight. It was lightyears beyond Zoe's. Clearly, I'd underestimated the complexity of the task. On top of that, Sam knew her stuff. I hadn't thought my balloon could be deflated any further, but Sam had just succeeded. "Okay. Apparently, Benji trusted the wrong person with deciphering his little secret message."

She studied the crazy jumble of letters, rubbing a crease in her brow in frustration. "There's another problem. Without the algorithm —that's the set of rules we'd use to decode the message—this means nothing. The original might help, but what we really need is a codebook and a key."

My shoulders slumped. That's basically what Zoe had said, too. "So, for now, you can't do anything, right?"

"Exactly. Without the decryption key, it could take years to decipher the message, even with a supercomputer. There's no good starting point. There's not even a single-letter word in this message to get us started. If you can get me that original document and the key, then we might have a shot."

"There's only one problem. I've got the original, and I can bring you that, but I don't have the key. That's why I came to you."

Sam chuckled. "You thought I could work some kind of magic. Didn't you?"

The blush kicked in. My face and chest felt like they were on fire.

"Don't worry about it. Unless they're in the business, most people don't realize the importance of attention to detail and the potential consequences of overlooking even the tiniest thing. In a forensic investigation, every piece of evidence needs to be examined and analyzed carefully to ensure that nothing is missed." She took a sip from her mug, smacked her lips, and laughed. "And it's super helpful if you have the knowledge and the tools I've got here. And good coffee."

Why had Benji selected me to figure out this message? Maybe it wasn't because I was an expert, but because I knew how to find them. I scanned the room. How over my head I was in this world—just as Sam might be in mine. But maybe that's why Benji's choices made sense. He'd sent Hilda to me because he knew I was tenacious. He'd told Sam to give me the keyring because he knew I'd put together the bigger puzzle. The keyring was simply a way to spark my curiosity. If I was right, my job was to solve the more basic puzzle—where would Benji hide the cryptogram key?

"Benji asked me once if I was familiar with cryptograms," I said. "I told him I'd always had an interest in them. What I didn't tell him was that the ones I worked on were super simple. Shift the letters of the alphabet a few spots, and voila, instant coded message. You don't think this is anything like that?"

"If Benji was going to the extent of creating an encrypted message, you can bet he'd do something that would be, for practical purposes, unbreakable. Benji knew enough to use a polyalphabetic substitution."

Sam must have seen the blank look on my face because she quickly explained.

"In layman's terms, that means his letter replacements are based on multiple substitution alphabets and formulas." She went on to explain the difference between simple Caesar and more complex Vigenère ciphers.

I snickered. "My assistant called it a Vigilucci code."

Sam barked out a laugh, then said, "Say what? Isn't that a restaurant or something?"

"Yeah. Zoe was sure the type of code started with the letter 'V.' I guess she got that right. Anyway, forgive me for being dense, but you've totally lost me."

"Okay. Here's a simple example." She flipped over my copy and wrote the words HELLO and KEY in block letters. "Let's say we want to send the message 'HELLO,' and we're going to encrypt it using the keyword 'KEY.' The first letter, 'H,' is shifted forward by 'K' positions in the alphabet, the second letter, 'E,' is shifted forward by 'E' positions, and the third letter, 'L,' is shifted forward by 'Y' positions. For the fourth and fifth letters, we return to the start of the keyword and do the same thing until we have the final encoded message."

"Oh. I get it. What you're telling me is that until we find the equivalent of the word 'key' in your example, we're totally screwed."

"Even once we have it, it will take some time to decode the message. It's not that hard, and I can do that part, but you'll have to find that key first. And I don't think he included it with the encrypted message itself."

Looking down at the two simple words she'd written with the last of that wonderful caramel macchiato still in my mug, I realized what a daunting task I had ahead of me. After finishing the last of my drink, I said, "It's almost like Benji dumped the pieces of a jigsaw puzzle out on the table, and now it's my job to put it all back together. I agree that he's hidden the key. And his message to find the stone has got to have something to do with it, but where did he hide the stone?"

Sam's expression fell, the enthusiasm she'd demonstrated a few seconds before as she'd explained the process of encoding a message now gone. "You don't even know where to start?"

"I didn't say that. I think the place to begin is with the most obvious location—at home. That's where I'd hide a secret if I knew I was going to die. Basically, I can broaden the search as I go. Right now, I'm convinced that I need to talk to Clara Thompson."

Enthusiasm crept back into Sam's face. "Of course! She's got to know something, right?"

"I can't be certain, but it's worth a try. I'll call her and see if she'll talk to me today. If I'm right, Benji might have left a clue in his home office. If that doesn't work out, I can get Clara to let me into the store."

After confirming that Clara was home and willing to see me, I got in the car and headed out, calling my dad once I was in traffic. I'd probably see him soon for dinner, but this was about the time Mom usually started cooking. If my timing was right, I could avoid having Mom join the conversation without hurting her feelings. Dad answered his cell on the first ring, which I assumed meant he was bored to tears. "Hey, Dad, are you alone?"

"Your mom's in the kitchen. Is this about work?"

"How'd you know?"

He laughed. "Honey, I know you. About the only time you call during the day is when you have a question about a case. And, since you're calling when you know your mom will be busy, it's almost a sure thing you want to talk shop. What's all that noise?"

"Some old guy in a blue minivan is blasting out an old Dire Straits song. He's so into it that he's using his steering wheel as a drumset."

"Sounds like 'Money for Nothing.' Tell him to crank it up."

I rolled my eyes, realizing too late that Dad loved those old 80s rock songs and would probably get along really well with the noisemaker. The light, which had been red for an eternity, turned green. Cars began snaking forward. The old guy was still busy playing the drums and not paying very close attention, so I hit the gas and cut over to keep him behind me. Checking my rearview mirror, he seemed unfazed by the quick lane change.

"After we're done, you can go put on some of your favorites, but right now, I have a question for you about Leo Baxter."

"Leo? Oh, sad case. He was a top-notch police chief for a long time. But he was forced to retire when his behavior became erratic."

I would have asked what Dad meant by that, but he continued without prompting. "Leo became extremely forgetful and moody. Things all came to a head when he threatened the mayor and a couple of council members during a City Council meeting. It turned out he was having a bad reaction to a medication he'd been given after a stroke. But the damage had already been done. He's not involved in one of your cases, is he?"

"Indirectly. He was at Benji's funeral. He came up to me and told me that there were a lot of unsavory characters at the funeral."

"Are those the words he used, Jade? Unsavory characters?"

"Yes. Is that code for something?"

"In a sense, yes. Leo and I worked on an art theft case a long time ago. This was back before he was Chief of Police. I was working for a client who'd had a painting stolen. It was before Leo had his stroke, too. The police investigation was stuck, and so was mine, so we decided to pool our resources. Unfortunately, we couldn't prove anything, so in that case, the bad guys got away."

"What was the case?"

"We were after a group that called themselves The Guild. As near as we could tell, the group was run by a mastermind they called Valkyrie. They also had a professional thief, an art restorer, a lawyer, and an appraiser. Five specialists who worked together. All for the common goal of making tons of money in stolen and fake art. They were very successful, and, somehow, they always stayed one step ahead of us."

"How is that connected to unsavory characters?"

"That's what he called The Guild. He always referred to them by that term."

"Could it be a coincidence? Maybe he meant something else?"

"Not likely."

"That's pretty cryptic, Dad. And exactly how is this connected to Benji's funeral?"

"We always suspected Benji was a member."

"What?"

"Benji wasn't always the friendly art dealer you knew, honey. At one point, we believe he was the one who moved the stolen art for The Guild. Leo and I also think he may have had a change of heart and realized how much suffering he'd brought to the people he'd helped steal from. That, quite likely, is why he's dead."

A picture of Detective Des Martini at the funeral flashed in my thoughts. Something told me Hilda Bauer's request was not nearly as straightforward as she'd indicated. What in the world had I gotten myself into?

Chapter 10

CLARA THOMPSON LIVED IN A small Craftsman home on a side street just a few blocks from Benji's store. If Benji had been a successful jewel thief, as my dad had suggested, he certainly hadn't put his money into his home. Then again, with small fixeruppers now selling for over a million dollars in Carlsbad, who was I to judge?

From the street, the house looked like most of its brethren on the block. Nothing ostentatious. White picket fence. Manicured front yard. The subdued blue-and-gray color palette had been updated a few years ago. This was a perfect example of a normal house owned by a sensible man and his sensible wife in a humdrum neighborhood. In some ways, this was exactly the kind of place I'd live in if I were a retired jewel thief. I could envision Benji deciding to create a gorgeous backyard and leave the front as plain as possible. Who would expect them of anything other than wanting to live a quiet life under everyone's radar?

In a true case of bad timing, my phone rang as I knocked on the front door. I checked CallerID, saw that it was Ethan, and sent him to voicemail before I pocketed the phone. Connection or not, adding a relationship to my life would only complicate matters. Forget that—at least for now.

Having second thoughts, I pulled my phone from my back pocket and contemplated the screen. Who was I kidding? Complicating my life had nothing to do with my reason for not wanting to talk to Ethan. Gina had clearly expressed her feelings about him. I was too confused even to know what mine were. It was best if I kept my distance. Letting things play out between those two before I got into the mix was the right thing to do. It was best all the way around. I shoved the phone back into my pocket and knocked again.

From inside, I heard Clara call out that she'd be just a minute, so I took the time to inspect the front of the house. The paint looked like it was in excellent condition. No flakes or chips. The windows were retrofits, the same kind Mom and Dad had installed while I was off at UCLA getting my Criminology degree. They'd never told me how much the windows cost, but Dad had once hinted I shouldn't plan on a lavish wedding anytime soon. Of course, after I'd found my ex with a bimbo yoga instructor in our own bed, my wedding plans had gone out the window. Lavish wedding or not, I'd rather shoot than marry Jason the Slime.

The front door creaked open, jarring me from my fantasy of what I should have done when I'd discovered Jason cheating on me. Clara's smile was a fleeting shadow, heavy with unspoken sorrow. She asked if I wanted to come in and, to a small degree, I felt like a rat as I accepted her invitation. Not only had I never been here before, but now I was going to grill her about her dead husband.

Clara led me into the living room, where my feelings of guilt were displaced by awe. The room was a veritable museum of history, each piece telling a story from a different corner of the globe. An intricately carved mahogany table from the heart of Africa served as the centerpiece, surrounded by chairs upholstered in rich Persian fabrics.

Along the walls, shelves groaned under the weight of antique books, Chinese porcelain vases, and brass lamps from India. The air was thick with the musk of aged wood and leather.

Across the room, Clara was already sitting in one of those magnificent chairs. She gestured at another nearby. My breath caught. Was I dressed well enough to sit there? I stammered, "I shouldn't. I'm wearing jeans and a tee shirt."

Putting her hand to her mouth, Clara shook her head and suppressed her laughter. "Jade, it's not a museum. Benji and I spent years traveling and collecting, but we always said we would never do anything but live in this house. Now, sit. Please."

She gestured again at the chair near her, and the feelings of guilt haunting me for being here on business came rushing back. Now, I would grunge up her furniture and ask impertinent questions. Mom's Social Graces 101 told me I deserved a good, solid rap on the knuckles. I apologized silently to Mom, but I couldn't let my personal hangups get in the way. I sat where I was told.

Leaning forward, I took Clara's hands in mine. Her eyes were rimmed in red. There, I saw pain but also a strength deep down that I thought would carry her through. "Clara, I'm so sorry for your loss. Benji was such a dear man."

"Thank you, Jade. I appreciate you coming by. But it wasn't necessary. Really. Benji's death was a shock—I always thought he'd die on that stupid surfboard of his. I had this gnawing fear, a mix of dread and resignation, knowing each wave he chased could steal him away forever." She stopped, looked vacantly across the room, and silently snorted. "And then the man died changing a stupid lightbulb. Can you believe it?"

I didn't dare tell her what I knew—or suspected. Not yet, anyway. "Life's funny that way, Clara. I remember all the times Mom worried about Dad when he was working on a case. I guess we can never foresee how the end will come."

She didn't flinch or look away but nodded thoughtfully as though I'd said something incredibly profound. To me, though, it felt cold and heartless.

"It doesn't seem fair," I said. "Benji was so full of life."

Clara nodded, then looked at me directly. "Actually, there is something I've wanted to ask you. I've been thinking of calling you."

"Anything I can do, Clara. Just name it."

"I think Benji had gotten involved in something illegal. As I was going through his things, I found some documents in his office that didn't make sense to me. And then there was the phone call." She reached for a tissue and dabbed at her eyes. "He had a secret cell phone, one I never knew about. And two days before he died, I overheard him talking in his office. It was late, and he couldn't sleep. Of course, when he couldn't sleep, neither could I. He got up and went to his office. I'm ashamed to say that I eavesdropped. He was talking to a woman named Ashley."

I couldn't have asked for a more perfect opening. I'd come here wanting to see Benji's home office, and now I had a gold-plated ticket. "Clara, I can certainly check those things out for you. The best place to start would be in Benji's office."

"Okay. But if he was doing something illegal, do you really think you'll find evidence just lying about?"

My heart sank as I listened to her words. I, myself, had just discovered how wrong I'd been about Benji. If it was true that Benji called another woman in the middle of the night, it was highly possible he was having a romantic affair. He certainly could have been conducting illegal business, but when someone made a surreptitious call in the middle of the night, my money was on the lover.

"I don't know what to do," Clara continued. "I'm scared, and I need your help."

A shadow of anxiety seemed to drift across the room. Fear showed in Clara's eyes, and I knew she was serious. "Of course, Clara. Whatever you need."

She looked away, her eyes focused on some unseen object. Or maybe a memory? "I found one of his business cards in his wallet with a number written on the back. I don't know for sure, but I have a feeling it might be this Ashley he was talking to on the phone that night."

"Can I see it?"

She stood, crossed the room to the mahogany table, and returned not only with a business card but also with a cell phone. She shoved them both at me as though trying to rid herself of something evil.

The phone was a Nokia 6300, a popular burner choice. Simple and durable, the phone was a classic. The card was from Timeless Treasures. Benji had given me one the first time we met. I turned it over and read the neatly printed phone number on the back. "This doesn't look like it's local," I said. "Have you tried calling it?"

"It's disconnected."

Again, the shadow darkened the atmosphere in the room. "I can see why you'd be concerned, Clara. Do you have any idea what Benji was involved in? I hate to ask this, but have you considered the possibility he was seeing another woman?"

Clara shook her head adamantly. "Benji would never cheat on me."

"So you're convinced he was into something illegal?"

"How could it be anything else?" Clara croaked, tears welling up in her eyes.

We sat in silence for a couple of minutes—she caught up in questioning her husband's dealings while I wondered what she wasn't telling me. I hoped a few of the obvious questions might net me more information. "Did Benji have any enemies? Anyone who might want to harm him?"

Clara shook her head, her expression pained. "I have no idea. As far as I knew, Benji was well-liked by everyone. He didn't have any enemies." She paused, gritted her teeth, then croaked, "But that phone call. The disconnected number."

A phone call and an old phone number were hardly the stuff of vendettas or conspiracies. Affairs, though, that was another story. But then there was the cryptogram. Hilda Bauer's references. Leo Baxter's warnings. Detective Des at the funeral. A sea of red flags now surrounded me.

I summoned my most consoling and confident inner self and told her about A Mermaid's Allure and why I'd come here. When I finished, I said, "Let me look at his office. Maybe I can get to the bottom of this."

"Thank you," Clara said, relief lacing her voice.

"One thing that would help me is if you could get me a list of Benji's contacts."

"You mean the people he did business with?"

"Those, yes, but I'm also interested in his personal ones. If I'm looking for some kind of illegal business activities, I'll probably have to look beyond his traditional business contacts."

Clara turned her attention to the Chinese vase. With its fine lines and perfect glazing, the vase was a gorgeous example of Ming Dynasty craftsmanship. Assuming it was real. Given the museum aura hanging in the air, I had no doubt it was.

"You mean the enemies you asked about earlier," Clara said bluntly.

"I'm sorry, but yes. Let's face it, Clara. The statistics overwhelmingly favor someone being murdered for personal reasons rather than a bad business deal."

"So you think if he was doing something illegal, that's who killed him."

"Let me be clear, Clara. You're not hiring me to find his killer. That's a job for the police. However, I may determine who that person is during my investigation."

"I understand. Thank you, Jade. I truly appreciate you doing this. Of course, I'm willing to pay for your services. I can't ask you to do this for free. But right now, I have to leave."

Thirty seconds ago, she'd been in no hurry at all. Now, all of a sudden, she had to rush off? Seriously? "Do you have an appointment?"

"Yes. I'm sorry to rush you, but maybe you could look at his office when you bring the contract."

"Of course." I stood, still trying to figure out what had changed. "Let me write up an investigation agreement. The contract outlines the terms and conditions of the investigation, including the scope of work, fees, and confidentiality clauses. Can I come back tomorrow?"

Clara asked that I call first, but thought she'd be available most of the day. We said our goodbyes, and she, once again, told me how much better she felt because I was helping her. The fact was, though she might feel better, I had chills going down my spine. Whatever Benji had been into, it couldn't have been good. It might have even gotten him killed. And now Clara was acting strange. I wanted answers. And closure. For Clara. For Hilda. And for my own peace of mind.

Walking back to my car, I thought about Ethan's phone call. I supposed I should at least see what he wanted. My insides stirred at the sound of his deep baritone in my ear.

"Jade, this is Ethan. Call me back, would you? I have a lead that I think you'll be interested in. It's about Benji's final hours."

Chapter 11

SINCLAIR'S WAS ONE OF DOWNTOWN Carlsbad's hoity-toity restaurants I never envisioned myself walking into. And forget dining there. I couldn't afford those prices. They used linen tablecloths, real polished silver, and had an outdoor dining area cordoned off by a waist-high wrought iron fence. Though someone could easily step over the fence, it did its job of keeping the riffraff out. That would be people like me. The ones who were too cheap to lay down a hundred bucks for dinner.

The restaurant had been around for as long as I could remember. I'd walked by Sinclair's many times and had always ogled the amazing concoctions on the patrons' plates. Ethan's invitation to meet here for dinner was enough to make me wonder how much money he had, whether this was a business meeting or a date, and what I'd do if it actually was the latter. Butterflies flitted around my stomach at the very thought. They went into overdrive when I saw Ethan.

He sat at a table on the border of the outdoor dining area. The restaurant's meticulous attention to detail was painfully obvious and reflected the establishment's commitment to providing an exceptional dining experience, one I was about to partake in. I felt like a bum as the hostess seated me. Her long, blonde hair was pulled back into a perfect ponytail. At least I'd pulled mine up into a loose chignon. But my tee shirt and jeans were no match for her perfectly pressed white shirt, black vest, and black slacks.

Ethan stood when he saw me and waited expectantly as the hostess led the way to the table. "Thanks, Jessica," he said.

"Of course," she said with a smile that could have come off the cover of any fashion magazine. She laid a menu on my side of the table and sauntered away. That girl might be ten years younger than me, but she had class in spades. Ethan leaned forward and hugged me. I couldn't stop myself from melting into his embrace.

Though brief, I realized halfway through the hug how much I was relishing every second. I cursed my weakness for wishing he'd never release me, and when he finally did, an ache for his warmth and closeness clung to my heart.

He stepped behind me, pulled out my chair, and flashed me a smile that made my stomach flutter. "You look great, Jade."

"I should've changed, but I ran out of time."

"Don't be silly. This is Carlsbad—anything goes."

I sat without saying another word, keeping my attention on my place setting. Oh, my gawd. What was I doing? Gina wanted this guy for herself. But my mind was a storm of conflicted emotions. The initial flush of warmth from Ethan's hug still lingered on my skin, but what worried me most were the feelings deep inside. A strong physical and emotional attraction made me want to be close to him. Those emotions battled against my sense of betrayal to Gina. Despite the sounds of the city around us, a silent battle raged within me, pitting my loyalty against my heart's whispers. How could something that felt so right simultaneously feel like a transgression?

Ethan sat across from me, leaned forward, and asked, "Jade, are you okay?"

"Yes. I'm fine. Do you come here a lot?"

"No," he chuckled, then whispered, "I can't afford restaurants like this. I work at Anchor & Ale. We're more of what you would call maritime historical meets cozy pub. It's a lot more fun than places like this."

I put my hand over my mouth to stifle my laugh as our server, a middle-aged man graying at the temples, appeared at our table. He introduced himself as Foster, asked if we'd like to start with a cocktail or a bottle of wine, and graciously left when Ethan told him we needed more time. Foster took up a position about twenty feet away, standing ready to fulfill our every dining whim.

"I thought maybe you came here all the time," I said.

Ethan shook his head. "Why?"

"The hostess. You knew her name. It was like you were old friends or something."

"Jessica? I've known her for years. She still takes a few shifts at the bar, but this job was a great step for her. She's saving up to go to law school."

"Law school?" I peered across the restaurant at the girl, unable to believe she was old enough to attend law school. "She looks like she's in high school."

"She's twenty-four."

A groan escaped my lips.

"What?" Ethan laughed.

"My mom's been on my back lately about skin-care routines."

Ethan shook his head. "Don't worry about it. You're gorgeous."

Luckily, I managed to catch the words "so are you" before they slipped out. "Thanks," I said, my face feeling as hot as a poker just pulled from the fire.

He cleared his throat. "Sorry. I embarrassed you. I didn't mean to make this sound like a date. I asked you to come here because Chef Pete was friends with Benji."

Friends? How close? I'd wondered why Sinclair's had catered Benji's reception. To my knowledge, Sinclair's didn't cater. But I guess I'd been wrong. Apparently, if you had enough money—or the right connection, or maybe both—they would do it. Forget the date thing; I had questions. Serious questions about this newfound connection.

"Well, I appreciate the invitation. I worked with Sam earlier, and I'll be out there again in the morning. So, you're saying the two of them were friends? Were they close?"

"Close enough for Chef Pete to volunteer to cater Benji's reception without Clara having to ask."

"Wait. He volunteered? How do you know that?"

"I have my sources." Ethan winked at me, then added, "The next thing you're going to want to know is why he'd do that."

Indeed, it was. Although the guy facing me radiated heat like a smoldering ember, my focus now was to get an answer to that question. Which made me wonder how you approached the owner of one of Carlsbad's best restaurants and question his motives for doing something nice. "Got any ideas on how we should handle this?"

"I was hoping you'd have some thoughts on that. You're the professional, right?"

One thing I love about being a PI is that you get to think outside the box. It's not just about following the obvious clues; it's about seeing the connections others might miss and using creative problem-solving to uncover the facts. This was my opportunity to do just that. I was determined to learn the truth about Chef Pete and his connection to Benji's reception, no matter how awkward or uncomfortable it might be.

"I wish I'd have known this a couple of hours ago. I could have asked Clara." Nevertheless, she had volunteered to pay for my services, so I would have another opportunity to ask. "I suggest we have dinner, then see if we can speak with the chef. When he comes out, we can compliment him on his food and then casually bring up the topic of Benji's reception."

"Sounds like a plan to me," Ethan said, a small smile forming on his lips. "By the way, I lied earlier. This isn't all business. At least, I hope it's not. Maybe this could be sort of a pre-date. You know, a chance to get to know each other better."

I must have looked like a complete idiot sitting there with a stupid grin on my face. But I didn't care. He liked me. To avoid acting like a total schoolgirl with a mad crush, I raised my menu, licked my lips, and looked through the options. I snuck a peek at Ethan over the top of the menu, feeling an electrifying rush of joy coursing through me. "Sounds like a plan to me, too."

While we ate, the mayor and Luna Martinez showed up with two men in suits. I was surprised to see Luna with the mayor, but she did have tons of money and was probably one of Mayor Amy's big donors. I noticed that Jessica sat them immediately and then left them alone. While we were now splitting Foster with three other tables, they had their own private server.

The food was nothing short of amazing. It was even more delicious than what had been served at Benji's reception. The service from Foster and the other staff was perfect. The atmosphere and the companionship couldn't have been better. This was a case where it would be easy to shell out a list of compliments to the chef—assuming I left off the part about the companionship, of course.

When Foster showed up with the check, I asked if we might have a word with the chef. He did a double-take but quickly recovered and was again the consummate professional. "Was something wrong? I can take care of anything you need."

"Oh, no, everything was perfect, Foster," I said. "The fact is that Chef Pete catered a reception for a friend of ours, and we just wanted to tell him how wonderful it was. As was everything here."

"Chef Pete does love talking to satisfied customers. Let me see if he's available. It's not too busy yet, and I don't think he'll mind breaking away. It shouldn't be a problem."

Across the room, a man wearing a white chef's coat chatted with the power diners. Come to think of it, he was the man I'd seen working with the waitstaff at the reception. He stood about six feet tall and had a sturdy build that probably came from years of physical work in the kitchen. His unkempt, dark hair was complemented by a three-day scruffy stubble that men—and maybe the women in their lives—found so popular these days.

Foster went to the group, spoke quietly with the man, and then waited patiently until the conversation ended. Foster returned in the lead with Chef Pete right behind him.

"Chef, this is Ethan and Jade. They were at Benji's reception yesterday." Foster stood to one side and made room for his boss.

"The food was incredible," I said.

"Thank you so much, I really appreciate that." Chef Pete's face lit up with pride. "I'm glad you enjoyed it."

"We more than enjoyed our meal," Ethan added. "The pasta was cooked to perfection. Yours, too. Right, Jade?"

"I agree. You have a real talent. Have you owned the restaurant the entire time it's been here?"

"Oh, no. My father opened Sinclair's when I was just a boy. He'd bring me here to do my homework. When I finished with that, he'd let me do little things. Eventually, the little things became bigger things. He passed about five years ago. That's when I took over."

"I'm sorry about your father," I said. "But it sounds like we have something in common. I took over the family business, too."

"Really? What do you do?"

"Jade's a PI," Ethan said proudly.

I flushed a little at his enthusiasm and added, "Beachtown Detective Agency. It's just a few blocks away."

Chef Pete pursed his lips and studied me with a spark of interest. "I dare say your business has to be more exciting than mine."

I avoided the cynical retort about his being more profitable. "Perhaps. Can I ask you a question? We were just talking about how you catered Benji's reception. Do you do that often?"

"No," Chef Pete said. "I only cater for friends."

"So Benji was a friend of yours?"

"He was in here all the time. He was very close to my father. In fact, Benji had his last meal here. He and Clara came in for dinner the night he died. They were here until closing. I didn't realize he was going back to work. If I'd known he would be climbing a ladder, I'd never have let him order a bottle of wine with dinner." Chef Pete clucked a few times, then sighed. "I'm going to miss him. Benji was a great customer."

Across the table, Ethan's eyes were wide with surprise. And I, I had warning bells going off. If this man had known Benji well enough to prevent him from ordering a bottle of wine, I had more questions for him. Starting with, what exactly was the nature of the relationship between the two men?

I also made a mental note to see if I could get a copy of the autopsy report. Maybe there had been more for dinner than just what was on the menu.

The power meeting broke up, and, to my surprise, Mayor Amy made a beeline for our table while Luna and the two men said their goodbyes. Chef Pete turned to the mayor, asked if she was leaving so soon, and seemed pleased by her excuse that she needed to return to work.

"You're Jade Cavendish, aren't you?" Mayor Amy asked.

"I am."

"I thought I recognized you. I hope you don't mind my asking, but you're not investigating Benji's death, are you?"

The tiny hairs on the back of my neck rose. What the heck? "I'm sorry, Mayor, but I can't really say one way or the other."

"I'll take that as a yes," she said firmly. "I was hoping you'd turned down Mrs. Thompson's request. I hate seeing my constituents waste their money on fruitless endeavors. Ms. Cavendish, do Mrs. Thompson a favor. Close this out quickly. Don't take too much of her money. Good day."

I watched her go, my mind reeling with disbelief. Did she think I was some kind of scam artist? Did she just expect me to walk away from Clara and her grief? And if I didn't drop the case, would she try to tarnish my reputation?

"You might want to think about that," Chef Pete said. "She's a powerful person in this town. Anyway, thank you for coming in today. I'm so happy you enjoyed your meal."

When Ethan and I were alone, he lowered his voice. "Don't let all that cloud your judgment, Jade."

I finished off my glass of water and placed the empty glass back on the table. "Actually, it's done exactly the opposite. There is definitely something going on here, and I'm going to get to the bottom of it."

Chapter 12

ETHAN STOOD, TOSSED HIS NAPKIN on the table, and motioned with his head toward the exit. "Come on. Let's get out of here. There's a great ice cream shop just down the street."

"Oh, wow. I haven't been there in ages." In fact, the last time was with my ex. We were there exactly once when we first started dating. He spent more time checking out the girl behind the counter than the ice cream. At that point, I should have known he would eventually cheat on me. I should have cut him off that day and saved myself the heartache.

As we walked, I couldn't help but think about the conversation with Mayor Amy. She clearly didn't want me involved in Benji's case. Why? Was there something more to his death that she didn't want uncovered?

"Hey, Jade. Are you okay with this?"

I looked into those blue eyes. I knew I really shouldn't. I had work to do. But I couldn't resist. Offer me ice cream, especially the good stuff, and I'll follow you anywhere. Near the corner of State and Grand, we sidestepped an oblivious, scruffy young man with an equally scruffy dog, And when Ethan gently put his hand on the small of my back, my breath caught. I hadn't needed the reassurance, but his tenderness touched my heart.

We walked side-by-side, my heart lifting at the sound of water burbling from the fountain at the town's small transit station. Somehow, the sky felt bluer, the palms overhead greener, and the storefronts along the street more charming. I pulled my hand away when Ethan's accidentally brushed mine. I looked sideways at him. He smiled. And I felt foolish. I wished I could turn off these feelings for him. If only.

As we approached the ice cream shop, I spied a line of customers out front. My mouth started watering as the old memories came flooding back. "My mom and dad brought me here when I was little. I was addicted to chocolate chip in those days."

Ethan nudged my shoulder with his and turned on that wicked smile. And, yeah, my heart melted like a scoop of chocolate chip on the sidewalk on a hot summer day. I think my brain did, too, because I knew he'd asked me a question. Something like, was that still one of my favorites?

"It's still in my top ten." Somehow, I had to steer this conversation away from me and back to Benji. "When we met, you said that Benji never drank. I also saw the look on your face when Chef Pete said Benji ordered a bottle of wine with dinner. He never drank at your bar? How did you two meet?"

"Benji first started coming in maybe two or three years ago. Once or twice a week, he'd show up and order a club soda with a twist of lime. I just assumed he was a teetotaler. He usually sat at the counter, and we'd talk about art and history. Every once in a while, he'd run into a client, and they'd get a table. We had some deep conversations after he started trying to find my grandmother's brooch."

I gaped at Ethan and this latest revelation. "You and Benji? The two of you talked about art? I didn't realize you had that kind of knowledge."

"Actually, Oma taught me a great deal about art and history when I was growing up. She took me to museums and seminars. To be truthful, I didn't always appreciate what she was teaching me, but I loved being with her. I suppose I soaked up the attention and learned a lot in the process."

"How did Benji get started on this search for your grandmother's brooch?"

"Hold that thought," Ethan said and stepped up to the counter. "What's your pleasure?"

"I'll have the Mocha Fudge Swirl. A single in a cup."

He frowned and peered at me. "You don't like cones?"

"They get kind of messy."

Ethan made a humphing sound and sighed. "I feel exactly the same way. Make it two," he said to the girl taking the order.

We were silent while she prepared the two cups and finished the transaction. After taking a bite and letting the sweetness of coffee and chocolate coat my tongue, I started to walk. Ethan immediately fell in step with me, almost as if he'd read my mind. "I hope this is okay," I said apologetically.

"More than okay. Exceptional, I'd say."

I fought back a smile and jabbed my spoon into the ice cream. "You were telling me how Benji started helping your grandmother."

"Oh, right. Benji was trying to help people recover art pieces that had been confiscated during the war. My oma had tried to find her family's brooch when she was younger, but she gave up about five years ago. She said she'd run out of leads. And then, out of nowhere,

Benji started coming into the bar. He and I got into a discussion of the Holocaust. I told him what Oma had said, and he promised to look into it."

"Did he?"

"It took a few weeks. To be truthful, I thought he'd forgotten all about the conversation. But then he showed up and said that he had a lead. He said it would take some time because he needed to be extremely cautious, but he'd get back to me. Over the course of the next year, he gave me periodic updates. The last time, which was a couple of nights before he died, he handed me the envelope with the cryptogram and gave me your name."

"That's it? He didn't say anything else?"

"There was one other thing. It still doesn't make any sense to me. He said that the message wasn't the key, but the key was in the message. How's that for bizarre?"

I stopped, scraped the last of my ice cream from the paper cup, and tossed it into a nearby trash can. "Not bizarre, Ethan. Brilliant. It's a clue as to where we'll find the key that will help us solve the cryptogram."

Ethan's eyes lit up. He followed my lead by tossing his paper cup in the trash, then looked at me and asked, "Great! So what's it mean?"

"I have no idea."

His face fell. "But you said it was a clue."

"Exactly. A clue that will eventually lead us to an answer."

"Okay. So what's next? How do we find out what the clue means?"

"I don't know that, either."

Ethan pursed his lips. He seemed lost in thought for a second, but his smile quickly returned, and his voice turned even more persuasive. "What do you know, then?"

That I find you incredibly hot seemed totally wrong under the circumstances. Then again, had he been flirting with me? No. I was a professional. At least until this case was over—or until Gina said she really wasn't interested or until any one of a half dozen other excuses I could think of came to be. We both needed personal space. Boundaries. We had to have them.

I shrugged off the question and tried to sound nonchalant. "Not a lot. I know I'm at that stage of an investigation where there are way more questions than answers. I know I don't like being warned off of a case by someone who doesn't know what they're talking about."

"Mayor Amy?"

"Exactly."

"She was just protecting Clara, that's all. Clara's a constituent. And a friend. Mayor Amy just wants the best for a grieving widow."

Suddenly, my throat parched as though an unseen force had whisked away every drop of moisture, transforming it into a tiny, barren desert of unease, where each breath felt like swallowing sand. Why was Ethan defending the mayor? He'd been there. He'd seen the whole interaction. And maybe that was the problem.

Coincidence was a pill I found hard to swallow. My dad often said that in the vast medicine cabinet of investigative work, coincidence was a drug you shouldn't take without a glass of hindsight. That Mayor Amy just happened to go to dinner at the same restaurant and the same time that Ethan had invited me to meet him felt less like chance and more like a chess move. Was there something calculated and deliberate about that entire dinner? This walk? The ice cream? And, yes, even the flirting?

I turned away from Ethan, feeling frustrated and unsure about what to do next. The truth was, I needed time to clear my head. To sort out Leo Baxter's warning from the emotional soap opera churning inside me. Figuring that out was like picking gummy bears out of a salad.

To get there, I needed an answer to one critical question. Could I trust Ethan?

Chapter 13

THE THUD-THUD-THUD OF hip-hop blasting from an old Chevy vibrated the air and jarred me from my thoughts. Ethan stood next to me, his bright smile replaced by a frown. "What's wrong, Jade?"

How did I answer that? Sorry, buddy, but I don't trust you? Unsure of what to say without sounding paranoid or crazy, I went with avoidance. "I don't know. Everything feels way too convenient. Like Mayor Amy showing up at the same restaurant and the same time we were there."

I left off the part about the walk. I couldn't shake the feeling that Ethan was hiding something.

He brushed away my statement with a nonchalant wave of his hand. "It was just a coincidence."

"Sorry, Ethan, but in my line of work, coincidences don't exist."

Ethan sighed, and his cheeks tightened. "I get it. You're having doubts about my intentions."

"What makes you say that?" I asked innocently.

"Oh, come on. Ten seconds ago, we were having this connection. Then, we started talking about the mayor, and you shut down. I shouldn't have defended her."

I crossed my arms and looked away. "Let's just say this whole dinner date is starting to feel awkward."

"It's that Baxter guy, isn't it? He told you not to trust me. Didn't he?"

Who was being paranoid now? "What makes you think he did? Is there a reason?"

Ethan ran his fingers through his hair. "No, not really." He stopped, made a face, then blurted, "He doesn't like me."

How many times in my life had I heard that line? The guilty used it as an excuse to hide what they'd done to others. The innocent used it to gain sympathy. The Chevy pulled away from the stop sign, taking the heavy bass with it. I watched it turn at the next corner, all the while trying to decide which category Ethan fell into.

"What about you?" he asked. "Do you like me?"

My defenses crumbled at his playful tone. "I suppose that depends on how much trouble you'll get me into."

Ethan grinned, dimples appearing on his cheeks. "Well, that depends on how much you want to get into. Right?"

"Yeah, I guess so. What about Leo? You said he doesn't like you. Why is that?"

"I got in some trouble when I was in high school. My mom and dad had just divorced, and I wasn't handling it well, so I started doing some crazy stuff. Leo Baxter was the police chief, and he wanted me tried as an adult. The DA decided my case was better suited to juvenile court. Leo doesn't like being told he's wrong, so he holds a grudge against me."

I wasn't sure if I believed him, but his vulnerability pulled at my heartstrings. "That must have been tough for you."

Ethan twisted his cheek in a casual attempt at indifference, though his jaw subtly tensed. "Like I said, I made some mistakes. Looking back, it was all pretty stupid. But you can't always escape your past in a small town like this."

"True."

I didn't know what else to say. Plus, I still didn't know whether I could trust Ethan. What I did know was that I needed more information, and he was a source. As my dad would say, it was time to go fishing. Cast my line and see what I got. Would I find the truth? Or a lie? There was only one way I'd ever know.

"The cryptogram," I said. "You never did tell me why Benji gave it to you."

"Honestly, I don't know." Ethan raised his hands to his sides, palms up. "We had some deep conversations about art and history, but we were far from confidants or anything like that."

I leaned forward, my curiosity piqued. "But if this cryptogram really is what you say it is and can lead us to the brooch, why would Benji trust you with it? Why wouldn't he have just told your grandmother where it was? Why wouldn't he have just given the cryptogram to me himself? It doesn't add up."

"I can't answer any of those questions. I've asked myself the same things a thousand times since he passed. Benji was a brilliant but eccentric guy. He had his reasons, I suppose. Maybe this all happened because he'd been working with my grandmother."

"I suppose that's possible." But then again, why not deal directly with Hilda? I needed to approach this with caution—trust but verify. But how did I verify a motive for a dead man? It could be we'd never know unless I solved the cryptogram and found the brooch.

"Benji was always a few steps ahead of everyone else. It wouldn't surprise me if he had a plan all along," Ethan said.

I straightened up. Cursing myself for having been so slow. Of course, I shouldn't be relying on Clara for information about the business; I had to wade through the details myself. In addition to sifting through Benji's home office, my investigation required me to find a way into the store. Maybe I could find something other than the list of contacts Clara was working on. For instance, was Benji's death truly accidental or not?

"Somehow, I need to confirm that the police are looking at Benji's death as a homicide," I mused, half to myself, half to the ocean breeze.

"No! You can't go to the police. We need to keep the entire investigation quiet."

"Ethan, that's not possible. My job is to ask people questions. At the same time, I can't be interfering in a police investigation."

"Please, Jade. Just don't go to them yet. If word gets out about the brooch, it might disappear again."

I didn't like it, but he had a point. It was best to keep things quiet for now. But I couldn't let it rest completely. "Alright. We'll keep this on the down low for the next day or so. But if I come across something that will help the police, I'm going straight to Detective Des. And I'm continuing to gather information. Maybe I can start connecting some of the dots."

"Okay. I understand." Ethan drew in a long breath and let it out slowly. "I'll do whatever I can to help you."

"Thanks, Ethan. I'll be in touch." Flashing him a polite smile, I turned away and strolled to the office. On the way, I breathed a sigh of relief. At least Ethan and I had boundaries. I hoped. Either way, I had a plan forming. That plan began with a service agreement for Clara. It also involved digging into Benji's life and business. I was hoping to find something that would give me more insight into the cryptogram, the brooch, and his death.

To my surprise, Zoe was still in the office. She started firing questions at me the moment I walked through the door. How was dinner? Are you seeing him again? Zoe's official duties not only involved maintaining the agency's blog but also filing and answering the phones. Occasionally, she served as my sounding board. And she always spent time in her unofficial role of Meddler in Chief. Yes, she was as bad as my mom when it came to helping me find Mr. Right. Hence, the questions.

"Come on, Jade, spill! I stayed late just to find out what happened with you two." Zoe parked herself on the edge of my desk. She planted one hand at her side and gave me her I'm-not-letting-this-go look.

"There's not much to tell, Zoe. Ethan is a source. He brought me the cryptogram, remember?"

"Yeah, but he's also incredibly hot. I can see why you like him. Gina showed me a photo of him and her together."

The hairs on the back of my neck tingled. I hated feeling jealous, especially because I wasn't even sure Ethan and I had any kind of real connection. I made the incredibly stupid move of asking Zoe which photo she was referring to because she launched into an explanation that included all of the details—including that the photo had been taken at the reception by one of the servers.

Determined to get myself off the hot seat, I cleared my throat. "Not to change the subject, but how's the blog doing?"

"Awesome. I'm working on a post about the importance of shredding documents."

"Great. I'll look forward to seeing it. When can you have it ready? I might be out of the office a lot this next week."

"I'm almost done. I could finish tomorrow. How come you're going to be out a lot?"

"Field work for a case."

"What about that secret code? Do you want to work on it again?"

"Thanks, Zoe, but I found an expert to do that. It's getting late. Right?" I shot a subtle glance at the front door.

"Oh, right. Gotcha." Zoe quickly packed up her stuff and said goodnight, urging me not to stay too late myself.

The big benefit to business being good is that it forces you to systematize the things you do. To that end, I'd created a boilerplate service agreement several months ago. Within twenty minutes of starting, I had listed everything I expected to be doing for Clara. To avoid overlapping with Hilda's case, I restricted my activities for Clara to investigating Benji's business dealings and that mysterious phone call. I also capped the contract at $3,000.

With Clara's agreement completed, I folded the document and stuck it in an envelope, then put the envelope into my laptop case. Tomorrow morning, I'd get her to sign. I then turned my attention back to what had been bothering me since the conversation with my dad.

Going to the files to check my hunch, I discovered that my dad had done surveillance on Benji. That didn't answer the question of if he'd ever worked for him, though. Dad hadn't said anything about Benji ever being a client, but I hadn't asked that particular question, either.

The only case reference on Benji's rolodex card was Hilda's case, and there was no file under Benji's last name. Still, I couldn't shake the feeling there should be a file on Benji somewhere in this office. The question was, where?

I had two choices—spend the evening searching or call Dad. Why not save myself some time? I dialed Dad's cell, and he answered almost immediately.

"Hey, honey, you missed dinner. It's kind of late for you to be at the office. Isn't it?"

"Clara's hired me to look into Benji's business dealings. It's looking like a homicide, Dad."

Dad groaned and then asked, "What makes you say that?"

"What I didn't tell you before is that Detective Des was at Benji's funeral in what looked like an official capacity. Leo suspected that Benji had been murdered. There's nothing concrete, and so far, there's no proof. I suspect it may have been related to his role in The Guild."

"I wish I could help you, honey. But I tried every trick in the book to dig up Benji's past. I even went so far as to buy jewelry from him for your mother on several occasions. Nothing worked. He never disclosed a thing. Do you want to go over it?"

"Sure." I explained what I'd done so far, but his only suggestion was to keep pushing. He liked the idea of me working for Clara and thought it might eventually bear fruit.

"If you've got access to his office files, honey, maybe you can finally answer the question Leo and I always had. Was Benji innocent or an expert at hiding his past?"

"I'll keep you in the loop. But there is one more thing I've been wondering about. Did you ever do any work for Benji?"

My dad cleared his throat. "He asked, but I never took the job. Let's see, it was last year. He wanted me to do a background check on someone. A former client."

"Let me guess. Hilda Bauer."

"Yes. He also wanted me to check out her grandson—Ethan Harper. I told him no because I thought it would be a huge breach of client confidentiality. Not to mention the fact that I still had my suspicions about his background."

"Thanks, Dad. You've explained a lot."

"Oh, like what?"

"Like why Benji started going into the Anchor & Ale so he could become friends with Ethan. How he got himself hired to return the brooch to Hilda Bauer. I think Benji was a very patient man who was excellent at working people. I'm guessing he's dead because whoever is in charge of The Guild discovered what he was up to."

After a long pause, my dad said, "Be careful, honey. You don't know who you're up against—literally."

"I know. And that's what worries me."

Chapter 14

I BEAT ZOE INTO THE office the following morning. It wasn't a particularly difficult feat—Zoe wasn't a morning person. With only two things to do—pull the original cryptogram and send Sam a copy of the brooch photograph from the files, I was in and out in fifteen minutes.

My goal was to get in a workout at X Factor Defense before I drove to Sam's office. On my way to the gym, I texted Clara to ask when I could stop by with the service agreement. Clara didn't answer right away, which made me hope she was out doing something she enjoyed rather than lying in bed grieving.

By the time I left the gym, the damp and heavy air was giving way to the cool crispness of a coastal morning. The first thing I noticed when I entered Sam's office was a sweet floral scent. A tropical bouquet bursting with a kaleidoscope of colors, anchored by the majestic presence of a plant with velvety petals, a radiant mix of purples, pinks, and whites, in the center, dominated Sam's desk. The entire presentation exuded both elegance and exotic allure.

To say I was envious was an understatement. My ex had never been much of a flower guy. The best he'd ever done was bring me a mostly wilted bouquet from the supermarket. The worst part was that he inadvertently admitted he'd been guilt-tripped into buying the flowers by his mother because he'd forgotten my birthday. As my mother so eloquently put it, the guy was a peach. Now that the pain was gone, I was happy he was, too.

"Those are gorgeous," I said after greeting Sam. "What's the occasion?"

Sam beamed at me with blue eyes and black hair that coordinated perfectly with her teal wool cap and matching sweater. "They're a 'just because' present. My boyfriend sent them. Look at the note! Isn't that sweet? 'I'm thinking of you and want to make sure you're thinking of me, too.'"

"Wow. Hang onto that one." I went on to tell her the story about Jason. "It was painful at first, but I finally realized I could do much better."

Sam rolled her eyes and assured me I was better off without him, and then her lips curled into an impish smile. "Ethan stopped by."

"Why?" I asked and scrunched up my face. My suspicions from last night came flooding back. "He wasn't asking questions about the investigation, was he?"

"No. He's the one who delivered the flowers. He told me he showed up at the same time as the delivery guy, but I saw his car in the parking lot before that. The poor guy must have sat out there for thirty minutes before he decided to come in. Anyway, he said he was hoping to run into you."

My eyebrows raised slightly as I peered at Sam. Something wasn't tracking here. "Sam, I don't know if we can trust him. Last night, he defended the mayor after she told me to drop my investigation."

Sam began twirling a lock of dark hair, and her impish smile returned. "You really don't get it, do you? He likes you, Jade. A lot."

"I don't think so. He had dinner with me last night just to get information from me."

"You are totally clueless. The guy came out here, sat in his car for half an hour, then interrupted a flower delivery guy so he'd have an excuse to talk to you."

Eager to deflect the attention away from my personal life, I told Sam I didn't have time for a relationship right now and asked if she'd received the photo I sent.

"Wow. You're totally closed off, aren't you?"

"I've got two cases," I said defensively. "Hilda's and Clara's. I'm sure they're tied together, but I can't figure out how."

Sam scrunched up her face and pulled me into a hug. "Okay. I get it. I'll lay off."

"Thank you," I said as I pulled away. "What about the photo?"

"Yes, I got it. It was a huge help. It's the same one I already had, but it got me thinking about doing an image search. I found several references to it. I'm not a hundred percent on this yet, but it looks like your piece was stolen by an international band of art thieves about twenty years ago. It had been in several private collections after World War II, but it disappeared after the theft."

"So, it's been missing for twenty years?"

"Not exactly. Let me show you something." I followed Sam to one of her worktables, one that looked like it was covered by a tablecloth made of documents and photos. "This is my timeline. That photo in the upper left corner is a print of the one you sent me. It came from your dad's files?"

"Yes. I got it from a file at the agency. My dad had been working on a case involving Hilda Bauer, and that's where I found it. Darn. I didn't think to ask him how he got it."

Sam nodded thoughtfully and touched her chin with a white-gloved finger. "My guess is that it's an enlargement made from a negative by a commercial lab. I can't tell without the actual photo, but it looks like that."

Although I knew in my head that dealing with Sam would be different from dealing with Zoe—I should expect a professional answer from Sam, not so much from Zoe—I couldn't help but cringe mentally. "Go on, give me the bad news."

"Huh?" Sam craned her neck forward and shook her head. "It's not bad news. But it is interesting. After the brooch was stolen, copies of it showed up. From what I can determine, three, to be exact. One was sold at auction, a second was the subject of a magazine article published about five years ago, and a third recently found its way into a museum."

"That's a lot to unpack."

"I know. But there's a pattern here. The piece sold at auction was handled by a proxy. That typically means the seller wants to remain anonymous. That's a dead end. The magazine article covered the return of the brooch to the original owner's daughter—Hilda Bauer—and how she discovered it was a fake."

"What? She never told me about any of that."

"I'm not surprised. Mrs. Bauer was super-embarrassed because she almost believed she had her mother's brooch back. Rather than trying to force her to talk about it, I think the one that went to the museum is the better option. It might work for us."

Dare I hope these fakes could ultimately lead us to the current owner of the brooch? It seemed a long shot, but what if we could solve the case without the cryptogram? That would be awesome. It wasn't the way I'd expected to do this, but I'd be happy to take the win. I scanned the images on the workstation as Sam continued.

"The thing is, museums hate being scammed. And the fact that the copy they bought had been authenticated looks really bad. It's only because I've worked with Jonathan Prescott before that he's willing to confide in me."

"Alright, so what do we have to do? Is there a way I can talk to this guy? Maybe get more information?"

Sam held up her hand with her fingers splayed. "Already covered. Believe me, he wants to talk to both of us. He did his due diligence and followed the museum's protocols to ensure this didn't happen. He thought he had the original in his collection, but when I started asking questions, we both realized what had happened. He is so not happy. He's driving up from San Diego, so he should be here any minute."

Her explanation was interrupted by the swishing of the front door. She started to stand but stopped halfway up and whispered, "He's in a bad mood. Be nice."

Turning her attention to a man with salt-and-pepper hair and a scowl that could curdle milk, Sam extended her hand and greeted him cheerfully. She then introduced us and explained my role in the search for the missing brooch. I made nice, gave him my most winning, yet professional, smile, and gushed about how I wished we were meeting under other circumstances.

That helped to soften the scowl. "I can't believe this has happened," Jonathan said, running his hand through his hair in frustration. "We spent so much time and effort trying to acquire this piece, only to learn that we were scammed." He grunted. "Lends new meaning to Pablo Picasso's feelings about art."

"I'm not sure I understand," I said.

"Pablo Picasso once said, 'Art is a lie that makes us realize the truth.' This deception I've encountered, much like a meticulously crafted piece of art, has laid bare a truth I was unprepared to face. It's a stark reminder that even those of us who devote our lives to beauty and authenticity can be misled by artifice." Jonathan's voice was somber as he spoke, revealing his deep passion for art and his disappointment.

Sam clucked a few times and then reassured Jonathan. "Don't worry. We'll get to the bottom of this. Of course, it will be up to you to make sure it doesn't happen again."

"That's the problem, Sam. We followed all of the protocols. On the drive up here, all I could think was that this looked very much like an inside job."

"Jonathan, I don't think Jade's familiar with the steps you took to authenticate the piece. And you know our business. Our lifeblood is getting things right. Given its history, especially being confiscated during the war, how were you convinced of its authenticity?"

"As usual, we took a multifaceted approach. Initially, we placed significant trust in the provenance documents supplied by the seller. They appeared comprehensive, detailing the brooch's journey through various hands post-war. Additionally, we also depended on the expertise of a jewelry historian familiar with that era's craftsmanship. And, of course, we compared the piece against known photographs."

"That seems very thorough," I said. "You said you thought this might have been an inside job?"

He pushed up his tortoise-shell glasses and let out a long sigh. "Young lady, I've spent my life making career-focused choices. Those choices have led me to the pinnacle of my profession. They have also forced me to make personal sacrifices that included spending less time with my late wife and postponing starting a family. At times like this, I truly understand how Van Gogh felt."

When I didn't react, he let out another deep sigh. "Vincent van Gogh once wrote, 'I feel that there is nothing more truly artistic than to love people.' In moments like these, when the silence of my own company becomes deafening, I'm reminded of the artistry in connections—in the simple act of loving and being loved. In these times of solitude, I understand Van Gogh's yearning and relentless pursuit of connection through his art. And yet, I work daily surrounded by masterpieces but devoid of the very connections that breathe life into them."

The man still hadn't answered my question, but I now knew a little more about fine art. And Van Gogh. I guess that was some consolation. I still wanted an answer, but at the same time, his words resonated deep inside me. Perhaps that was the reason I'd had such a strong reaction after my dinner with Ethan. I thought I'd found that connection, but then discovered it might not be real. "I get it, Mr. Prescott."

"Jonathan, please. We're all working together here."

"Okay, Jonathan, can we go through the steps? Maybe try to figure out where that internal breakdown took place?"

"Of course. We knew there were inherent risks, given the brooch's value and historical significance. It appears we might have been too reliant on the documentation, which, in retrospect, could have been part of an elaborate forgery."

"Who was the seller?"

"It supposedly came from the estate sale of a Swiss banker who passed about five years ago. His name was Lukas Müller."

"Scamming a museum requires extensive planning," Sam said. "It could mean you were targeted deliberately. How did you hear about the estate sale, Jonathan?"

"The museum has an ongoing Holocaust display. We're well known amongst the dealers we work with. One of them called me and said he'd been contacted by a provenance researcher he knew and was asked to broker the sale of Herr Müller's collection. He said that when he learned A Mermaid's Allure was part of the collection, he immediately thought of us. The piece fit well with the others in our display, so I told him I might be interested. Everything appeared above board. I knew the provenance researcher from previous transactions."

"Who was the broker?" I asked.

"Benji Thompson. We'd also worked together before. It seemed like a safe and easy acquisition."

"Wait! Benji was the dealer who brokered the sale of the fake to your museum?"

"Yes. He was. And now, he's dead, and I might lose my job."

And I had tons of questions, including, what else had Benji been involved in?

Chapter 15

THEY SAY THAT A PICTURE is worth a thousand words. But sometimes, that same idea applies to a look. After the question of Benji's honesty surfaced in my mind, Sam and I exchanged one of those looks that was charged with unspoken understanding and depth. She, too, was undoubtedly wondering about the man we'd known as a friendly art dealer. If there was one thing I was learning about Benji Thompson, it was that he'd had his fingers in many different pies. I found it hard to believe that a man who'd seemed so kind and honest had also been a crook.

"So Benji trafficked in fake art? I never realized how good of a conman he was." I said.

"Who did the provenance, Jonathan?" Sam asked.

"A woman in Berlin. Her name is Michelle Wolfe. She used to work for a large auction house before she went out on her own. That was about ten years ago. I worked with her before she went independent. She was quite good and, I thought, above any type of criminal activity." Jonathan reached into his jacket pocket and pulled out an envelope. He gripped it tightly as if he were reluctant to let the contents out of his sight.

"Is that the letter of provenance?"

"The original, as you asked."

"Good." Sam raised her eyebrows and reached for the envelope Jonathan still clutched. It almost looked like they would have a tug-of-war over it until Sam asked, "May I?"

Jonathan pulled his hand back slightly. "Leonardo da Vinci said, 'Details make perfection, and perfection is not a detail.'"

Oh, brother. This guy loved to quote dead artists, didn't he? I didn't think I could put up with him all day, but his quotes didn't seem to bother Sam.

"Jonathan," Sam said patiently, "da Vinci understood the importance of every stroke in a painting and every observation in science. As do you and I. I agree that it's important to maintain the integrity of this evidence."

"Sam, handing it over without ensuring it's properly preserved could be akin to altering a masterpiece. Once the original state is compromised, its true value and meaning might never be fully recovered or understood."

"You know me, Jonathan. I'm not about to break the chain of evidence. I'll document everything, just as I normally would. I'll give you a receipt for it, of course. But if you're not comfortable having me look into this for you, that's okay. You also know that trying to investigate this kind of fraud, which probably began with that document, requires the originals. Otherwise, you're asking me to authenticate the Mona Lisa from a photograph."

I groaned because this was like a verbal duel between two art geeks. Next thing you know, they'd bring out their paintbrushes for a battle royale. I cleared my throat. "Jonathan, are you thinking Ms. Wolfe was working with Benji to sell the museum the fake?"

Jonathan didn't answer, but Sam did. "It's the most likely scenario."

Sam turned back to Jonathan and raised her eyebrows. Reluctantly, Jonathan handed her the original. Sam then faced me. It was time to decide. Jonathan had just committed completely to having Sam help. Was I about to do the same?

"Did you bring the original cryptogram?"

"I did."

If Sam was legit, this was the best thing I could possibly do. If she was crooked, Jonathan and I had both just handed her a golden ticket to freedom. I pulled the envelope from my purse and handed it to her.

While Sam looked over the cryptogram and the letter of provenance, I drummed my fingers on the tabletop. The gloves she wore suddenly made sense. She was leaving no trace that she'd touched those documents. Smart.

If Ms. Wolfe had been here in the US, finding information about a possible criminal record would have been easy. But in Europe? Where would I even begin? "Sam, is there a way to verify the credentials of this woman? Maybe see if there are any complaints about her work?"

"Sure. I'll look into her educational background. Look for degrees and specialized training, but I'm guessing Jonathan's already done that. Right?"

"Of course. It was part of my initial evaluation. She has degrees in both fine art and contemporary art practice from Harvard University. Her education is above reproach."

Sam skimmed the letter of provenance again, her lips barely twitching as if daring it to surprise her. "I'm probably rehashing Jonathan's work, but I'll also check for references, publications, and professional affiliations. I'm not hopeful. I'm sure they will look perfect."

"They will," Jonathan said. "As I told you, I checked her out thoroughly."

He started to go on, but Sam cut him off. "Which means that I need to go deeper. That includes looking for the things we don't normally look for."

I chuckled. "You're going to the dark side."

"I do have another persona," Sam admitted with a slight smile. "I also have a brother-in-law who's one heck of a hacker. If I can't find the dirt on her, I'll bet he can."

Jonathan had started looking extremely uncomfortable as soon as talk of the dark web and hacking started. He probably wanted to keep this whole investigation at arm's length. My suspicions were confirmed when he opened his mouth. "Is there anything else you need me for? I've scheduled an emergency meeting with my board for this evening, and I really must get going."

While I found this kind of investigation fascinating, I supposed that in Jonathan's line of work, even the possibility of being associated with 'that kind of thing' might damage his career. We said our goodbyes, and Sam promised to keep him updated. When he was gone, I asked her what was next.

"You'll need to let me handle this side of things," Sam said. "Sorry, Jade, but I don't want any witnesses to what I'm about to do. Besides, if this blows up, you don't want to be part of it. By leaving now, you'll have plausible deniability."

As much as I hated to admit it, she was right. But then again, in my line of work, it could sometimes be helpful to step outside the box. And if I could learn some of her tricks, it might help me in future cases. "Sam, I'm a professional investigator. To find the truth, I sometimes need to do things that fall into the big gray area we all like to avoid. How about you let me stick around? You might teach me a few tricks."

The dark blue in Sam's eyes hardened. The corners of her lips, which almost always curved up into the hint of a welcoming smile, turned down. "Sorry, Jade, but I've spent years building that alternate presence. I sometimes have to give out a little professional advice to newbies to keep my reputation."

I brushed a stray strand of hair behind my right ear, partly to move it away from my face but even more to allow me time to process Sam's revelation. "You're a consultant to wannabe art thieves?"

Sam's lips turned up again, and her laugh took me by surprise. "Don't worry, I never give them anything valuable. They could find anything I give them elsewhere if they were willing to do a little digging. Most of them are too lazy and will only get themselves in trouble. It's amazing how many people think they want to be big-time criminals and don't realize how easy it is to get caught if you don't know what you're doing."

I supposed that was some consolation, but I now understood Jonathan's reluctance to stick around. "Is that why Jonathan left? Because he knows what you're doing is illegal?"

"That's the thing. I don't cross that line. Or, at least, I try not to. But just in case, you don't want to be near this. Now, before you go, let's look at the letter of provenance. It may provide us with some clues." She handed me a pair of gloves. "Put those on. I don't want you contaminating the evidence."

"Got it. Leave no trace. Look at us. Pulling tricks from the same investigative toolbox."

"Don't get too cocky, Jade. This is very serious business."

I didn't bother with a retort. I knew all too well how serious my job could get. After pulling on the gloves, I turned to Sam, trying to keep my tone neutral. "I'm curious. You've made it clear that you're walking a fine line when you help some of these people. But tell me, does helping them ever bother you?"

Sam paused, her focus momentarily drifting away from the letter of provenance to meet mine. "Jade, every job has its gray areas. Yes, I hover in them more than most. But think about it—the art world is no stranger to controversy. My role, as peculiar as it sounds, ensures that some semblance of balance is maintained. As Jonathan pointed out, details are critical. And my job sometimes makes sure that the integrity of the art itself is preserved so it can eventually find its way back to its rightful owner."

I couldn't decide if her justification made her actions any less dubious. "Does that mean you help the cops, too?"

Sam chuckled, her eyes twinkling mischievously. "I'm not a snitch, but whenever they need my expertise, I don't hesitate to lend a hand."

Obviously, Sam lived and worked in a world where blacks and whites were in the minority and grays dominated. I wasn't sure I could ever fully embrace that idea, but I could certainly use her help.

"About the letter of provenance. What exactly should we be looking for? Clues that point to the brooch's last known location or something more incriminating?"

"Both," Sam replied as she led me to a magnifying lamp. "We need to establish the letter's authenticity first and foremost. Once we've done that, any detail—no matter how small—could guide us to where your brooch might be. And who knows? Maybe along the way, we uncover something unexpected." Her voice trailed off, suggesting mysteries yet to be unveiled.

Sam pointed to the first paragraph. "The person who wrote this obviously knew what they were doing. They gave us the who, what, why, and when and a classification into the Art Deco period in one short paragraph."

This document serves as the official letter of provenance for "A Mermaid's Allure," an exquisite, beguiling brooch crafted in the year 1927 for Simone Dubois. This piece clearly illustrates the unparalleled elegance and artistic innovation of the Art Deco period, embodying the era's fascination with geometric designs and luxury.

"Now, look at the photo you found," Sam continued. "Compare that to the rest of the description. See how they listed the material— sterling silver? The person who wrote this also emphasized the value of the black opals."

I read through the description. It called the brooch magnificent and described how the opals had been positioned to serve as the mermaid's eyes, inviting onlookers into a world of wonder and mystery. "This is incredible. 'The setting around these gemstones mimics the delicate features of a mermaid's face, with flowing lines that suggest her hair moving in the ocean currents and the subtle hints of scales around the edges, sparkling with smaller gemstone accents to catch the light.' Is that normal for these letters?"

"This one is more flamboyant than most," Sam said. "Look at the photo. You can see how the piece incorporates fluid lines and symmetrical patterns characteristic of the Art Deco movement."

As I followed Sam's glove over the photo, I understood why the description emphasized the movement of water around a mythical mermaid's face. I still didn't understand why Hilda hadn't given me a photo or told me how she'd been scammed, but I was beginning to get a picture of her, too. Perhaps she was simply too proud to admit a mistake or a transgression.

After the flowery language part, the description became more factual, going into some of the more mundane aspects of the brooch. It closed with a comment about the clasp mechanism having been affixed to ensure security while maintaining the piece's aesthetic integrity.

Pulling my phone from my back pocket, I snapped photos of each page of the letter.

"Just don't print those," Sam said.

"Why? You're not afraid that someone would steal a copy, are you?"

"Let's just say that there are two people I trust right now. You and Jonathan. And I'm not even one hundred percent on him."

"But he brought you the original letter. Why wouldn't you trust him?"

"I'll trust him once I examine this document for any changes. Besides, the question isn't whether he brought me the letter or not. The question is, why did he agree to do it? Was it because he wanted to help us find the original brooch? Or is he trying to cover his tracks? Trust nobody, Jade. There's a ton of money involved here. And if this brooch somehow got Benji killed…"

I finished the sentence for her. "Then whoever killed Benji might strike again."

Chapter 16

IN ADDITION TO WHAT SAM had called the flamboyant description of the brooch, the letter of provenance also detailed the owners. Everything began, of course, with Mademoiselle Simone Dubois, who had commissioned the brooch during her height as a wealthy Paris socialite. Upon her untimely death, it had been sold to Hilda's father. The brooch disappeared for several decades after that, eventually surfacing in the collection of Lukas Müller.

I felt a lump form in my throat as I imagined what it must have been like for Hilda when she'd been sent off to America. She'd been just a child and had been forced to leave behind everything she'd ever known. "It's no wonder Hilda is so strong today. How do you suppose they got her out of Austria?"

"I don't know, and I can't think about that. I have to focus on the art, Jade. Sorry, but I just can't go there." Sam shivered, then pointed at the next line in the letter. "I wonder how many hands it went through until it showed up in the estate sale of Lukas Müller."

"And that's where Benji comes into play. Maybe what I should do next is go through Benji's records. I might be able to find some connection to this Michelle Wolfe. He may have worked with her before."

Crossing her arms over her chest and leaning with her hip against the table, Sam gazed down at the letter. "This is going to take some time. If we knew what Benji's previous connection to Michelle Wolfe was, that could be a huge help. Why don't you check out that angle while I work on this?"

"We each play to our strengths?"

"Exactly."

Sam and I exchanged a fist bump. The simple ritual gave me hope that our collaboration had promise. On my way down the stairs, my phone rang. It was Gina calling. Guilt rushed through me. I tried telling myself I had nothing to feel guilty about, but the hormone rush during dinner with Ethan felt like a huge betrayal to my friend.

"Hey, Gina. What's up?"

"I wanted to ask you something." Gina's breath came in quick gasps, each word spilling out with an undeniable urgency. Not good.

"What is it, Gina?" I asked tentatively.

"Are we okay?" she asked in the high-pitched, little-girl voice she used when she was upset.

"Of course. Why wouldn't we be?"

"I talked to Zoe. She said you had dinner with Ethan."

Oh, gawd. How did I not see that one coming? Of course, Zoe blabbed. Why hadn't I warned her to keep it quiet? "It was business, Gina. That's all. We talked about his grandmother and the brooch."

"That's all? You're not interested in him?"

"No, no. Not like that." Oh, man, that sounded totally fake. "He's just a resource for finding his grandmother's brooch." Even worse.

Gina's sigh of relief came through loud and clear despite the background noise on her end. "Good. I was worried for a second there."

"Yeah, well, no need to worry. He's just a resource. That's all."

After hanging up, the guilt still lingered. Maybe it wasn't about betraying Gina's trust but more about not being honest with myself. Something about Ethan made my heart race and my palms sweat. I pushed those thoughts aside and focused on the task at hand—finding Hilda's missing brooch.

Rather than calling Clara to see if I could stop by, I drove home. With guilt closing in around me like a suffocating blanket, I needed someone to serve as my sounding board. Sam's comment about only having two people she could trust suddenly hit me. Did she not have family she could talk to? Thank God for Mom and Dad. At times like this, they were my lifeline to sanity. They probably would be until I could come clean with Gina about my dinner with Ethan.

As I drove, the memories of that dinner came flooding back into the soundtrack playing in my head. The way he looked at me with those intense blue eyes, the sound of his melodic voice as he talked about his grandmother's brooch. There was something about him that drew me in despite my best efforts to keep things strictly professional.

When I got home, I found Mom in the kitchen. She took one look at me and picked up her phone. "I'm texting your dad. He's out in the garage." She laid down the phone and pulled me into a hug. As her hand rubbed my back, I felt like I was seven all over again and had had a bad day at school. With Mom hovering, sharing what I found in the files with Dad was not an option, effectively squashing any plans to discuss the case.

I was pulling away from Mom when Dad came into the room. "Uh oh. Jo, I think we're going to need some of those chocolate chip cookies you made."

Mom quirked her cheek at my dad. "Thomas, don't be using your daughter as an excuse."

I sniffled and rubbed my cheeks. "You made chocolate chip cookies? This morning?"

With a roll of her eyes, Mom turned away and huffed. "Fine. Your dad's probably right. These will make you feel better."

"Way better than a half gallon of ice cream," I laughed.

Mom pulled the cookie jar from the countertop and opened it. She held it out for me. I grabbed two. It might be early morning, but if I was getting sympathy cookies, I was going to make the most of it.

Dad tried to take three, but Mom slapped his hand. "You know your limit, Thomas."

"One more than Jade gets," he said confidently.

"Wrong." Mom pulled the jar away. "Two. That's it." She took one for herself. "Now, Jade, what's wrong?"

I bit through the crunchy crust. The chewy texture of the inside, along with the soft chocolate chips, melted in my mouth. "Mmmm. These are delicious."

Dad winked at me as he took a bite of his. "I taught you well."

Mom made tea, and then we sat at the kitchen table, talking and savoring the snack as I told them all about Ethan. From the guilt of keeping my dinner with Ethan a secret to the overwhelming feelings that seemed to be growing every time I saw him.

"Follow your heart, Jade," Mom said. "Just make sure you're honest with yourself and those around you."

Dad agreed, then said, "Think about Gina's background, honey. She had a privileged childhood. She married a man she thought was her soulmate, then discovered he was defrauding her."

"Your point, Thomas?" Mom huffed.

I remembered the first time I'd met Gina. How I'd fangirled over her presence in my office. How gorgeous she was. And when reality eventually set in, I saw a different Gina. One much more broken than I'd ever imagined.

"Actually, I think I get it, Mom. Gina's not really prepared for emotional attachments. She tends to think she's falling in love with every guy she meets. She sets herself up for failure in her relationships because she can't see past the surface. And I'm not sure it's healthy being around someone like that."

"My point, exactly," Dad said, then gave Mom a mock sneer.

I could only hope I ended up with a love like theirs. Something that would stand the test of time and any challenges that came along. Whether that would be with Ethan, I didn't know. What I did know for sure was that the weight of guilt was lifting from my shoulders. My parents had once again helped right the ship, as a sailor might say. They'd helped me through my breakup with Jason, and they'd probably have to help me again.

"Thanks, guys," I said, feeling better.

"Don't forget who you can always count on," Mom said, giving me a knowing smile.

I nodded and hugged her tightly. "Love you both."

By the time I left, I'd added three items to my list of "things I knew for sure." One, steer clear of Gina, at least until the smoke cleared on this case. Two, get into Benji's business records. And third, whether I wanted this one or not, I would avoid Ethan Harper. The guy was not only bad for my clarity of mind but also might be part of whatever conspiracy I'd stumbled into.

Chapter 17

AFTER LEAVING HOME, I SWUNG by to check on Clara. Although it was midmorning and the clouds had burned off, lights glowed from behind the off-white curtains. I pushed through the pristine white picket fence gate, admiring the classic charm of the home. The well-manicured front yard, with its carefully tended array of shrubs and flowering plants, showed tremendous homeowner pride and attention to detail. Once again, I wondered if this was the home of a kindly shop owner or a criminal mastermind. Not to be crass, but I was dying to know.

Halfway up the walk, my phone rang. Dad. Wonderful. As long as Mom wasn't standing next to him, I could ask about the files. The fact that he was calling right after I'd left the house did have me curious, though. "Hey, Dad, what's up?"

"Jade, I didn't want to say anything while your mother was around, but I'm worried about you investigating Benji's death, it could be dangerous. You should turn this over to the police."

"That's not my case, Dad. I'm looking into his business dealings for Clara."

"Really? Because from where I stand, the two look remarkably similar."

I turned so my back was to the house and kept my voice low. Parental concern was one thing, but trying to keep me from doing my job was another. "You know I can't back off. Clara hired me to do a job. That's what I'm going to do. Besides, you never backed off of a case when you ran the agency."

"That was different."

"Really? How?" I demanded.

"Well, it just was."

I reminded myself that he was calling only because he cared. A confusing mix of determination and doubt churned within me. The weight of his concern clashed violently with my unwavering resolve to get to the truth. "Dad, I appreciate your concern, but I'll be careful. I promise."

I heard him blow out a long breath. I could almost see him standing there in the garage, the one place he knew my mom wouldn't interrupt him, running one hand through his hair, trying to decide whether or not to push the issue. He'd always been good at that, weighing both sides of an argument. He must have been very worried for him to make this call. Or something else was going on.

"Did Mom make you call me?" I demanded.

"She's just worried. You know how it is."

And there it was, Mom's fingerprints all over my life again. "You know I can't let this go, Dad. You trained me to always find the truth."

He hesitated a long time before finally saying, "All right. But be careful. And keep me updated."

I crossed my fingers, forced a smile to brighten my voice, and said, "I will. But now, I have a question for you. When we talked about Benji, you led me to believe you were working with Leo Baxter. You never told me that you were hired by Hilda Bauer."

"Oh. Did I not mention that?"

"Please don't patronize me, Dad. Why did Hilda hire you to investigate Benji? Why didn't you tell me?"

"The truth is that Mrs. Bauer wasn't that great of a client. She had money, but when I presented her with an invoice, she became a different person. I didn't know if she was still the same, and I didn't want to influence who you worked for."

Oddly enough, the explanation made sense. It wasn't like he'd tried to destroy the files or anything. "So you didn't want to sour my relationship with Mrs. Bauer? That's why you didn't say anything?"

"Exactly. And before you have to ask, that photo you found did not come from Hilda Bauer. Leo got that. And he never would reveal his source."

"What? Leo had the photo? How?"

"He would never say."

"Did you show that photo to Hilda?"

"Nope. After she terminated our agreement, I saw no reason to go back to her."

"So she doesn't know about it."

Dad hesitated, but when he spoke, I could sense the resolve in his voice. "No. And I don't think you should show it to her. That's just my personal opinion."

Holy cow. Now, I was being warned about my own client. "This isn't like you, Dad. What are you not telling me?"

"Mrs. Bauer never paid my invoice. She stiffed me for half a week's worth of work. In the end, I decided to walk away rather than get into a mudslinging contest with a client."

The woman who had handed me a $10,000 check before we had a contract hadn't paid my dad's invoice? What else wasn't Dad saying? "Is there anything else I should know?"

"Not that I can think of. But I promise that if you have other questions, I won't hold back. I'm sorry I did."

As I hung up the phone, I couldn't help but feel a sense of guilt wash over me. My parents had always been my biggest supporters, and here I was, challenging my dad and treating him like an adversary. I would have loved to have taken him at his word, but I also kept hearing another voice, the one who had pounded the trust but verify mantra into me. Sorry, Dad, but I think I've got to make sure you're not holding back on me.

But what if he wasn't the one holding back? What if it was me? Was I lying to myself about Clara's case? If I found Benji's business partner—assuming he was involved in something illegal—I would probably find his killer.

Turning around, I went up the stairs and knocked on the door. It took Clara less than a minute to answer, but that minute felt like a lifetime. So many thoughts raced through my head as I waited. Now, on top of needing to decode a secret message to find Hilda's brooch, Clara was asking me to look into Benji's business. I was becoming convinced that was simply code for finding Benji's killer. Somehow, I managed to put on a smile just as Clara opened the door.

My heart broke at the sight of Clara's anguish. She'd obviously been crying. Her face was a poignant canvas of raw emotion and vulnerability. Her eyes were glazed with the sheen of tears, and there was the faintest smudge of mascara on her flushed cheeks. Her eyebrows lifted when she saw me. "Jade. You're back."

"Is this a bad time, Clara?" Of course, it was. They would all be bad times for a while.

"No, no. It's fine," she croaked.

"I brought the agreement. Would you like to look it over?"

A shrug. She held out her hand. I gave her the document and asked if she wanted a few minutes before she signed.

"I guess. Would you like to look at Benji's office while I do that?"

"If it's okay."

Her mouth quivered, probably from the aftershocks of sobbing. Her lips parted slightly as if the words she intended to say had considered emerging but thought better of it. She stepped aside to let me enter.

Clara closed the door when I was inside, then gestured down the hall. "You know where it is," she whispered.

Actually, I didn't, but the snoop in me liked the idea of roaming freely. I assured Clara I would be fine, and then I reached out and pulled her into an embrace. She let me pull her close, and I waited until she backed away to release my hold.

"Thanks," she said, the corners of her mouth curling up into the semblance of a smile. But the smile didn't reach her eyes and seemed to require more energy than she could muster.

"My mom always says hugs fix everything."

The smile grew, and Clara nodded. "She's a smart woman. Let me know if you need anything."

The first room I passed was a guest bedroom. The second looked like an office, and the third was the master bedroom. A photo album lay open on the bed. My breath hitched at the thought of being able to sneak a peek at it. I slipped into the master to check out the album, my hand twitching with anticipation.

Chapter 18

THE FIRST PHOTO IN THE album was of Benji and Clara, who looked like they were in Hawaii. They both wore flowered leis, and Benji wore a tropical-print shirt that matched Clara's dress. I'd heard about those matching aloha outfits. Although I had a job to do and a purpose for being here, I became entranced by the photos.

As I flipped through the old album, a loose photo fell out. Unlike the others, it hadn't been put into a sleeve. A vibrant snapshot, it looked like it had been taken in the late 80s or early 90s. It was completely different from anything else I'd seen. In it, a much younger version of Clara stood confidently in neon-colored spandex workout gear, the bright hues of pink, green, and yellow clashing in a delightfully retro way. Her tight, curly perm added an extra layer of volume, framing her face with bouncy curls. She'd struck a playful pose, one hand on her hip, the other giving the camera a thumbs-up. Her expression was comically exaggerated, with wide eyes and a tongue sticking out, capturing the spirit of carefree fun. In the background, a classic boombox and a few colorful exercise mats completed the nostalgic scene. I couldn't help but burst into laughter, charmed by the sheer exuberance and boldness of the era captured in that single frame.

I don't know why I couldn't put down the album, but I took it with me to Benji's office. The room was a study in organization with everything in its place. It was so clean that any self-respecting speck of dust would be afraid to enter. It was evident that Benji took pride in his workspace. As I looked around, I couldn't help but think about Clara and the pain she must be going through.

The absence of clutter created a serene workspace conducive to concentration and creativity. The only items on the top of the desk were Benji's laptop, his phone, and an organizer with pens, notepads, and a tube of lip balm. Benji had also attached a monitor stand to the far right corner. The wires disappeared into a compact hole with a rubber grommet, then popped up at the back of the laptop. I admired the slick arrangement, which confirmed my impression that Benji had an obsession with order.

Rich, solid wood dominated the space, from the sturdy oak desk that anchored the room to the built-in bookcases that lined the walls, their shelves neatly arranged with books, periodicals, and a few tastefully chosen decorative objects. Natural light filtering through the stained glass windows complemented the wood's deep tones and cast colorful patterns on the polished hardwood floor, enhancing the room's cozy ambiance.

Clara poked her head in the door. She had our agreement in her hand, which she laid on the desk. "I signed it. I haven't had a chance— oh, my God. Where did you get that?" She pointed at the photo album.

Biting my lower lip to suppress the smile, I spun the album around so she could see the photo of her in neon spandex. "I love this photo! You looked so carefree."

Clara approached the desk slowly, unable to avert her eyes. "You...you don't think it's...embarrassing?"

"Oh, good grief, no! Photos like that are priceless. Did Benji like it?"

"It was one of his favorites. I have a confession to make. Yesterday, the reason I chased you out of here was because that photo was on Benji's desk in a frame. It's silly, but I didn't want you seeing it." She hugged her arms to her chest and avoided looking at me.

"I get it, Clara. No worries. I think it's a fabulous photo and that you should put it back in its frame and cherish it always."

She nodded, muttered a weak "I will," and then apologized for not having the list of contacts ready.

"It's okay. I know this is a tough time for you. I can try to find what I need. Don't worry about it."

After confirming that Clara had signed the contract in the right place, I also signed it and promised to send her a copy. Given the circumstances of Benji's sudden death, I waived the deposit and progress payments. After the conversation with my dad, I felt like not getting money up front was a colossal mistake. On the other hand, given Clara's state of mind, I didn't want to push her.

After a brief hesitation, Clara asked, "Can I sit in here while you work? I don't want to be alone right now."

"Take a seat and make yourself comfortable." I gestured to the plush leather chairs in front of the desk. Clara sat opposite me, almost melting into the chair. She began looking through pages of the photo album, and the weight of her troubles visibly lifted from her shoulders.

I fired up Benji's computer. The dreaded login screen came up. "Do you know Benji's password?"

"It's in the top drawer. He kept it there so I could use his computer for the banking. I never wanted a computer. They intimidate me. Most of the time, Benji wound up doing the banking anyway. I suppose I'll have to learn how to do that now."

I was struck by how familiar the scenario sounded. Mom and Dad had their domains. Mom handled all things related to food, and Dad was still searching for his passion after retiring. But at least they were both familiar with the money side of running the house, and if something happened to either of them, the other would get by.

As I entered Benji's password and logged in, I couldn't help but feel a pang of sadness for Clara. Learning to navigate personal finance accounts in a technological world would be tough. "Do you have someone who can help you figure it out?" I asked.

"Our daughter. She's a nurse. She was at the funeral, but I guess you didn't meet her. Unfortunately, she was called away because her little boy got into some trouble at school." Clara's shoulders shook with a little laugh. "Kids. They pick the darnedest times to do things."

I smiled sympathetically. "Well, if you ever need any help with anything, feel free to call me. I'm not a whiz at banking and finances, but I can always lend an ear."

"Thank you," Clara said gratefully. "It's nice to have someone who'll listen, but I've bent your ear enough. I'll let you work in peace and quiet." She stood, clutched the photo album to her chest, and left.

The first thing I checked on Benji's computer was his program for contacts. There were tons of them. Far more than I could ever justify calling. However, I still wanted to know who these people were. It took me a few minutes, but I figured out how to export all the information and email it to my address.

With the exporting of contacts completed, I looked for Michelle Wolfe. Sure enough, she was listed with a Berlin address and a telephone number. I checked the international code, confirmed that it was for Germany, and then looked up the area code. It was for Berlin. I contemplated calling but decided I didn't yet have enough to go that route. However, Sam might want this information, so I texted her with what I'd found.

As I pushed the button to send the text, a single word on Michelle Wolfe's contact card caught my eye, "Mystique." What did that mean? Was it related to something? A painting, perhaps? Or some other type of art? I sent Sam a follow-up text with those questions and suggested she see if her hacker brother-in-law could help.

Turning back to Benji's computer, I did a global search for the word Mystique, and one document came up—an obituary. I read slowly, still dumbstruck by the presence of yet another highly suspicious coincidence.

Michelle Wolfe, an art historian and provenance specialist, tragically passed away on June 16, 2022, at the age of 48, in an auto accident while touring the Alps. Born on January 5, 1974, in Boston, Massachusetts, Ms. Wolfe was deeply influenced by her father, a history professor, and her mother, an artist. She earned a Ph.D. in Art History from Harvard University and spent over a decade with a prestigious auction house in Germany, where her meticulous and ethical work earned her widespread respect.

In 2017, Ms. Wolfe founded her own consultancy, providing provenance and authentication services for high-profile clients. Her dedication to uncovering the hidden histories of artworks made her a distinguished figure in the art world. She left an indelible impression on all who met her.

Ms. Wolfe's death is a profound loss to the art community and all who knew her. She leaves behind her mother, siblings, countless friends, and colleagues. A memorial service will be held at St.

Peter's Church in Munich to celebrate her vibrant life and enduring legacy. In honor of Ms. Wolfe's memory, donations can be made to the Museum of Fine Arts, Boston.

I groaned as I finished the document, pulled out my phone, and sent Sam another text telling her not to bother asking her brother-in-law to look for Michelle Wolfe. Another door had just slammed in my face.

Chapter 19

THIS WASN'T THE FIRST TIME I'd been shut out, and it wouldn't be the last. If anything, this roadblock only fueled my resolve because I viewed challenges like this as tests. I was determined to pass this one. I did another search, this time for 'Mermaid's Allure.' Nearly a dozen documents filled the search screen. One was a spreadsheet that Benji had named 'Acquisitions.'

I opened the spreadsheet which was a list of 34 items, each on a separate row. Each row began with the piece's name and was followed by a column with a link to another document on Benji's computer. The link for A Mermaid's Allure led to a password-protected folder.

"Really, Benji?" I muttered. "Now you're password-protecting a specific folder? It must be important. I mean, like, really important. What kind of sensitive information have you got in there?" I typed in the password for the computer, but my entry was rejected.

"Oh, now you're switching it up on me, are you?" I made a face at the computer and tried again. It was always possible I'd typed a letter incorrectly, so I typed more slowly this time. I got the same result. What the heck? "There's more than one way to deal with this," I said and returned to the search results and clicked on a link in the list.

There had to be another password. Something in his desk. The top left drawer contained an envelope with my name printed on the front. The bulky envelope looked like it contained far more than just paper.

I reached for the ivory letter opener on the desk. My fingers curled around the intricately etched handle. It was truly marvelous craftsmanship. Why should I expect anything less from a fine art dealer? Picking up the envelope, I slid the letter opener under the flap and sliced it open. Inside was a single sheet of white stationery from Timeless Treasures and a small black stone about the size of a quarter. It was smooth and polished with rounded edges. A hole had been drilled through one end.

The font on the note, which had been written in blue calligraphic ink, was reminiscent of something written hundreds of years ago. But the message was as current as it could get.

Congratulations, Jade. You've found the stone. Solve the riddle to find the key.

Five lines of computer-generated text were printed beneath the note.

Born from the heart of chaos, yet smooth as evening silk,
I am a child of fury, darkness made in ilk.
Holding the night's sharp edge within my glassy sheen,
They shape me into tools, where my fractured gleams are seen.
What am I?

I practically wadded up the paper to throw it away. I had enough enigmas and mysteries to solve. I didn't need another of Benji's little games. But then I stopped and read the words again.

This message was addressed to me. And referred to a key. It must hold a clue about the cryptogram. Was that what this treasure hunt was all about? Finding the cryptogram key? Or was it about Benji's death? Or was it his password?

I folded the letter, put it back in the envelope, and stuffed it into my bag. Then, I pulled out the keyring Sam had given me and held it next to the little stone. The smaller loop was a split ring. It seemed perfectly sized to go through the hole in the stone. I pressed the split ring inwards and guided the metal ring through the hole. I'd been right. It was a perfect fit.

"Damn you and your puzzles, Benji," I muttered, then pocketed the keyring and returned to the search results. I clicked on a link in the list. The document opened immediately to a news story about the passing of Lukas Müller. The story included a commentary on his art collection, which had been quite substantial. Some of the collection was purported to have been smuggled out of Germany during the war. The article included pictures of pieces he'd owned.

I scanned the pictures, stopping when I came across the same brooch photo in my dad's files. The one he'd gotten from Leo Baxter. Was this how Leo had gotten the photo? At the end of the article, Michelle Wolfe's name was listed. Apparently, she'd been selected to establish the provenance of the jewelry in the collection.

The other documents I'd found all opened with no problems. The password-protected folder was the only one I couldn't access. Who knew how much was in that folder? With my curiosity truly running on overload, I went to the living room.

I found Clara still going through the album. She glanced up and raised her eyebrows. "Find anything?"

"Maybe. Do you know anything about a folder on Benji's computer for acquisitions?"

Clara sat motionless, fixated on the wall, the world around her seemingly fading into a soft blur. "Why would Benji do that? He always said he kept his work files at the store."

"Are you sure, Clara? I found a lot of stuff that looks work-related."

"That makes no sense. He kept information about the store's artwork and ours in an inventory management system. He always insisted it was an easy way for him to track everything he'd acquired."

Clara was missing the one big caveat in that statement. A computer program could only work with the information given, which meant the program would track everything Benji wanted it to track. Was there more? Was that what was in the password-protected folder? Somehow, I had to crack that folder's password.

I pulled the envelope with the riddle from my bag and showed the note to Clara. The way her head tilted to the side and her eyes widened as she read told me everything I needed to know. I knew there was no point in showing her the keyring. She was clueless. "It's okay, Clara. I'll figure it out."

"I've never seen that before, Jade. Honest. What was my husband up to? Why would he leave you that? What's it even mean?"

All questions I was asking myself. Including another. How in the world was I going to figure it out? After refolding the letter and putting it back in my bag, I returned to Benji's office. I spent the next thirty minutes searching for something, anything, that might shed light on my questions. I came up with nothing. Exasperated, I asked Clara when I could go to the store. She said she wasn't up to that yet and needed more time. I wasn't happy about another delay, but I also wanted to respect her feelings—so I agreed to check back with her later.

The one thing I knew for sure was that I would follow Sam's lead. I would limit what I shared to those I trusted. One would be Sam; the other would be my dad. And for now, my dad could wait. I called Sam and asked if I could stop by so we could talk. Alone.

The drive back to Art Restoration Specialists went quickly. For a change, I caught a string of green lights, and the freeway wasn't jammed. Walking into the office, the scent of the bouquet—rich and sweet—had become overpowering.

"Oh, my God, That scent is intoxicating."

"I know. It's good my boss is on vacation this week. He hates heavy scents."

"Not a guy who would want to walk through an orange grove, huh?"

Sam brushed back a lock of dark hair and laughed. "I'm sure he'd hate that. But that's not an experience most people have. I certainly never did."

I smiled as the memory came rushing back. "I was seven, and my dad took me on an interview with the owner of an orange grove. When the owner saw me, he insisted we walk through some of the rows. The memory's so vivid because it was like being in a world of green and orange with the freshest air I've ever breathed. It was incredibly quiet inside the grove, except for the voices of my dad and the owner."

"Wow. Your dad was a PI. And he took you on a case?"

I made a face to indicate it wasn't a big deal. "It was only an interview with the owner to discuss whether he wanted to hire my dad to do a background check on a possible business partner." After a short pause, I snickered. "He did take me on what he told me was a stakeout once."

"For real?" Sam's eyes widened.

"No. It was all a setup. I was five and thought my dad's job was the coolest thing ever. One night, just before bedtime, he told me he wanted me to go with him. He brought snacks and hot chocolate, and we watched some random house until I fell asleep. I was in college when my mom and dad told me the truth." I bent over the tropical bouquet. "This is a beautiful arrangement. I can't get over the scent."

"That's the Cattleya Orchid." She fingered a small card attached to the orchid and showed it to me.

The card described the orchid as the Queen of Orchids. It was a name the flower fully deserved. With its distinctive, frilled lip and contrasting colors—lavender and white mixed together—it could only be described as a stunning display.

Leaning closer, I took in the scent one last time. That's when I saw it. A small, almost imperceptible cylindrical device buried in dark green foliage. Its sleek, black exterior almost disappeared in all that dark green. But now that I'd seen it, it stood in sharp contrast to the soft hues surrounding it. Ingeniously disguised as a part of the bouquet, it was no larger than a pea, but its presence transformed my mood from almost buoyant to guarded.

I straightened up and pressed my index finger to my lips, then motioned for Sam to look deep into the bouquet. Her face twisted into a frown as she complied, and then her jaw fell, mouth hanging in disbelief.

Cocking my head, I had her follow me across the room. As we walked, I said, "You're so lucky to have a boyfriend who sends you such gorgeous flowers. He must love you very much."

Sam had a puzzled look on her face, but she played along. "I know. We've been together for a few months now."

Silently, I grabbed a notepad and wrote, *That looks like a bug. I have some equipment in my car that can help.*

I needed to buy time to retrieve my surveillance equipment. The lie I came up with wasn't great, but I hoped it sounded plausible. "Oh, I forgot to bring in the poem my boyfriend gave me." I handed the riddle to her and mouthed that I'd found it in Benji's desk. "I'll run down to my car and get that poem."

Sam cleared her throat as she read the riddle, her brow creasing with concentration. "Okay, I'll make us a couple of macchiatos," she said, sounding upbeat despite the sudden cloak-and-dagger atmosphere surrounding us.

I hated leaving Sam alone with this new worry, but if I was right and someone was listening to everything that went on in her office, it could raise suspicion if we both suddenly left. Hurrying down the stairs, I went to my car, pulled the surveillance kit from the back end, and lugged it upstairs.

In the kit, I not only had my own set of bugs but also a spectrum analyzer. It was about the size of a small tablet and weighed less than 2 pounds. I silently thanked Dad for always being one to stay up with technology.

As I closed the door behind me, I called out to Sam. "Got those coffees ready, girlfriend? I found the poem in my car." I winced at how fake the whole scenario sounded, but to my surprise, Sam played right along and set two coffees in a clear space on the closest worktable.

"We are, kind of, aren't we?" she said and gave me a hug.

I flushed and bit my lip. I hadn't really thought of us getting close, but maybe we were. At least, that's what I hoped. She was quickly turning into a trusted friend. And that meant I didn't want anything bad happening to her—especially if I was the one who caused it to happen.

Chapter 20

BASED SOLELY ON THE BUG'S size, it appeared to be state-of-the-art. There was no way to determine its sensitivity or capabilities without a make and model, but no matter how rudimentary or sophisticated it was, removing it from the bouquet to inspect it would be a dead giveaway to whoever had planted it that they'd been found out. The only option was to pretend we didn't know about it. With my instincts in high gear, I silently relocated to a spot across the room to take countermeasures.

The spectrum analyzer was compact but powerful and new enough to detect almost any nearby transmissions. I powered it on and methodically began scanning the immediate vicinity. Keeping my voice light and cheerful while I worked, I did my best to sound like Sam's newest and nosiest friend. "So tell me about your boyfriend, Sam. It sounds like he's the real deal."

Sam must have understood my signal, making little circles in the air with my free hand, because she forced a smile after sipping her macchiato. She did an admirable job of acting excited to talk about the man in her life despite the obvious angst on her face.

"His name's Isaac Johnson, and I'm telling you, he's awesome. He's an attorney. He's got a Catalina sailboat he likes to take to the Coronado Islands down in Mexico. I was super worried the first time because I'd never been on a sailboat. I thought I might get sick, but I didn't. Isaac said I have great sea legs."

I gave Sam a thumbs-up as I mentally cataloged the signals around the office. "Looks to me like you just have great legs, period."

We both laughed, and I windmilled my hand again to keep Sam talking as I moved in on the bouquet. I half-listened as she pointed at a picture of a sailboat anchored off a coastline of steep, rocky cliffs that plunged into the ocean. Sam told me Isaac's drone had taken the photo while they were having lunch. She prattled on about the secluded cove they'd visited and how they'd taken a break on a small sandy beach accessible only by boat.

While she talked, the digital display lit up with a strong RF signal from the bouquet. "Sounds awesome," I said. I looked down at my mug, which was still almost full. I think I'd taken one sip. Sam and I should plan our next move, but we couldn't do it in this room. "Hey, can I get another macchiato?"

"Sure. I'll make it for you while you tell me all about Ethan. I saw the sparks flying between you two."

I followed her to the back room, grateful for the excuse to get away from the bugged bouquet. I couldn't believe how strong the RF signal was. Fortunately, there were no signals in the back room.

After closing the door, I turned off the spectrum analyzer and considered our next steps. "Has anyone been near those flowers since I was here?"

"No." Sam gritted her teeth. "I can't believe Isaac would do this to me!"

"Isaac? What about Ethan? You said he's the one who delivered them."

Sam drew in a sharp breath, her eyes widening with disbelief as she slowly shook her head, the movement a subtle dance of frustration and resolve. "Oh, my God. He said he came out here because he wanted to talk to you. Do you think he lied to me?"

"Sure seems that way. His being here is too coincidental."

"But how would he know about the flower delivery?" Sam asked.

"Good question. I'm not sure how he'd know when the delivery was being made. Unless he's the one who placed the order—have you talked to Isaac?"

"No."

"For now, let's assume we have two suspects—Isaac and Ethan. It must be one of them because no reputable florist would put a bug in a bouquet. At least, not knowingly. At this point, I don't think we can rule out any of the possibilities."

Sam stared absently at her high-tech coffee maker, her hand poised over the start button.

"Are you okay?" I asked.

"Why would he do that?" Her voice cracked, and she brushed at her cheek with her fingers.

I pulled her into a hug. "We don't know for sure that Isaac planted the bug. Whoever it was, we'll flush them out and find out what they're up to."

"How are we going to do that?"

"We'll have to Sherlock this."

Sam's expression brightened just a smidge. "Oh? So we're calling on our deductive powers to find the rat?"

"Exactly. Are you up to calling Isaac's office?"

"I am so up for that." She pulled out her cell and placed the call.

Sam let me put my ear close to the phone so I could listen in. The answer we got didn't help Sam's mood at all. Isaac was in court and had meetings all afternoon. The receptionist didn't think he'd get any messages until almost five.

If Isaac was that busy, how had he found time to send flowers? Even more importantly, how had he had time to plant the bug? But in my head, I heard my dad's voice asking what about the other side of that coin? Many executives relied on their staff to do the more mundane tasks so they could focus on the critical items. Was Isaac that way? "Sam? Is it possible Isaac had his secretary send the flowers?"

"Maybe." She scrunched up her face. "I don't know which would be worse. The fact that he didn't send them at all or that he had her send them so they could spy on me."

"When you put it that way, Isaac doesn't sound much like good boyfriend material. Sorry."

"It's okay. I just have to accept that he's not who I thought he was."

"You deserve someone who will treat you right and respect your privacy."

Her lips curled into a fragile smile, yet her eyes glistened with unshed tears. It was clear she'd invested time and emotion into her relationship with Isaac.

"Why don't I call the florist? I might even have to go in, but I'll bet I can find out who sent the bouquet."

"I don't know which florist sent them, Jade. There was only the note and the card explaining about the orchid. I just assumed they came from Isaac."

"What? So there's no way to trace these back unless we go to Ethan and ask him what company the delivery guy worked for?" The thought of doing that after the way things had gone at dinner made my stomach clench into little knots. What if he'd been the one to plant the bug? What if he hadn't? I couldn't decide which alternative I hated more—the thought of the first man I'd been attracted to since breaking up with Jason being a crook or the idea that Sam's boyfriend was one. Either way, somebody was going to end up hurt.

Sam nodded, her eyes still filled with pain. "I guess that's our only option."

Already dreading the conversation with Ethan, I sighed. My emotions changed nothing. What I was about to do was necessary. We couldn't ignore someone eavesdropping on us. Or worse, hope it wouldn't happen again. "Unless—maybe there is another way. What if we lay a trap?"

A smile spread across Sam's lips. "More Sherlocking? I like it."

Fortunately, we determined that we didn't need to do much in the way of damage control. We were too early in the investigation to have anything concrete. The only thing of substance was that the spy knew we had Jonathan's letter of provenance.

Our next task was to brainstorm ideas on how to catch whoever was behind the bug. What we came up with was basic, but it would do the trick. Our intent wasn't to catch the culprit—all we wanted to do was identify him. And the way we intended to do that was to leave the bait in the office while we left. If I was right, whoever was behind the bug would break in while we were out in hopes of seeing what we were talking about. Once we'd identified our rat, we agreed it would be easier to control the situation.

We went back into the other room and began our little charade. While we talked about how the cryptogram might help us determine the actual location of the brooch, I extracted a miniature wireless camera from my surveillance kit and set it up so that we could have a clear view of the room. The camera had its own transmitter, but to be safe, I used a WIFI repeater to boost the signal and convert it to a format that could be sent over the Internet to my cell phone. That way, we could get away from the office, and I could watch the action without having to lug around more equipment.

"Here's my plan, Sam. Look at this." I picked up a blank piece of paper and drew a tic-tac-toe grid, then put an X in the lower-left square. "In the letter of provenance, there's this gap. See?"

I handed the pen to Sam, who drew an O in the center square. "Sure. I agree with you, Jade. That's probably the best place to start."

We continued our banter, playing out the game and making it sound like we had a solid action plan. When the tic-tac-toe game was done, I packed up my equipment. It was time for part two of the plan. "Let's go to lunch. We can leave that here and pick this up when we get back."

"Sounds like a great idea. I usually just have lunch here at my desk, but there is an awesome little sandwich place down the street that I sometimes go to. It gets busy, though, so it might take a while."

"No worries. I'll buy. It's the least I can do to thank you for finding this lead."

Sam left a decoy copy of the letter of provenance on the table, and we dropped the tic-tac-toe game in the recycle bin on our way out. Before she locked the door, I made sure my phone had a solid signal from the equipment I'd set up. On the way down the stairs, I asked Sam if the place she'd told me about was real.

"Of course, it is. I don't joke about good lunch spots. They're too hard to find. It's only two blocks. We can walk."

I checked the signal, noting that it was excellent. The repeater was working perfectly. Now, we could easily watch to see who, if anyone, showed up at Sam's office.

It didn't take long.

Chapter 21

WE WEREN'T EVEN A BLOCK away when a man wearing a loud, outdated suit and a worn fedora opened the front door. He went straight to the alarm keypad and punched in the code to disable the alarm. Sam's mouth dropped open as she watched the video on my phone.

"Who is that guy?" Sam gasped.

"I don't know, but I intend to find out."

The intruder's face was sharply defined, with a five o'clock shadow that would make any caveman proud. His suit, rumpled as it was, made him look like he'd just rolled out of bed.

"I locked the door on the way out! How'd he know the code?" Sam hissed.

"I don't know. But while he's looking around your office for this nonexistent plan, let's get some information on him. I want to see what he's driving."

We doubled back to the parking lot but stayed out of sight of the office. An old Chevy van was parked in the lot next door. I couldn't remember seeing the van when I'd scanned the area on our way down the stairs, but that meant nothing. Those nondescript white vans were everywhere. They were the standard for any business that made deliveries. Even my dad considered buying one for surveillance at one point. The presence of the van told me two things. First, our spy had to stay close to pick up the signal from the bug. Second, whoever was behind this, whether it was Ethan or Isaac, had more resources than I'd anticipated.

I took a photo of the back of the van, then we went and hid behind a large stand of bushes. If I was right, this guy knew he had limited time and would be in and out in five minutes or less. Actually, it was four minutes and thirty-two seconds.

"He's good," I whispered, almost in admiration.

Sam nudged me in the side. "But you're better. Right?"

"Absolutely." Unfortunately, the confidence in my voice was more false bravado than true confidence. The big problem was that we still didn't know who we were dealing with. "Come on. I'd love to confront this guy, but if we do that, we lose our edge. There's nothing new he's going to find, so let's go get that lunch. I'm starving."

Using the buses for cover, we circled around the van and headed off to lunch. We'd let the guy in the bad suit chill in the parking lot while we ate. At lunch, we decided the easiest way to get rid of the bug was for Sam to take it home and dispose of it. Even if whoever was spying on her was listening, when the device stopped working, our spy would probably assume it was out of range and give up. We also talked about changing the locks and the alarm code but decided it was probably a waste of money. If they'd broken in once, it would be easy to do it again. Right? Besides, changing the locks would also let the spy know we were onto him.

When we returned to the office, I again swept it for bugs while I had Sam check her wifi network admin page for unauthorized connections. The last thing we needed was for the bad-suit guy to be tapped into the network. Sam found nothing, and there were no new bugs, so I brought up my laptop and logged into the agency's database service to check vehicle registration records. The vehicle was registered to Marlough Private Investigations from Los Angeles.

"Seriously?" I said, biting back my laughter. "Is this for real?"

"What's that?" Sam asked.

Realizing that this Marlough character might be listening to us, I said, "Oh, it's just this funny cat video that Zoe showed me. It's called Space Cats: A Galactic Litter Odyssey." I quickly found the video and started playing it. "It's a sci-fi adventure featuring a crew of intrepid cats in a cardboard spaceship. Isn't it awesome how they decorated the living room with LED lights and a starry background?"

Sam looked at me like I was crazy. I pressed my finger to my lips, then scratched out a note. *Going to turn the tables on this guy.* "Keep that playing," I mouthed.

After getting a nod from Sam, I bolted out the door and scanned the parking lot for the white van. I spotted it between the trees in the next parking lot over. It was in the shade. I doubted that he could see me, so I hurried down the stairs to my car.

I retrieved my Glock and a tracking device from the back of the car. I didn't intend to use the Glock, but I wouldn't hesitate if this man turned out to be dangerous. Judging by his clothing choices and the agency name, he was some second-rate clown I could dispose of quickly. That changed everything. I fully intended to outfit his van with a GPS tracking device and send him running back to his boss before he hightailed it out of town.

I hadn't wanted to tip our hand, but with a name like Marlough Private Investigations, how could he be anything but a joke? if I could dispose of the problem easily, why not? I went around the building and past the parking lot, where our spy was probably snoozing in the van.

Again, made use of the large landscaping in this part of town to hide my approach.

From my vantage point, I could see the guy with the loud suit sitting in the front seat with the windows open. He had his head back and his eyes closed. He looked bored to tears as he listened to the final music on the cat video.

At the back of the van, I inhaled deeply and considered the legal and moral implications of attaching a GPS tracking device to a vehicle without the owner's knowledge. True, I could get in some serious trouble for this, but this guy had started things off by bugging Sam's office. I admit it was reminiscent of fourth grade when Wally Eggleston taped a 'kick me' sign on my back. My reaction this time might carry more severe consequences than a trip to the principal's office, but I told myself Wally had deserved the broken nose I'd given him. And this guy deserved to be tracked.

The other problem was that this situation could go sideways in a split second. After reminding myself one last time what a bad idea this could be, I slipped around to the driver's side and was at the door in three long steps. The guy's eyes widened as he stared down the barrel of the Glock.

He raised his hands. His voice contained just enough gravel to give him a roguish charisma that was hard to resist. "Whoa. Easy, lady."

"Who are you?" I demanded.

"Jake Marlough." He reached out as if he wanted to shake my hand. "My friends call me Slick."

"I'll call you an ambulance if you move like that again."

Marlough's cheek crooked up into a lopsided smile. "You're pretty hot. And feisty. I like that. What do you say we…"

"Put your hands on the door frame, Slick." I practically sneered the last word, and Marlough winced.

"Why did you bug my friend's office?"

"Me? I think you got the wrong guy, lady. And, while we're at it, why don't you put down the piece and tell me who you are? I won't call the cops if you don't."

"Funny you should mention that," I snapped. "Look familiar?" I pulled my phone from my pocket and played the surveillance video. He made a face as he watched himself enter the alarm code.

"That is called breaking and entering," I said. "If the police see this, you'll be arrested. Plus, the Bureau of Security and Investigative Services takes a dim view of PIs who break the law. Just in case you don't know who they are, they're the ones who could yank the PI license you probably bought online."

"My license is perfectly legit."

I ignored his indignation. I was on a roll and wasn't about to let up on Not So Slick. "And let's not ignore the fact that your client will not be happy with you, and you'll probably lose any professional credibility you currently have. Limited as it may be."

Marlough's cheeks screwed up. "Look, lady, I've worked hard to build a reputation. I get things done."

"Apparently, you don't care what those things are," I shot back.

"Hey, that's not fair. I like to see justice served. That's why I do this. I may not be the most honorable guy, but I'm pretty damned effective." He paused and gave me another roguish smile. "Excuse my French."

I had to admit Jake Marlough was certainly a charmer. He might be sleazy, but he had a way of making you want to like him. His confidence and smooth demeanor were hard to ignore. But I wasn't about to let his charm distract me from the truth—this man had broken into my friend's office.

"But what justice did you serve by committing a felony? And don't try to deny it. I've got the video of you breaking into Art Restoration Services."

With a casual laugh, Marlough gave me a nonchalant shrug. "Hey, my client only said he needed to know what your little friend up there was finding. That's all. Can I take my hands off here now?" He started to lift his palms from the doorframe.

"No!" I snapped. "Who's your client?"

"Chill, lady, no need to get all hyped. You know I can't tell you who my client is. Besides, I don't even know your name. We can't hardly be swapping secrets if we don't even know each other, right? I'm Slick."

"So you said."

He lifted his right hand about an inch from the doorframe but put it back when I motioned with the gun.

"Here's how this is going to go, Slick. You're going to tell your client you came up with nothing. You're going to tell him that Sam has run into a dead end and is going to have to give up the search because she's got paying clients that her boss wants her working for. If you don't do that, this video is going to Detective Des Martini of the Carlsbad Police. If you think I'm cold, you'd better think again. Detective Des is the Ice Queen. She wouldn't think twice about turning your charming smile into a mugshot."

Marlough's eyebrows rose, and then his right cheek curled up into a crooked smile. "You think I'm charming?"

My finger slid over the trigger.

"Okay, okay. What are you, the Queen of the 'Not Today' Club? Got it. You make my ex look like Nancy Nice. So what you want me to do is tell my client I'm off the case and walk away? Seriously?"

"Yes. Oh, and one more thing." I snapped a photo of him, making sure to get his hands on the doorframe and the look of surprise on his face. "That photo just went to my cloud account. I already have your vehicle license number and now, your photo. So if something happens to me, Detective Des will find you before you can even finish saying, 'I didn't do it.' Got it?"

Marlough let out a heavy sigh, and he nodded quickly. "You got yourself a deal, lady. So, who are you? Not many women can bust my —"

"Never mind!" I glared at him, but he didn't flinch.

"Come on. Give a poor guy a break."

His rakish grin returned and for some stupid reason I couldn't fathom, I said, "I'm Jade."

"More like, Jaded," he quipped.

An involuntary breath caught in my throat at the name my ex had used for me after I'd found him cheating on me. I lowered the gun slightly, not trusting Marlough completely. "And by the way, if I see you again, that will also cause me to send the video to the cops and let Detective Martini be the one to make you wish you'd never taken this case."

Marlough raised his palms and smirked at me playfully. "Nice meeting you, Jade. Hey, you know, you're quite a looker. You sure we couldn't—you know?"

I jerked the Glock back in Marlough's direction and snapped, "No!"

Marlough sighed and said, "Oh, well. Can't blame a guy for trying."

He started the van and drove toward the street. After he'd made a right and was caught up in traffic, I checked my phone. The tracker was working perfectly. With any luck, it wouldn't be long before I knew who Jake Marlough was working for.

Chapter 22

I SECOND-GUESSED MY DECISION to confront Jake Marlough all the way back to Art Restoration Specialists. In retrospect, gambling that he'd go straight to his boss was probably a bad bet. He could just call. Or, he might just run—assuming he was as slimy as I judged him to be. What if I was wrong? And what if his boss sent someone more competent? I told myself what was done was done as I climbed the stairs.

Still irritated with myself, I burst through the door, went to the flower arrangement, and pulled out the bug. I dropped it on the floor, smashed it with my foot, then huffed. "Take that, Slick."

Sam stood next to me, looking at the shards of plastic and shattered electronics. She crossed her arms over her chest and grinned at me. "Wow, that guy must have totally pushed your buttons."

I rolled my eyes despite the unexpected jolt of exhilaration coursing through me. "Let's just get back to work. Okay?"

"Works for me," Sam said, the hint of a smile still playing at the corners of her lips.

We turned our attention to the riddle I'd found in Benji's desk.

Born from the heart of chaos, yet smooth as evening silk,
I am a child of fury, darkness is my ilk.
Holding the night's sharp edge within my glassy sheen,

154

Crafters shape me into tools, where my fractured gleams are seen.

What am I?

Sam screwed up her cheek and threw her hands in the air after a few minutes. "Jade, I'm terrible at these stupid things."

I gaped at her. "But you do all this technical work. You solve ancient mysteries involving art. And you said you could solve the cryptogram!"

"I said I could try to solve it. That's basically a mathematical process, but I totally suck at riddles," she said flatly.

I blew out a frustrated breath. "I'm beginning to feel the same way." I reread the riddle for what felt like the fiftieth time and sighed. "Let me think about this some more. My mom's pretty good at these kinds of things. I just hate to involve her in my cases. She gets a little overprotective."

"My mom is like that, too. But if you're right and that riddle is a clue that Benji wanted you to have, then maybe you need her help. Where did you say you found that?"

"In his desk drawer. I was looking for one of Benji's passwords. Oh, my God. I'll bet this riddle will tell me what it is. Sam, I need to leave. Now that I've blown up this whole surveillance thing, do you want me to call a locksmith before I leave?"

"To be honest, I never liked the idea of not doing that."

"You're right. It was a bad idea. I've got a guy I trust. I'll call him."

I placed the call, and my locksmith friend told me he could be there in about an hour. With that handled, I headed home. Mom was sitting out on the front porch alone when I arrived. She was in her regular Adirondack chair, a tall glass of lemonade on the side table next to her.

When she saw my Prius, she waved and went inside, probably to get me a glass of my own. By the time I reached the porch, Mom had returned carrying a glass, beaded with condensation and filled with a translucent, yellow liquid.

She handed it to me, then sat and patted the chair next to hers. "Try that, honey. I'm thinking it might need a little less sugar."

All of my taste buds jumped alive when the refreshing and tangy lemonade met my tongue. "Mom, this has major pucker power. It's like summer in a glass. Where's Dad? I'm surprised he wouldn't want some."

"He's having lunch with a friend. If he were here, he'd have to have a cookie to balance out the tartness."

Mom and I laughed. That was so true. For Dad, a cookie was the perfect complement to almost any food.

I leaned back in my chair. It felt nice to take a break and relax with Mom. It was something we hadn't done in ages.

"So what brings you home in the middle of the day, honey?" Mom asked, taking a sip of her lemonade.

I told her about the riddle and that it was a clue to Benji's password.

"That's incredible! You're so smart."

"I don't know about that, Mom. I can't solve the riddle. That's why I'm here. I know you love those."

Mom's eyes lit up. "Oh, I do. honey. Let me see what you've got."

"Which? The stone or the riddle?"

"Both," she sighed.

I handed her the little black stone and the paper with the riddle. She briefly scanned the sentences and said, "Obsidian."

"How did you do that? You barely looked at the words!"

"I didn't," Mom said, holding up the small worry stone. "That's what this is." Then, she read Benji's riddle and nodded. "That's the answer to your riddle, too. It's a good description of obsidian. There's some poetic license taken, but that's the answer to your riddle. I'm positive."

"How do you know about obsidian? I've never even heard of it."

"Oh, of course you have. You studied it in fourth-grade science class. It's a type of volcanic glass. You even had a little rock collection."

"I did?" I remembered a lot from my childhood, but rock collections? No. Definitely not.

"Well, actually, your grandmother gave you the rock collection because she was convinced you would grow up to be a geologist."

"Why would she think that?" I sputtered.

"Because your grandfather had a rock collection when he was that age, and you were still kind of a tomboy. You were also really interested in the agency, and your grandmother and I wanted to discourage that. For all the good it did."

Now I got it. I remembered why that birthday had been such a flop. "It's okay, Mom. It all worked out. You said Dad's having lunch with a friend?"

"Yes…he is."

Why was Mom suddenly so guarded? Going for innocent, I asked, "Anybody I know?"

"Nobody in particular. More lemonade, honey?"

Oh, no. What was Dad doing? "Mom, is Dad interfering in my case?"

Fortunately, Mom had never been a good liar, so when she tried to be evasive, I zeroed in on the obvious.

"He is, isn't he? Who's he having lunch with?"

"Leo Baxter," she huffed. "Honestly, honey, I don't see why you're getting so worked up about this."

"Because we set boundaries, and Dad turned the business over to me. Where are they?"

That earned me another huff, but I got my answer. It was one I should have known. Dad was at a taco place downtown that he loved. After thanking Mom for her help and assuring her I'd play nice when I caught up with Dad and Leo, I left.

My dad didn't even look surprised when he saw me approach. Contrite, perhaps, but he'd obviously been expecting me. He gestured at the open chair next to him. "Lunch is on me."

"Don't think you can buy me off with a free lunch. You broke our deal, Dad."

"This is just a little research. I got curious about something and called Leo. Here's ten bucks. Go get yourself a couple of tacos, and I'll explain everything."

I placed my order, brought it back to the table, and sat. A tense silence hung over the table as we ate, but when I finished, Leo said, "I understand you've got a cryptogram you need some help with."

Seething, I glowered at my dad. "You told him about that?"

"Relax, honey. Leo does cryptograms for a hobby."

"I started studying World War II cryptography when I retired. I found it incredibly fascinating. Did you know that Polish cryptoanalysts were working on cracking Germany's Enigma machine as early as the 1930s? Show me what you've got, and I'll see what I can do."

My heart beat faster in my chest, and I felt suddenly nervous. Leo was the one who'd told me to be cautious. And now he wanted me to share information that could be central to my case? What if he had the key? "I don't have it with me," I said cooly.

"Is it back at the office? Because we could walk over there and take a look."

Leo's eagerness was making me super nervous. This was wrong on so many levels. "Leo, do you have the key for it?"

"I don't know. Maybe. I'd have to see the cryptogram to be sure."

"Dad? Did you call Leo? Or did he call you?"

My dad frowned. "What are you implying, Jade?"

"Just answer my question, please." I planted my elbows on the table and began a mental count to ten.

"I told you; I called him," Dad confessed. "I'm worried about you. This case is dangerous."

"I'm a big girl. Dad, you entrusted me with the agency. Now you need to trust that I know what I'm doing. And you, Leo. What are you trying to pull? I think you have a good idea of how much money's involved here."

"Jade, I've known your dad for decades. I've known you almost your entire life. All I'm trying to do is keep you safe. Your dad and I have dealt with these people before."

"What people?"

He groaned. So did my dad. "Your dad told you Benji wasn't always an upstanding art dealer. We believe he was involved with an art theft ring known as The Guild. These people are ruthless and will stop at nothing if they see you as a danger. Do you understand what I'm saying?"

"Perfectly. And let me make this crystal clear for both of you. I'm running this investigation. I'll use whatever resources I have available to solve my client's case." I stood and looked down at them. "And, quite honestly, I'm just as worried about having you two involved as you are about me. You're both retired. Enjoy it, and stop meddling."

I turned on my heel to leave but bumped into a homeless guy. He grunted something unintelligible before he pawed me as if he were a blind man trying to find his way out of a room, then stumbled away. Even though I felt sorry for the guy, I also felt like I needed a shower to wash off the cooties. That's totally fourth grade, but I couldn't escape the involuntary reaction.

A wave of apprehension washed over me a few steps later when I saw a white utility van exactly like Jake Marlough's. It was parked about two blocks ahead. Had I misjudged him? Maybe the guy was more dangerous than I'd realized.

I jumped when a large hand gripped my shoulder. I spun around, ready to take on whoever it was.

Chapter 23

THE GOOD THING ABOUT SELF-defense training is it not only teaches you how to fight but also increases your self-confidence and attack timing. I was thankful for that restraint because the person who grabbed my shoulder was my dad. I faced him, glad I hadn't reacted before seeing who was there.

"Whoa, Jade. Sorry. I shouldn't have surprised you like that. I also shouldn't have talked to Leo about your case without discussing it with you first."

Deep furrows puckered my dad's forehead. I could see how much I'd upset him. "Sorry, I overreacted. You were just trying to help."

Down the street, the white van pulled out. Maybe it hadn't been Marlough after all. There were hundreds of those in this area. I dismissed the van and faced my dad, wanting to reassure him that we'd get past him reaching out to Leo. What I did not want to do was tell him my concerns about Marlough. There was no need to reinforce his worry.

"You're right, Dad. You shouldn't have. When I asked you about Leo before, you told me his behavior had become erratic because of a medication he was on. Do you think it was just the medication?"

"What are you getting at, Jade?"

"Can I really, really trust him? And before you answer, consider the danger you warned me about. With all that in mind, would you trust Leo with my life?"

"I'd trust him with mine," he croaked, but then the color in his cheeks drained. His jaw tightened as he grappled with the gravity of the question. "I don't know, honey. I'd like to think so. Let's just say I would trust him if you were in mortal danger and he was there to help. But that's not the situation, is it?" He took a long, slow breath. "I'll tell him I made a mistake in reaching out to him."

"Before you do that, I have one more question. Do you really think Leo could decipher Benji's cryptogram? Be honest, Dad."

He shifted his weight from one foot to the other. Back at the table, Leo sat tossing tortilla bits to a group of pigeons who fought for a crumb. He smiled weakly and said, "I'll give him the bad news."

I hugged my dad, who awkwardly patted me on the back as we went our separate ways. I wasn't sure what to believe about Leo anymore, but I knew for certain that something was off. I checked the GPS tracker I'd put on Marlough's van. Sure enough, it was a few blocks away. So he had been here. The good news was that the van was headed for the freeway, which meant he was leaving town. For now, I put Jake Marlough out of my thoughts.

Back at the office, th door was locked, and Zoe was gone. Since she only worked part-time, we'd agreed when I hired her that she could keep her own hours. The arrangement had worked out well so far—Zoe could continue working on her journalism degree, and I had someone to handle the mundane office tasks.

I sat at my desk and considered the questions that were stacking up. Complicated seemed to be the watchword for my life lately. Hilda Bauer had asked me to find her brooch. That seemed simple enough.

But nothing else about this case had been simple. Even my connection with Ethan had been complicated by Gina's interest in him. And now I wasn't sure I could trust Ethan. Was he truly out to find the brooch because he loved his grandmother? Or was he using her and me to find the brooch and make a ton of money?

What about the letter of provenance? Was it legitimate? Had Sam even determined that yet? And what about her boyfriend? Could we trust him? Had he hired Marlough to spy on us? Or had that been Ethan? I put my hands behind my neck and paced the floor. All I could do was hold my head at the contradictions.

So many questions. This case was beginning to feel like one big riddle. I stopped pacing and grabbed my phone. This was doing me no good whatsoever. I told myself to focus. Think about what information was missing. At the top of that list was the question of access to that password-protected folder on Benji's computer. I dialed Clara's number. She answered right away and told me I could stop by.

Clara met me at the front door, greeted me with the same sadness she'd been wearing since Benji's death, and said she'd be in the dining room if I needed her. It surprised me that she wasn't interested in seeing if the password would work, but then I might do the same thing in her shoes.

I realized the fallacy in my plan as soon as my butt hit the chair—passwords were case-sensitive. What were the odds I'd get it right on the first try? I went with all lowercase—fail. The same thing happened when I tried all caps. But as I looked at the envelope with my name on it, I realized it wasn't addressed to Jade Cavendish but to JD Cavendish. On a hunch, I tried 'OBSidian' and held my breath as a little wheel spun round and round.

When the screen opened, I let out a little whoop of joy—and then my shoulders slumped. I'd been so focused on accessing these files that I hadn't thought about how to proceed once I got in. I leaned back in the chair and studied the jumble of documents on the computer desktop.

"Well, White Rabbit," I said, "begin at the beginning."

I started by checking the names of the files and folders, hoping for something obvious like my name or 'cryptogram.' No such luck. Next, I opened the Documents folder. In a folder called Acquisitions, I discovered another folder for nearly a dozen different pieces. One of those was A Mermaid's Allure.

The first file in the folder was titled Acquisition Checklist. It began with details about the brooch, including its name, description, condition, and more. There was also a section titled Interested Parties. Hilda Bauer's name was there, along with a link to a scanned copy of letter she had written to Benji. The letter was basically the same story she'd told me when we'd first met. The only difference was that she included a more detailed history than she'd given me.

Somewhat miffed that my own client hadn't given me a copy of her research, I continued on. But as I read, I noticed details in the history of ownership that differed from the letter of provenance Jonathan had given to Sam and me. Whereas Jonathan's letter of provenance stopped with the estate sale of Lukas Müller, Hilda's letter included the sale of the brooch to Valkyrie Collections. Behind the name was a note in Benji's handwriting indicating the sale had been brokered by Obsidian Collections.

The implication of those words drove a cold chill down my spine. Was Benji the dealer behind Obsidian Collections? Was that why he'd been killed? And if he had brokered the deal to this Valkyrie Collections, where was the brooch now?

"Clara!" I called out and headed to the living room.

I practically ran her down as she hurried toward Benji's office. "What's wrong? Did something happen?"

Ignoring her questions, I responded with one of my own. "What do you know about Benji's acquisitions?"

"I know about our personal ones. But there were times when he'd say what he was working on at work was too complex, and I wouldn't understand. That was when I thought he considered me a complete idiot. It was infuriating."

"Did you ever tell him that?"

"I tried. Once."

"What happened?"

"Benji hardly ever got angry with me, but he did that day. He was furious and told me there were things I wouldn't understand." With a subtle shake of her head, she focused on an unseen point across the room. "I never tried again. It wasn't worth the argument."

"I think I understand what he was saying, and it's not that he thought you were stupid. In fact, it might be exactly the opposite. Are you familiar with a letter of provenance?"

"Of course. We have those for all of our artwork."

"Good. Come with me."

We returned to Benji's office and I showed her the letter from Hilda. Pointing at the screen, I said, "That transaction in 2012 is not on the official letter of provenance for A Mermaid's Allure."

"Was the letter of provenance produced by a reputable source?" Clara asked.

"Until I found this, I thought it was. Now, I'm not so sure. What about that name? Have you ever heard of Obsidian Collections?"

Clara shook her head and made a face. "No. Who is it?"

"What about Valkyrie Collections?"

"Jade, I have no idea what you're talking about. Are these art dealers?"

I showed her the list of passwords I'd tried. "I think he brokered a deal in 2012 for Mrs. Bauer's brooch."

The color in her cheeks, which were already sallow from days of grieving, seemed to pale further. "What in the world was my husband into?"

"I don't know, Clara, but I can assure you I intend to uncover the truth. I'll have to ask my art restoration specialist if she has any suggestions on how to identify this Valkyrie."

Clara frowned, and as she did, she rubbed her temple with her fingers. "I don't know if it's of any help, but Valkyries were powerful female warriors who served the Norse God Odin. They were tasked with choosing who lived and died in battle and then escorting the slain to Valhalla."

I paused for a second to comprehend what she'd said. To be fair, I wasn't exactly expecting a history lesson right now. "Just curious, but how do you know that?"

"Benji and I traveled extensively over the years. We took a trip in 2012 and spent nearly three weeks exploring Norway, Sweden, and Denmark. Near the end, Benji added a stop in Switzerland. He said he had to attend a last-minute art auction while we were there. What was odd was that he refused to let me go with him. He said it was going to be very boring and he wanted me to do something fun. I spent the day going to museums and galleries, but Benji seemed distracted for the rest of the trip."

"That is interesting," I said, making a mental note of it. "I'm pretty sure Benji was somehow involved with Obsidian Collections. He had to know who this Valkyrie was. Clara? Did you meet anyone while you were on that trip?"

Clara nodded absently. "Benji did. He was working, so he had several meetings while we were gone."

"Did he attend any other auctions during the trip?"

"No. Only the one."

My breath quickened as my mind began spinning theories. The one that dominated everything was enough to make my stomach churn with a clay-like heaviness. Was this some sort of conspiracy? I swallowed hard.

"When I met Hilda, she and her grandson handed me a cryptogram they said Benji wanted me to solve. Then, the way I got to the password was through Benji's riddle. Now, this strange name. If Benji brokered a deal for this Valkyrie, they must have been working together."

"Oh, my God," Clara said. "I'll be right back."

She stood, left the room, and returned a few minutes later carrying a photo album. She began thumbing through pages. It seemed like an odd time to be searching for a photograph, so I asked what she was looking for.

"That." She jabbed her finger at a photo of her and Benji standing next to a painting of a beautiful woman sitting on what looked like a castle. A soft light shined down on her from above. "That painting is called 'The Valkyrie's Vigil.' It was at an exhibit Benji insisted we see while we were on the trip. He said he was taking the photo for an associate."

"Valkyrie," I said softly. If my dad was right and Benji had been a member of The Guild, I now knew the name of a second member. Which led me to another, even bigger question—was Valkyrie the person who had hired that ridiculous Jake Marlough character? Great. All I had to do now was accomplish the impossible—find out Valkyrie's true identity.

Chapter 24

I STOOD OUTSIDE THE FRONT door of Anchor & Ale. My head was still spinning. According to the tracker I'd planted on Jake Marlough's van, he had never left town but had come here about half an hour ago. That could only mean one thing—Ethan had hired Marlough to spy on Sam and me. By extension, did that also mean Ethan had murdered Benji? Was that how he'd gotten the cryptogram? And he was now using me to solve it? My gut twisted at the mere thought.

The bar's interior was a harmonious blend of rustic charm and nautical elegance. Ethan was right when he'd described it as maritime heritage meets cozy pub. Why did he have to be the one who'd hired Marlough?

The polished wood bar gleamed from the soft, ambient lighting overhead. Behind the bar, exposed brick walls glowed from the recessed spotlights in the ceiling. Ethan stood, talking to a man who sat at the bar, a half-eaten sandwich of some sort on his plate.

Ethan looked to see who had entered, and his face lit up. "Jade! Welcome to my world." He spread his hands wide, then motioned at one of the barstools.

The sinking feeling in my gut deepened with every step I took. I couldn't believe this man I'd fallen for had betrayed me. Then again, so had my ex. Maybe I was destined to always choose the loser.

"What's the matter, Jade? You look like something's bothering you."

"Where's Marlough? Why'd you hire him?" I blurted.

The shock on Ethan's face gave way to a broad smile. "No way. Slick and I go back a ways, but he's not working for me. Wait a second. Did you think I hired him to background check you or something?"

"Don't lie to me, Ethan. I know he's here. And I know he was hired to spy on Sam and me. He didn't name names, but his van is parked about a block away. The game's up. I busted his little spy scheme. Where is he?"

Ethan blinked, then shook his head. "What do you mean, his little spy scheme?"

"Oh, please. I found the bug in the bouquet that you delivered. Are you going to tell me the florist was spying on us? Give me more credit than that."

The more I talked, the angrier I became. The fact that Ethan wouldn't fess up to what he'd done was beginning to irk me—and convince me he had murdered Benji. I also knew that if I didn't get my temper under control—if I didn't stop feeling so hurt because I'd trusted this guy—I'd say something I'd regret. But with the pain of betrayal burning inside me, I wasn't sure I even cared about that.

Planting his palms on the bar's dark wood, any warmth or color in Ethan's face drained away, leaving a stark, unyielding mask. "I see. I guess it doesn't matter much what I say. You've already made up your mind."

My insides still trembled from the anger burning inside me. I shot back a terse, "Fine. You want to explain? Explain."

"That's okay. I think you've made yourself clear." He picked up a white towel from behind the bar and absently polished the already gleaming wood. "Anything else, Jade?"

Seeing his reaction—the hurt in his eyes—the chill of misgiving almost made me shiver. Could I have been wrong? I steeled myself against the feeling. I'd been fooled by my ex one too many times to back down now. I'd started this case telling myself to avoid an emotional connection to Ethan and had ignored my own advice. Now, I was relegating him to the source or suspect pool. Either way, I still needed information from him.

"You claim that Marlough isn't working for you. Then why was he here?"

"Slick and I have known each other for years. He came in for lunch yesterday because he was in the area."

"I don't care where he had lunch yesterday. Why is his van parked down the street?"

"Now?" Ethan asked, then shook his head. "No idea."

"Why was he in the parking lot outside Sam's work this morning?"

"Don't know."

"If he's not working for you, who is he working for?"

"No clue."

"Did he say anything about your grandmother's brooch?"

"No."

Terrific. I'd totally burned this bridge. I could kick myself or, at least, my emotions. "How's your grandmother?"

Ethan stopped wiping the bar and grimaced. It was like a shadow crossed his face, and he suddenly regretted his part in this whole interaction. "She's doing well. She asked me to follow-up with you about the cryptogram."

"We're making progress," I said, trying to sound noncommittal. If Ethan was behind the bug, he already knew that. How could I have been so blind? What if he wasn't? "What we need to solve it is the key. Did Benji say anything that would help me to find it?"

"No. Like I told you when we first gave you the cryptogram, he was confident you could handle this."

I was glad someone had faith in me because right now, it felt like I was burning bridges faster than I could build them. The frustration of working on two separate cases and making zero progress on either of them was getting to me. My only hope was that Benji had been a member of The Guild and that something would break soon. I was feeling like I was trapped in a massive spider web of lies and deceit.

"He didn't give you anything else? Just the envelope with the cryptogram?"

Ethan frowned, then reached behind the bar to pluck a pen from the dozen or so in a beer mug on the countertop. "He gave me this. He said he'd just bought them."

Oh, my God. I had exactly the same pen back at the office. It was just lying in my desk drawer with a bunch of others. Benji had given it to me a couple of weeks ago. "Huh. Can I see that?"

He handed me the pen and watched closely as I unscrewed the top and bottom of the barrel and pulled them apart, half expecting a secret message hidden inside. My anticipation turned to disappointment when the only thing I found was a refillable cartridge.

"Oh, that's brilliant," Ethan said, his crooked smile returning. The hurt I'd seen moments before was still there, but at least now, there was also a sign of interest. "Classic spycraft. Hide the clue in an everyday item you can pass off without raising suspicion. You know, he gave my grandmother the same kind of pen. Maybe we should talk to her."

Once again, Ethan had surprised me. He'd dropped the information about spycraft without batting an eye. How had he known that? Not wanting to let on that I had mentally moved him back onto my list of what Leo would call unsavory characters, I returned the pen. "It's worth a shot. For now, I should get going. I have some other leads to run down. Catch up with you later about talking to your grandmother?"

"Sure." His smile fell, and he sighed as I stood. The customer at the end of the bar held up his hand. Ethan nodded and flashed him a thumbs-up. "I'd better deal with my customer. I'll see you. Oh, and one more thing. Jake is very, very good at what he does. Don't let his looks deceive you." He turned to his customer and smiled. "All done?"

I closed my eyes and hesitated when I pushed open the front door. Conflicted was only the beginning of how I felt about trusting Ethan—both emotionally and professionally. I needed time to think. To sort things out. Taking a deep breath, I pushed down the emotions raging inside and headed back to my office. Before I did anything else, I'd check out the pen Benji had given me.

I knew from experience that the only way out of a tangled web was to keep following each thread until the truth surfaced. I sat at my desk and pulled out Benji's pen. This time, when I unscrewed the two halves of the barrel, I discovered a small slip of paper rolled around the ink cartridge. My fingers quivered as I unrolled it. The paper contained only one word—must.

Why in the world would Benji put paper inside a pen? Ethan's comment about classic spycraft came back to me. Maybe Benji had written more on that paper than just a single word. I thought about all the subterfuge Sam and I had discussed. Could Benji have been passing me a secret message? The best person to help me figure it out, and the only one I trusted, was Sam.

Returning the paper to where I'd found it, I called Sam to confirm that she was still in the office. When she said she was, I told her I'd be there in twenty minutes. With Ethan's caution about Marlough running through my head, I suddenly wondered if our conversation was really private. Now, I had something else to worry about. Maybe I'd underestimated both Ethan Harper and Jake Marlough.

Chapter 25

I CHECKED MARLOUGH'S LOCATION AGAIN and saw that the van hadn't moved. It was still about a block from Anchor & Ale. If Marlough was still parked near the bar but wasn't with Ethan, he must be somewhere in the neighborhood. But where?

The truth was, I didn't know. Even worse, when I thought about the confrontation with Ethan and how he'd reacted to my accusations, I realized that his indignation had been real and my behavior completely out of line. In his shoes, I'd have reacted the same way. Maybe even with less restraint. I'd probably blown any chance at a relationship with him. After asking myself how I could have been so wrong about the guy around 20 times, I called Hilda. She answered, sounding excited to hear from me.

"Have you learned anything yet, my dear?"

"I'm making some progress. I still haven't deciphered the cryptogram, but I might know where the key is. Hilda, did Benji give you a pen?"

The line was deathly quiet for a few seconds, then she said, "Yes. He did. It was a cheap commercial advertisement, but it writes nicely."

"Do you still have it?"

"I do. It's in my desk drawer. Why do you ask?"

"I think that might contain a key to the cryptogram. Would you do me a favor?"

"Of course, dear. What do you need?"

"Unscrew the barrel and open it up."

"It's in my office," she said. "Hold on while I go there." A short while later, she gasped. "Oh my. There's a piece of notepaper inside. It has a word written on it—Guild. What does it mean?"

"I hope it means I'm getting closer to finding your brooch." Recalling Sam's insistence on having the original cryptogram, I added, "Give me your address so I can stop by and pick up that piece of paper."

Hilda lived in the Aviara Point development of Carlsbad. This picturesque neighborhood was known for its rolling hills and upscale homes. As I drove, the cityscape gradually gave way to perfectly landscaped roads flanked by mature trees and well-manicured lawns. The houses here were sprawled out, each more majestic than the last.

It was also a gated community with a guard. Fortunately, Hilda had cleared me already, so I was granted immediate access. Upon arriving at her house, I found her waiting for me at the door. Her eyes sparkled with enthusiasm. "Thank you for coming so quickly, dear. Here's the paper that was inside the pen. How exciting! Is this some kind of secret message?"

"I don't know yet, but to be thorough, I should take the pen, too." I took the paper from her and looked over the message. Just like mine, hers had also been handwritten.

She pulled the pen from her pocket. "Of course, dear. I thought you might want it. Keep Ethan updated, won't you? I must get ready for dinner with an old friend."

"Ethan? You don't want me to give you progress reports?"

"I trust Ethan implicitly." She smiled. "Now, I must go."

After putting the paper back inside the pen for safekeeping, I left Hilda's, baffled by how she'd delegated this entire case to Ethan. The elephant in the room, my suspicions about him, suddenly loomed larger. Hilda might trust her grandson implicitly, but I couldn't. Not yet, anyway.

I drove to Sam's office, trying to get my mind off of what was turning into my Hilda/Ethan problem. The subject I found was no less perplexing. Should I escalate things with Jake Marlough? It wouldn't be difficult to break into his van and plant a bug of my own. It was an option, just not one I felt comfortable taking yet.

The first thing I did when I got to Sam's office was check for bugs. Now that it had happened once—and having been warned about Marlough's proficiency—it would be prudent to be cautious. This time, the place was clean.

"Look at this," I said as I pulled Hilda's pen from my bag. "Benji gave that pen to Hilda Bauer. He also gave me this one. Unscrew the barrel."

As Sam unscrewed the barrel of Hilda's pen, I did the same with mine. When we had the two messages on the worktable, Sam cocked her head to one side. "Guild must? Do you think that's the key to the cryptogram?"

"Seems incomplete. Doesn't it? Maybe we're missing part of the message."

Sam studied the two pieces of paper. A few seconds later, her lips curled up into a smile. "Unless we're not."

I was annoyed with myself for missing the obvious when Sam moved Hilda's half next to mine so that the right edge of Hilda's was next to my left edge. I hadn't thought anything of it, but the right edge of Hilda's piece was ragged, as was my left. Once Sam had matched up the tear marks, the word 'Guild,' which was written on the right half of the paper, lined up perfectly with the word 'must,' which was written on the left half of my part.

"I think what we have here is the complete message, but the remaining words are invisible."

"Well, that's not very helpful, is it?" The breath I let out carried with it a wealth of frustration. Somehow, we had to find a way past Benji's bag of spycraft tricks.

Sam shook her head, the corners of her dark eyes crinkling with excitement. "On the contrary, Jade. I think this is the whole key. Look how the pieces line up. They're exact. And the outside edges are all clean cuts. Benji wrote the message, two words in regular ink, and the rest in invisible ink. Now, all we need to do is figure out how to make the invisible ink visible."

"If I remember correctly, there are several types of invisible inks. And don't you have to do something different for each type to make the ink appear?"

"Yes, and some of those tests could be destructive."

"In other words, if we choose the wrong one, we're screwed," I muttered.

"Not how I was going to put it, but yes. But think about this, Jade. From what I've been learning about him, Benji was an old-school kind of guy. He used a riddle in which he referred to the ancient way of making a stone blade. He wrote a note, tore it in half, and put the two halves in different pens. That's very old school. Why would he do anything different with ink?"

It made sense. And it tracked with what I knew of Benji. "What are you thinking?"

"A couple of times in our conversations, Benji told me he was fascinated by Pliny the Elder."

"Who?" I blurted.

"He was a naturalist and a philosopher who lived in the first century AD. Anyway, he described how the milk of the tithymalus plant could be used as an invisible ink."

"Wait. How many times did he mention this Pliny guy?"

"I don't know. At least twice."

Another clue? Another part of Benji's plan? "Even if you're right, where are we going to find this plant? Whatever it's called."

Sam brushed away my protest with a dismissive wave. "We don't need the actual plant. The point is that the milk of the tithymalus is a sap that reacts the same way as other organic inks. All we need to do is apply heat, and the ink will become visible."

It seemed brilliant. It seemed very Benji. And potentially risky. "Is there any downside?"

"Well, yeah. If I'm wrong, we might destroy the message."

I closed my eyes and took a long breath. Did I trust Sam? Did I trust my own assessment of Benji? "I assume we have the same problem with any method we use to reveal the message."

"Correct. It's not one-hundred percent, but there's a possibility that if we choose the wrong process, we'll destroy whatever Benji wrote."

"You said Benji mentioned this guy a couple of times?"

"At least. Benji was very impressed by him."

"Okay. Let's try it, then. If we've only got one shot, I'm going to trust that Benji had Ethan give me the cryptogram because he trusted me and my instincts. I'm also trusting that he told you about this guy for a reason. Let's go for it."

Sam immediately set to work, pulling what looked like a small hair dryer from a storage cabinet. "This should be gentle enough not to torch the paper but hot enough to reveal the ink if there's any to be shown," she explained, plugging it into a nearby socket.

"It looks like my hair dryer," I said with a grin.

"It's a hot air gun, but it's the same idea."

I held down the two message halves as Sam slowly waved the air gun back and forth. When nothing happened, my stomach did little flip-flops. But then, faint letters slowly emerged, growing darker as the heat continued to work its magic.

"It's working!" I leaned closer but was careful not to interfere.

Sam turned off the air gun and laid it aside. We both peered at the now-visible letters. The characters were still a bit hard to read, but clear enough to make out the entire message—*The Guild must pay*.

My heart pounded as the meaning of the key settled in. "I think this proves Benji made the mistake of crossing his old gang. It's what got him killed. You're sure that's the whole key?"

"There's only way we'll know for sure. We have to try it."

On a blank piece of paper, Sam wrote out the key as well as the text of the cryptogram. For both, she stripped out the spaces and aligned the letters. "Because there are more letters in the cipher— that's the text of the cryptogram—we repeat the key."

"Okay, what's that do for us?"

"Nothing, yet. Remember how I described shifting the letters in the encrypted message? For that, we need a Vigenère table. It's used to encrypt and decrypt messages." She pulled up a file from her computer and printed it. Sam pointed to the first column. "The table is a simple tool we can use for encrypting text. See how the alphabet is written across the top and down the side? Each row of the table shifts the alphabet one letter. So, the first row starts with A, the second row starts with B, and so on."

"Oh, I get it! The columns do the same thing."

"Exactly. It repeats all the way to the end of the alphabet. To use it, you find the letter from your message on the top row and the letter from your keyword on the side column. The point where these two letters meet in the table is the encrypted letter."

My lips parted, and I made an 'aha' noise. "That's why the keyword phrase is so important. It really is the secret code that helps us to unscramble the letters."

"Right. So we just keep repeating theguildmustpay until we have the same number of letters as we do in the message." She pointed at the Vigenère table. "To decrypt the message, we follow down the first column to the T. From there, we trace across the row to the X, which is the first letter of our encrypted message. Then we trace up to the very first row, and that gives us the first letter of our decrypted message."

This might be a simple process, but it sure was tedious. Just thinking about how long it would take was enough to put me to sleep. "Why don't we just use a computer?"

Sam rolled her eyes and smiled. "Where's the fun in that?"

Right. Sam was a self-professed nerd. This must be how they had fun. At least I knew for sure—I was not nerd material. Eventually, the encoded message became clearer, and my spirits rose. I swallowed hard when Sam wrote out the last letter and read, "Elizabeth Carter, Harris, Mitchell & Reynolds LLP, XRJETBASP."

"Who's Elizabeth Carter? And what is this Harris, Mitchell & Reynolds? It sounds like a law firm."

"And the code?" Sam asked. "Another cryptogram? I can't believe Benji would nest these. It must be something else."

My breathing quickened as I read the text again. My initial shock had worn off, but now this might actually make some sense. If Benji wanted to keep a secret from everyone, why not hide it with an attorney? And maybe the code was something like a password. Another layer of security to make sure only the person with the code could get access to whatever he'd entrusted to them.

"I think I know what Benji was up to." I pulled out my phone and did a search for Harris, Mitchell & Reynolds. When their website popped up, I wanted to do a little happy dance, but as I dialed, I wondered if it could really be that easy. My intuition told me the answer was most likely a no.

Chapter 26

THE OVERLY PROFESSIONAL RECEPTIONIST WHO answered the phone at Harris, Mitchell & Reynolds informed me that Elizabeth Carter not only worked there but was a senior partner. Good news, right? It would have been if Ms. Carter hadn't been out of the country until the end of the week.

"Can I make an appointment to see her?" I asked.

"She's usually booked about a month out. What's this about?"

Good question. Did I even know? "The death of a client of hers—Benjamin Thompson."

"One moment."

Before I could protest, I was listening to a soothing, soft jazz melody.

"What happened?" Sam asked impatiently.

"I'm on terminal hold." It ticked me off that the woman hadn't even asked if I could wait. But before I could get too worked up, she was back. "Ms. Carter has an opening on Monday, the 21st, at 8 a.m."

"I'll be there," I said quickly, but inside I was groaning over nearly a week's delay. When I disconnected, Sam was watching me expectantly.

"Well? When do you go see her?"

"The receptionist told me Ms. Carter was booked a month in advance, but she got me in next Monday. At least it's early in the day."

"That's impressive. Benji must have been one heck of a client. Do you have any idea why this attorney's involved?"

"In a word, no. All I can figure out is that Benji was obsessed with planning for his early demise. Whatever Ms. Carter can tell me must be important. At this point, I think anything is possible. Benji's surprised me every step of the way."

"Maybe she's got the brooch. Or maybe she knows where it is."

"Or maybe she's a member of The Guild. Anything's possible. I won't know until I talk to her."

"Benji wouldn't ambush you like that."

By sending me to a member of The Guild? Probably not. "I hope you're right."

"Jade, if you think meeting this woman is too dangerous, just walk away. You could tell Hilda about this lawyer and let her deal with it."

"It's not that simple. We've put something in motion, and it's too late to back away. I also don't think Ms. Carter will speak to anyone but me."

"You're probably right. Benji must have been obsessed with security. At least we're pretty sure Ms. Carter must know where the brooch is."

I shook my head. "I hope so. Unfortunately, we won't know anything else until I meet her. And, like I said, we've started something. I still remember this one case my dad had when I was about ten. Mom was worried about him, and so was I. When my mom told him he should walk away, he said he couldn't. When I asked him why, he said, 'Honey, once you've kicked the hornet's nest, the best you can do is keep from getting stung. They're coming for you, no matter what you do.' Think about it, Sam. Why else would Jake Marlough have bugged your office?"

The color drained from her cheeks. She grimaced. "So you think we've already kicked the nest?"

"Exactly. The trick is to find the remaining members of The Guild before they come for us. I have a start. I'm pretty sure it includes someone named Valkyrie."

"Did you say Valkyrie?" Her lips parted in surprise, and her eyes locked onto mine with a gaze that was steady and piercing.

"You know who Valkyrie is?" I asked.

"I don't, but I know someone who might. Let me show you something. Follow me."

She returned the hot air gun to its spot on the shelf, then went to her desk with me firing questions while I tailed her.

When she sat, I asked again if she knew who Valkyrie was.

"You mean other than as in Norse mythology?" She tapped the keys and made the kind of face I make when I can't find something,

"Not funny, Sam," I grumbled. "Yes, other than Norse mythology."

Suddenly, she spun her laptop screen around. "Look at that. It's a blog post written two years ago by a local blogger. Her name is Rachel Yang, and her blog is titled *Art for the Rest of Us*. She does art history tours."

I scanned the page. "How's she connected to this case?"

"She's also an avid historian. Her videos are totally starting to take off. Rach knows everything there is to know about local art. A few years ago, she got an anonymous tip about a theft at Jonathan's museum. The tipster told her some international gang was behind the job. Look at the image at the beginning of her post."

The image Sam referred to was a winged helmet. Based on what Clara had told me, it was the kind of thing you'd imagine a Valkyrie wearing in tales of old Norse legends. The wings arched gracefully from each side, suggesting both power and protection. I couldn't help but be drawn to it, and as I read the opening paragraph of Rachel Yang's post, I grew more certain that Valkyrie was the code name for the leader of The Guild.

"Wow. She really lays it out. She claims Valkyrie, Obsidian, and Mystique are all members." I was impressed by the matter-of-fact style of the prose, but, at the same time, I was wary. When Zoe and I first met, she was a blogger trying to make her name. She'd made some pretty wild accusations, only a few of which had been true. "Does this Rachel Yang do her homework?"

"Of course. Like I said, she knows everything about local art. She spent months researching that post. We became friends and stayed in touch. She's doing video blogging these days. She could be a good resource for us."

I let out a heavy sigh. "I don't know, Sam. Not only do we need to keep this whole operation quiet, but we also need to make sure we don't jeopardize anyone. Benji is already dead, and I don't want there to be anyone else."

"We're going to need help, Jade. Resources. People with knowledge. We have to start trusting a few people."

Thinking about the bridge I'd burned with Ethan, I said, "I know you're right, Sam. The problem is, who are the right people to trust? And who's going to double-cross us?"

"Are we still talking about Rachel?"

Ouch. Sam wasn't buying any of my BS. She was right. I was no longer thinking about the case, but I needed to. "You got me. I'm not being professional. Call Rachel. Let's see what she can tell us."

Sam left a message for Rachel Yang to return her call. I fingered the keyring in my pocket while Sam finished, suddenly realizing the one obvious place I hadn't looked for the key was Timeless Treasures. I called Clara, and she agreed to let me into the store. While I drove to meet her, I also called Hilda.

Upon hearing that I'd solved the cryptogram, she let out something resembling a childish squeal—perhaps the closest thing I'd heard to an emotional response since I'd met her.

"That's wonderful, dear. I knew you could do it," she said.

I resisted the urge to tell her I was glad one of us had that level of confidence. "There is something else that's come up. Hilda, in Benji's files, I found a letter you sent to him about A Mermaid's Allure."

"Oh, yes. I did send him a letter, dear."

"How did you know about Valkyrie Collections? And why didn't you tell me about it?"

"Ethan found a source at the auction house that handled the estate sale. The information had not been verified when I sent the letter."

Ethan? Again? Maybe I hadn't been so far off base in my accusations. "So you've heard the name Valkyrie before."

Hilda paused, and when she spoke, I heard notes of caution in her tone. "Benjamin confirmed when we first talked that Valkyrie Collections had purchased the brooch. He also indicated she was very dangerous and would stop at nothing to get what she wanted."

"You're saying he told you Valkyrie was a woman?"

"Never explicitly. Be careful, dear. I withheld the letter because I didn't want you searching for Valkyrie. I'd feel terrible if something happened to you."

My insides twisted as I debated why she trusted Ethan so much. Eventually, my inner cynic won out. He was her grandson. Of course, she trusted him. Whether he deserved that trust was another question. I ended the call by assuring Hilda I'd update Ethan once I knew something more. In my mind, that also included being sure I could trust him.

When I arrived at Clara's home, she was waiting for me at the door.

"Are you sure you're up to this?" I asked.

"I think so. I've got to face it sooner or later."

"Okay, then. Let's go."

Timeless Treasures Gallery was only a few blocks away, so we walked. On the way, I told Clara I might be closing on finding the brooch. She swiped away a tear, and a wry smile formed on her lips. "I'm glad something good is coming out of this. Maybe she'll finally get part of her family's legacy back."

We were silent the rest of the way to the store, at which point I snuck a peek at Clara's face. Her green eyes were clouded with a mixture of sorrow and determination. Though she was trying to hide it, deep down, I sensed a depth of pain that seemed almost unfathomable.

"Clara, you don't have to do this right now."

She shook her head, and her jaw tightened. "No, I must. For Benji."

I nodded in understanding, slipped the key into the lock, and we entered. A bell tinkled above us, announcing our arrival. Then, absolute silence. The emptiness felt otherworldly. It was as if I'd been transported to a place where time had stopped.

We walked through the store, looking at the different pieces of art and antiques that adorned the shelves and walls. As I walked, I realized the futility of my idea. Benji could have hidden a key in any of a hundred places in this store. While I stood, fixed in place and feeling overwhelmed, Clara was drawn to a hanging mobile. It featured sleek, dark stones suspended from delicate metal wires. Each stone was polished to a gleaming finish, creating reflections and shadows that danced with the slightest air movement. Clear crystals and brushed gold medallions accented the piece, catching the light in mesmerizing ways and giving it an aura of elegance and mystery.

Clara studied it intently for the longest time before turning to me, her eyes glistening and her voice little more than a whisper. "This was one of Benji's favorites. He actually bought it for home, but when I suggested he bring it here, he loved the idea."

I put my hand on her shoulder in support. "This is all yours now. You can do with it what you want."

"I suppose so. I have an appointment with the attorney next Monday to review the trust and Benji's will."

"Let's hope it all goes well for you. Clara, I have an appointment with an attorney that same day. Did Benji ever mention an Elizabeth Carter?"

She shook her head. "No."

"Harris, Mitchell & Reynolds?"

"Who are they?"

"That's what I'd like to know. I'll circle back and tell you if I come up with anything. This whole lead could be nothing more than a wild goose chase."

Clara nodded absently as she wandered around the store, a faraway look in her eyes. When I entered Benji's office, I went straight to his desk. There, in the middle of a jumble of papers, was a red file folder labeled 'Valkyrie.'

After donning a pair of latex gloves, I opened the folder. My eyes nearly popped out of my head. The photo showed a man smiling proudly as he held up a framed painting with a winged Viking helmet and crossed swords.

I'd found Valkyrie. And it was Ethan Harper.

Chapter 27

AFTER RECOVERING FROM MY SHOCK at seeing the photo of Ethan with the winged helmet, I checked on Clara. She was still wandering the gallery and looking at the various pieces on display. Slipping the door to Benji's office closed, I dialed Sam's number. When she answered, I told her about the photo.

"Jade, I'm sorry. I know you liked him."

"Part of me still doesn't want to believe he's the one in charge of The Guild. And part of me says it isn't possible. He's too young."

"Maybe this Valkyrie thing is like the CEO of a company. It could be he took over from someone else."

"It could be. And he was close to Benji. They'd talked a lot recently. Oh, God. What if you're right, and this Valkyrie title is a position—Ethan might have killed the previous leader. Maybe that's what kicked everything into motion, and Benji was trying to expose him."

"If that's the case, why would Ethan have involved you?"

"Because of his grandmother. She'd been talking to Benji, who'd told her Valkyrie was dangerous. You know what doesn't make sense? She also said Valkyrie was a woman."

"Did she ever tell you how she knew that?"

"She said Benji told her. As far as why Ethan got me involved, if he thought I didn't have the cryptogram key, he probably thought we'd never decode it. It was a perfectly safe move until I found the envelope with Benji's message. Even then, he could always get rid of me once I found the key." I sighed, wishing I could turn back time and unlearn the whole truth.

"I'm sorry, Jade," Sam said. "But at least you know now."

"Yeah, I do. And now, we can focus on finding out what he's planning next. Sorry, Sam, but I should check on Clara."

We disconnected, and I went into the front of the store. When I showed Clara the photo, she was lost. Apparently, Benji had never shared any part of his secret life with her. "Clara, are you still okay just wandering around? While we're here, I should look for something."

She shook her head. "No, I've seen enough. What are you trying to find?"

I showed her the keyring. "A key that goes to this."

Clara's jaw dropped, and then she laughed. "You've got to be kidding me."

"I wish I was."

She steadied herself with a long breath and straightened her shoulders. "I'll help you look. Where do we start?"

We began our search in Benji's office. Clara sifted through the drawers while I rummaged through the file cabinet. We examined everything meticulously, but we found no keys anywhere. By the time we finished, the air in the room was heavy with tension. Still, I couldn't shake the feeling we were missing the obvious.

The only thing we hadn't gone through was a box stashed in the corner. I picked it up, opened the box, and gasped. "These are old letters and greeting cards."

Clara took one look inside and threw up her hands. "I told Benji to throw this stuff away. It's all correspondence from when he was traveling." She picked up an anniversary card, and her eyes welled with tears. "I guess I'm glad now that he didn't. I think I'll take it home."

I understood completely. "Sounds like a great way to relive some of the good times you two had. I'll carry it for you."

"Thanks. I think I want to go home now. I'm getting very tired."

"Of course."

After packaging up the box, we headed for the front door, but as I walked, I still had a nagging feeling I'd missed something important. "Where did they find Benji's body, Clara?"

"He was changing one of the lightbulbs. Over there." She cocked her head to her left.

"Why was he on a ladder to change a lightbulb when he had a lightbulb changing pole in his office?"

Clara screwed up her face, looking confused. "What? Why's it matter?"

I went to stand where she'd indicated. "Here?"

"Yes, that's it. Come on, Jade, I need to leave."

"One second, Clara. We've been looking for our key in the wrong place." I pointed up to the ceiling. Clara's eyes widened as she gaped at the mobile.

I hurried over to the side wall and retrieved the ladder propped up in the corner. I set the ladder beneath the mobile and climbed up until I could poke my head through to the top. When I got up there, I could have kicked myself. These weren't just any black stones; they were obsidian. And taped to the top of the largest was a small silver key.

A confident grin spread across my face as I retrieved the key from its hiding place. At the bottom of the ladder, I showed it to Clara. "Obsidian strikes again. Of course."

After getting Clara and her box of mementos home, I returned to the office. I'd decided it was time to do a background check on Ethan. I started with the basics, but the more I learned about him—thirty-nine years old, bartender for about ten years, and never in trouble with the law—the more perplexed I became. There wasn't even a record of his juvenile incident. Could Benji have been wrong about Ethan? Or setting him up? My heart said trust, but my gut said verify.

What I did see was a linked record for a trip to Europe that had taken place a few years earlier. I called Clara to see if I could somehow connect the dots between Ethan's trip and the one she'd made with Benji.

"How are you doing, Clara?"

"Since I got home, I've just been resting."

"I won't keep you long. Can you tell me the dates you and Benji made your last few trips?"

"We'd been going once a year for the last few years. We went last May. The year before that, we went in July, and the year prior to that, it was March. Why?"

"Did you ever meet Ethan Harper while you were on those trips?"

"Yes. He and his grandmother were there during our March trip. Benji introduced me to them. Do you think you've got proof that Ethan is this Valkyrie?"

"I'm getting close. Thanks, Clara. I'll be in touch."

I decided to talk to my dad again, hoping he could shed more light on Ethan's involvement. I called and after the obligatory chitchat, popped the question.

"There's a lot involved to give you a complete answer, but to make a long story short, neither Leo nor I were ever able to positively identify any of the members of The Guild. The one exception was Benji, but even there, we couldn't prove he'd ever participated in any crimes."

"Then how did you identify him as a member?"

"A piece of artwork showed up in his store. We thought we had him, but he showed us a letter of provenance. Apparently, there'd been a mistake."

"Dad, that's not normal."

"I know, honey. But when we checked with the provenance researcher, she was as shocked as we were."

I had alarm bells ringing like crazy in my head. "Who was this researcher?"

"Michelle Wolfe. When we called her, she found the actual provenance for the piece. It also matched what Benji had shown us. It turns out there were two copies made, one with a fake provenance and one with the real. She had impeccable credentials, so we believed her when she said it was an honest mistake."

"She's the one Benji used when he researched A Mermaid's Allure. Dad, Michelle Wolfe is dead. She died last year. I suspect that she was part of The Guild."

"How did she die?"

"An automobile accident. I'm not so sure that it was an accident, though."

"Jade…"

"Don't say it. You want me to stay away from this case."

"No, that's not what I was going to say. In fact, you made a connection Leo and I missed. It's so obvious, too. The Guild would need someone to manipulate documentation. You've come this far. You shouldn't stop now."

A warm flush spread across my cheeks at my dad's praise, a blend of pride and embarrassment washing over me. His words had a unique way of making me feel both accomplished and bashful simultaneously. "Thanks, Dad."

"No need to thank me. You truly deserve it. So, what's your next move?"

"Have a talk with Ethan Harper." I told him about the photo in Benji's office, what I knew about Valkyrie, and how we'd discovered the undocumented sale of Mrs. Bauer's brooch in 2012. He responded by letting me know Ethan's name had never come up in their investigation.

To a small degree, my dad's comment reassured me that I might have been wrong about Ethan. But it wasn't enough. I still had my suspicions. I said, "I'm not trusting Ethan yet, but now that I know what I'm looking for, maybe I can suss out whether Benji was trying to right some old wrongs. It could be that's what got him killed."

"Be careful, Jade. I'm sure that Hilda Bauer and Leo are correct. These people are dangerous. And, with all the crimes they've gotten away with over the years, they're not going to want anyone messing with their lives. If they did kill Benji because he turned on them, I'm sure they'd do it again to protect themselves."

As I disconnected the call, I decided it was time to add a fashion accessory to my wardrobe. With the outside-the-waistband holster I'd bought after my last case, I'd have easy access to my Glock 43. If

Ethan Harper tried anything, he'd better be quick. The gun might be compact, but it could still drop a man in his tracks with no problem.

Chapter 28

DESPITE BEING RELATIVELY LIGHT, THE Glock felt heavy and
cumbersome in its holster. I knew from experience I'd soon forget it
was there, but in those first few minutes, I had to remind myself that
this was a necessary part of the job. I was preparing for my 'talk' with
Ethan when my cell rang with a call from Clara. In a frantic voice I
barely recognized, she said, "Someone's breaking into the store!
Help!"

What the heck? We'd been there less than thirty minutes ago.
Timeless Treasures was only two blocks away. It could take the cops
five minutes or more to get there. I could make it in less than one.
"Call the police!" I said and hung up the phone.

I ran the two blocks to the store. The front door was still locked, so
I headed to the back. The rear door was wide open. I pulled out the
Glock and approached cautiously. No would-be thieves came rushing
out, so I stepped into the back entrance.

The store was eerily silent. With my arms held out and two hands
on the Glock, I cautiously made my way through the darkened store.
Benji's office was undisturbed. Nothing had changed. Venturing
deeper inside, the hackles on the back of my neck rose. No paintings
were missing. A creak from behind me made me spin around. I had my

gun raised, but it was only the mobile catching the air movement from the open back door.

As my search continued, it became clear something was off. Other than the open door, I'd found no signs of a break-in or missing merchandise. Just as I was preparing to leave, two uniformed officers burst through the back entrance.

"Police! Freeze! Put down the gun."

"This isn't what it looks like, Officer," I said as I placed the Glock on the floor.

"Keep your hands up."

I did as I'd been told but continued trying to explain the situation. As I spoke, I also took in the names of the two men. The older was Officer Wilson, the younger, Jimenez. "My name is Jade Cavendish. I'm a private investigator. The owner of the store is a client of mine, and she called to tell me someone had broken in. My office is just down the street, so I rushed over here."

Officer Wilson, who was graying at the temples and had a tan that could earn him a spot on the cover of Beach Bum Magazine, eyed me. "Beachtown Detective Agency?"

"Yes. Thomas Cavendish is my dad."

"Do you have any ID, Ms. Cavendish?"

Despite the situation, I felt a flush of embarrassment. The last thing I wanted was a cop sticking his fingers down the front of my pants. I winced as I said, "In my front pocket."

The two men exchanged a look, then Wilson said, "Pull it out slowly."

"Thank you," I said, breathing a sigh of relief. At least I'd been able to avoid that embarrassment. I handed Officer Wilson my driver's license, PI license, and concealed carry permit. After checking the validity of my documentation, they allowed me to holster the Glock and explain why I'd been in the store with my gun drawn. But as I recapped the sequence of events before the police arrived, I realized something about Clara's call was bothering me.

"Let me call the deceased owner's wife. That's Mrs. Clara Thompson."

"Wait. This was Benjamin Thompson's art gallery?"

"Yes."

Officer Wilson looked at his partner. "Stay with her while I call Detective Martini."

"Why are you calling Detective Des?" I asked, dumbstruck.

Jimenez snorted, and Wilson's hand went to his mouth to stifle one of his own. "She lets you call her that?"

I gritted my teeth. I felt foolish for letting my private nickname for her pop out like that. "Not to her face," I muttered.

"I didn't think so," Wilson said, covering his grin with one hand. "Stay here. Detective Martini will want to interview you."

He went to the rear of the store to make the call. I spent the time trying to think of reasons Detective Des would be concerned at all with a break-in. The only thing I could come up with was that she was still investigating Benji's death. That was both good news and bad. Detective Des was a good cop, but even though I'd earned her respect on my last case, she would not tolerate anyone stepping on her size 8 Manolos.

While I waited for Wilson, I noticed Clara standing at the front door, key in hand. Officer Jimenez also spotted her and started to wave her away but stopped when I told him who she was.

By the time I finished, she was already rushing toward us through the front door. "What's going on, Jade? Why are the police here?"

I was tempted to say something snarky and remind her she was the one who'd called them but was saved by Officer Jimenez, who stepped in to take control. Silently, I thanked him. The woman was, after all, distraught.

Jimenez introduced himself, then said, "We received a call that someone was breaking into your store, ma'am. Did you call 9-1-1?"

"I most certainly did not. This is the first I've heard about a break-in! Was anything stolen?" Clara looked past the officer, skewering me with obvious irritation. "Jade?"

"Not that I can see, Clara. Didn't you call the police after you called me?"

Jimenez seemed to notice that something fishy was going on. Rather than interrupting, he stood, eyes watchful, pad and pen now ready.

"What are you talking about, Jade? The last time we spoke was when you called me!"

That made no sense whatsoever. Unless Clara had suffered a stroke in the last fifteen minutes, I couldn't see why she wouldn't remember our conversation. "No, Clara. You called me maybe ten minutes ago and told me someone was breaking into the store. You asked me to check it out, and I told you to call the police."

Clara crossed her arms over her chest and looked at me like I was crazy. "I'm not senile, Jade. And I did not call you."

Jimenez cleared his throat, drawing our attention back to him. "Ma'am, do you have any security cameras in the store?"

"Yes, of course. They're monitored by an alarm company."

Something still wasn't adding up. "Clara, if you didn't call the police, then why are you here?"

"Benji's phone started making a terrible racket. When I checked on it, I realized the store alarm was going off. I thought maybe we'd done something wrong when we were here. I came in to see if I could fix it."

I pulled out my phone and brought up my call history, then turned the screen so both Clara and Officer Jimenez could see it. "Clara, here's the phone call that came in from your number. You're saying you didn't make this call?"

Clara bristled, but Detective Des Martini's razor-sharp tones cut off any further discussion about a nonexistent phone call. "Ms. Cavendish? Why are you interrupting my day?"

Uh oh. The Ice Queen was peeved. I swallowed the lump in my throat. There was no point in going for niceties. Detective Des didn't do those. She stood only a few feet away, exuding an air of authority. She was dressed in an impeccably tailored, dark navy pantsuit that hugged her frame perfectly. The suit's jacket was buttoned neatly, accentuating her slender waist, while the trousers fell smoothly, ending just above a pair of immaculate, black leather pumps that screamed sophistication and expense. As my Scottish grandmother might have said, how the woman dressed like that was beyond my ken.

I turned the screen so the detective could see it. "I received this call. The voice sounded strained. At the time, I assumed it was Mrs. Thompson calling me because it was her number. Now, I'm not so sure."

"I most certainly did not call you, Jade." Clara looked about as indignant as a cat whose tail had been stepped on.

"Then how do you explain this call, Mrs. Thompson?" Detective Des raised one eyebrow and returned Clara's stare.

I reached out, took Clara's hand, and said, "I believe you."

Much to my surprise, Detective Des didn't have one of the cops haul me away for interfering in her investigation. Instead, she looked at me cooly and said, "Alright, Ms. Cavendish. You seem to have the answers. What's your theory?"

My gut twisted when I realized what I'd just done. If I'd kept my mouth shut, this whole thing probably would have been chalked up to an alarm malfunction or something equally unremarkable. But now that I'd opened the door, Detective Des was not going to let me go until I'd spilled my guts. I might as well just get it over with.

"I think someone spoofed her number. I also think this whole break-in was a warning to me to back off my current case."

"Which you can't talk about because of client confidentiality," Detective Des said in a bored-with-this-excuse tone. "So let me take a guess. You're trying to find a missing family heirloom for Mrs. Bauer. You're also working for Mrs. Thompson to find her husband's killer because the police are inept and can't find their way out of a paper bag. Am I correct?"

It felt like the temperature in the room had dropped about one degree for each word. My throat was so dry it felt like I was swallowing sand. "I never thought of the police as inept."

"Good to know," Detective Des said tersely. "Anything else you'd like to volunteer, Ms. Cavendish?"

That I was sorry for stepping on her size eights? That I was considering closing the business, moving to an isolated island, and becoming a beach bum? "Actually, my contract with Mrs. Thompson is only to look into her husband's business dealings. Are you convinced his death was a homicide?"

Her cynical smile made it clear she didn't believe a word about my contract with Clara. But I could almost see the wheels turning in her head, calculating what she might gain from answering. "Very well. Since Mrs. Thompson is here, you both might as well know that we've brought in someone for questioning."

Clara touched her fingers to her lips, then dropped her hand to her throat. She croaked, "Who?"

"Ethan Harper."

A torrent of doubts surged through my mind. They tumbled off a cliff, suspended in mid-air like a cascading waterfall, before crashing into a swirling, churning pool of confusion below.

"You look surprised, Ms. Cavendish."

The detective's dark eyes held mine as the churning waters sucked me in, and the seconds ticked by. Until Detective Des had said Ethan's name, I hadn't realized how badly I wanted to be wrong about him. I also didn't want to help the police make their case until I was sure of Ethan's guilt.

"I am. He doesn't strike me as a killer."

The corners of the detective's lips curled up ever so slightly. "That's naive, Ms. Cavendish. And you know it."

"What evidence do you have against him?" I asked casually.

Detective Des was all business again, the trace of a smile replaced by a cold-as-steel facade. "We're done here. Wrap it up, officers. And, Ms. Cavendish, you know how the game is played. If you want to know who triggered that alarm, contact the company." With that, Detective Des was gone.

"Is she always like that?" Clara asked. Poor Clara looked like she was still in shock.

Officer Wilson cleared his throat to avoid answering, then said, "Be sure to lock up when you're done and reset the alarm. Good day, ladies."

My phone rang. I saw that it was from Hilda Bauer. And there it was. The call I'd been expecting ever since I'd talked to Dad. Might as well get it over with.

"Do you think that young man killed Benji?" Clara asked.

I sighed before I tapped the screen to answer the call. "I honestly don't know, Clara. I hope not, but nothing would surprise me at this point."

Chapter 29

HILDA, IT TURNED OUT, DIDN'T want to fire me or get her retainer back at all. Instead, she wanted to know if I'd heard from Ethan. Technically, he hadn't called me, so I told her I hadn't. I wasn't about to break the news that he might still be with the police.

After finishing the call, Clara and I closed up Timeless Treasures. While I headed for X Factor Self-Defense, she promised to contact the alarm company as Detective Des had suggested. X Factor was my refuge, my place to think. Sometimes, I liked to surf to clear my mind, but the heavy bag was a better solution for me today.

I wrapped my hands tightly, feeling the rough texture of the cotton fabric pressing against my skin. With my knuckles secured for the intense session ahead, I approached the bag and pulled in a long, slow breath. Cool air filled my lungs. I exhaled, consciously releasing the tension inside me. The bag, an unyielding opponent, hung there waiting to absorb all the anger and frustration bottled up within me.

Ethan Harper. The man had certainly gotten under my skin. Although I was elated that the police had a suspect in Benji's murder, I couldn't shake the feeling that something about the police questioning Ethan felt wrong. The facts weren't adding up, and as a private investigator, it was my job to make sure they did.

A satisfying jolt raced through my arm and shoulder as my fist sank into the dense, unyielding surface of the heavy bag. Its leather shell and textile filling absorbed the impact with solid, reassuring resistance. With each punch and kick, I tried to piece together what I knew so far. Hilda had wanted her family's brooch back. Benji might have brokered the sale of it to someone named Valkyrie. The letter of provenance from Michelle Wolfe didn't reflect the full history. Someone had bugged Sam's office to track what we were doing. And Ethan had been the one to deliver the bug. I landed an especially hard kick and nearly lost my balance.

Kimberley Cosma, the owner of X Factor, smiled at me from about ten feet away. "Hey, Jade. You must have a lot of frustration built up."

"I'm trying to sort out some things." My chest heaved as I let my arms hang freely at my sides. I was grateful for the interruption but anxious to finish my workout.

"Guy trouble?" Kimberley asked.

The fact is, Kimberley knew me all too well. She'd been instrumental in helping me get through my break-up with Jason. She'd introduced me to the bag, which gradually helped me put my life back together. "Case trouble," I quickly added, "And I guess guy trouble, too."

Kimberley winced. "Ouch. The worst kind. Alright, get back to it. Work it out. The bag is your friend."

I returned to my workout, my heart racing and pumping. Adrenaline surged through my veins as my body's rhythm intensified. By the time I finished, I was dripping sweat but had a plan.

It was nearly five and I'd skipped lunch, so I went to my favorite free-food hangout, Sandy's Wiches. Just walking through the door reminded me of how much I'd relied on my network of friends post-Jason. Kimberley had been my source of inspiration to be strong, while Charlie, the owner of Sandy's, had been my emotional bedrock. A strong woman who'd survived and thrived after her husband's sudden death, Charlie had taught me to put one foot in front of the other. She'd also been tasked with picking up the pieces of my life far too many times whenever I'd stumbled.

Charlie waved and nodded when I motioned that I would have my usual California Sub with jalapeno chips. In her classic take-charge manner, she told one of her staff what to make and was at my table, sitting opposite me a few minutes later.

She pushed the sandwich, chips, and a tall drink across the table at me and sipped water from a cup. "You look like you just ran a marathon, Jade."

"I just came from X Factor."

Charlie nodded knowingly. "Guy trouble?"

"No!" I scrunched up my face and mock-glared at her. "Why does everybody ask me that?"

"Oh, I don't know. History?"

Frustrated with myself for not accepting my feelings about Ethan, I bit into the sandwich and thought about how to respond. The truth hurt. Charlie was right. My track record with men was not stellar. "Well, it's not exactly like that. Gina likes him, and so do I. But right now, he's a suspect in Benji Thompson's murder."

Charlie rolled her eyes as she shook her head. "You know how to pick them, don't you? Look, if you want, I can introduce you to plenty of guys."

"Yeah, you've got like, what? A thousand of them on the hook?"

"Hardly." Charlie deliberately looked away and watched her staff work. "Bobby will be starting kindergarten soon."

Never before had I seen Charlie even remotely uncomfortable in a discussion about men. She was drop-dead gorgeous, and much of her repeat business came from men—and even a few women—who came in mostly to flirt with her. Her husband, Shawn, had died a few years ago on a mission overseas. Since Shawn's death, she'd only dated a handful of times. And until recently, Charlie had always said Bobby was the only man in her life.

"Charlie? What's going on?"

She shook her head. "Nothing. I might be starting to think a little about something serious, but I've got Bobby to consider. What about you? How serious are you about this guy?"

"I'm officially in denial about my feelings for him," I laughed. "Besides, I'm pretty sure his grandmother will ask me to prove he's not a killer."

"Ouch. And I don't see you as the prison groupie type, so I guess you'd better prove this guy's innocent. Unless you believe he really is guilty?"

Without realizing it, Charlie had once again acted as my unofficial therapist, helping me sort through my life's complexities and get to the essentials. As much as I would have loved to share the details with her, the incident at Timeless Treasures made me realize just how far of a reach The Guild had. I was convinced that Valkyrie was behind that whole incident. And Ethan couldn't be Valkyrie because he'd been in police custody during the break-in. I finally got it. I couldn't share any of those details with anyone. Especially those I cared about.

I winced and shook my head. "Sorry, but I've already said too much. We shouldn't be talking about this right now. It's too dangerous."

Charlie gaped at me from across the table, a cup of water raised to her lips. Fear showed in her eyes—not for herself, but for me. "What are you involved in, Jade?"

"You know what? Just me coming in here might be dangerous for you. Until this case is over, I need to stay away."

Charlie grimaced but seemed to understand. After taking another sip from her cup, she stood. "I'll get you a bag. You're gonna tell me all about this when it's over. Right?"

"Totally."

I finished my sandwich back at my desk while I checked messages. Next, I logged into my computer and checked on Jake Marlough's location. Sure enough, he was still in Carlsbad. In fact, he was parked not far from where he'd been the last time, about a block from Anchor & Ale. That parking spot was only a fifteen-minute walk to Timeless Treasures. After the call from 'Clara' and the incident at the store, I wondered if Marlough might be involved. If so, he was way more talented than I'd given him credit for.

Rather than walking, I drove the few blocks to where Marlough's van was parked. I checked as I passed it, and the van looked empty. Possibly, he was in the back. That seemed unlikely since the windows were rolled up, and there were no exhaust fumes coming from the tailpipe. Today's temperature was only in the low seventies, pretty typical for this time of year, but the intense sun would turn the interior of that van into a sweatbox in minutes. I parked half a block away, then doubled back on foot.

After a quick walk around the van, I was satisfied it was empty. I jaywalked across the street, then hurried to Anchor & Ale, hoping that whoever was filling in for Ethan might tell me something valuable. My heart pounded as I stood with my hand just inches from the handle of the wooden door. When my fingers touched the smooth surface, a tingle surged through me. What if Ethan had been released and was back at work? I didn't expect trouble in a place of business, but stranger things made the news daily.

Anxiety gnawed at me as I pulled open the door and stepped into the dark interior. It took a few seconds for my vision to adjust. The place was mostly empty. A couple sat at a table in a darkened corner. They leaned into each other and spoke in hushed tones. The two men at the bar came in at the other end of the raucous scale, laughing and talking in obnoxiously loud voices. But there was no sign of Marlough. And no Ethan.

Somehow, I suppose I'd hoped to barge in on a clandestine meeting between conspirators. That would have made things easy, but nothing about this case was going that way. I slowly approached the bar, behind which stood a burly man with a thick mustache and a slick pate. He looked up as I approached.

I ordered an iced tea and sat on an empty stool, trying to remain inconspicuous while keeping an eye out for Marlough. As I sipped my drink, my mind raced with all the possible scenarios. I felt certain that something big was happening, but without Marlough or Ethan present, I was left with more questions than answers. Again.

Midway through my drink, the bartender asked how my day was going. I dodged the question. "Pretty good, I guess. I was actually hoping Ethan was working."

"I'm filling in for him. Cops hauled him in for some bogus questioning deal. All I know is he called in a panic and told me I had to get down here."

"Have you seen a man who wears loud shirts and maybe a fedora?"

He gestured toward the two men at the bar, then the couple. "They're the only customers I've seen so far."

"This guy would have been talking to Ethan."

"Oh, you mean Jake? They're friends from way back. I saw him yesterday when he came in for lunch. He's been doing some work down here for some attorney Ethan introduced him to." A second later, the bartender craned his neck back and focused on me. "You okay, Miss? You look kind of disoriented."

I scanned the bar again. If Marlough wasn't working for Ethan, then everything changed. Who was this attorney? Since Marlough's van was only about a block away, he must be within a few square blocks. And that meant Marlough would be with his real client.

A fleeting vision of the winged helmet image from Benji's desk folder crossed my mind. It had been so conveniently placed. There was no way I could have missed it. Had the entire incident at Timeless Treasures been choreographed to make me think Ethan was Valkyrie? To have me nearly arrested by the cops? And, yes, to send me a message.

Downing the last of my iced tea, I stood and dropped a five on the counter. "I've gotta go," I said. I had news for whoever was trying to manipulate my investigation. I wasn't backing off. I was determined to find Jake Marlough and his client. And maybe, Valkyrie.

Chapter 30

I BACKTRACKED TO MARLOUGH'S VAN. This time, a familiar figure leaned against the side. Marlough had his cell phone pressed to his ear, and he didn't look happy. Part of me wanted to confront him right then and there, but another part knew that strategically, it made sense to wait and see what he did next. It was the smart move and one he probably would never see coming.

After several minutes, Marlough ended his call and got into the van. I debated whether to follow or not. What the heck? I had the GPS tracker on the van. I could continue my search and catch up with the annoyance later. I started walking, checking each storefront and building for an attorney's office. It didn't take long to come across a familiar name. Isaac Johnson, Attorney at Law. I shouldn't have been surprised that the office was closed. It was, after all, after normal business hours. I suppose Johnson could have left via a rear door, but if he and Marlough had met here, maybe their conversation hadn't gone well. Could that be why Marlough looked so irritated?

I felt like a fool for not having connected the dots before. Sam's gorgeous tropical bouquet had come from her boyfriend. She'd even told me his name and that he was an attorney. I should have put everything together when Ethan's replacement told me Jake was working for an attorney. This had to be the guy I was looking for, but

I'd already jumped to far too many conclusions on this case, so I continued my search. I might as well be one hundred percent certain.

Over the course of the next few blocks, the only other attorney's office I found was a family law practice. It, too, was locked up for the weekend. I did a quick search, found the names of the attorneys in the firm, and ruled out all of them. None sounded familiar.

Next, I called Sam. It pained me to tell her my suspicions, but she deserved to know. "I'm afraid I have bad news about Isaac. I'm almost positive he's the one who bugged your office."

"Are you sure"

"I talked to a different bartender at Anchor & Ale. He confirmed that Ethan and Jake Marlough have been friends for a long time and that Marlough is working for a local attorney. The bar where Ethan works is an easy walk from Isaac's office. There's more."

I went on to tell her about the break-in at Timeless Treasures, the photograph of Ethan, and how the cops had caught me inside. By the time I was done, Sam was cursing Isaac and her bad luck with men.

"Looks like everyone's catching this bug lately," I said. "I'm sorry, Sam."

"It's not your fault. I should have known there was something off with him. We really connected when we were talking about art. He seemed to know a lot, and that totally impressed me. If he really is part of The Guild, that would make sense. What about Jonathan? Do you think he's in on it, too?"

"I don't know yet. For all I know, he and Isaac could both be members. What we need is information about all of Isaac's contacts." I couldn't believe what I was thinking. Was I really going to stoop to Marlough's level and bug Isaac's office?

Great. Just what I needed. A legal and moral dilemma on top of everything else. And should I get caught, the consequences would be severe. I'd have to regard planting a bug as the last step to take before everything fell apart. On the other hand, good old-fashioned footwork was certainly a legitimate option. I asked Sam if she could send me a photo of Isaac.

"What are you going to do?"

"I'm going to go the old-fashioned route and show his photo around."

"Good. I'd love to see you nail that slime's hide to the wall. One photo, coming up."

I had Sam's message in seconds and returned to Anchor & Ale. The bartender waved when I walked in and began polishing up an already spotless place at the bar.

"Another iced tea, Miss?"

"No, thanks. I have a question for you." I pulled out my phone and showed him the photo of Isaac. "Have you seen this man around?"

The bartender's eyes widened, and he slowly nodded. "Yeah, he comes in once in a while. Always seems to be waiting for someone."

"The last time he was here, do you know who he was waiting for?"

The bartender leaned in closer. "Sure. The last time he met with Jake. Before that, he came in to meet some Asian guy—gray hair, stocky, maybe medium height."

"This man?" I held up my phone to show him a photo of Benji.

His head and body nodded up and down in a singular motion. "Yeah, that's the guy. He comes in once in a while, too. Usually talks to Ethan. I told your partner that this morning."

My partner? Oh, he thought I was a cop. And he was willing to talk? I might as well play along. "Was that Detective Martini?"

"She's the Frost Princess, that one. Nothing like you. Why are you two working separately, anyway?"

"Detective Des and I have different ways of handling witnesses. You know how it is. People tend to forget things sometimes. But now that I'm here, this is your opportunity to bring those things up."

I looked at him and did my best Detective Des eyebrow raise. It seemed to work because he pursed his lips and nodded. "You know, I did forget to tell her I saw this guy you're asking about one other time. It wasn't here, though. I live about five blocks away and walk to work every day. I saw him on the sidewalk over on State St. talking to some woman. Older, graying hair."

He raised and lowered his hand in the air to indicate someone who was about five-foot-six. "About that tall, maybe." He nodded to himself and seemed satisfied with the estimate. "Yeah, that's about right."

His description could have matched half the population in Carlsbad, but there was one person I had in mind. I gave him a description of Hilda Bauer. He made a face, then said, "I don't know. Could be. Sorry, I can't be more helpful."

"No worries," I said. Not for him, anyway. Did my client know Isaac Johnson? If so, how well? Well enough to have him help doctor a letter of provenance? I left the bar with Leo's warning once again rattling around my head. "Don't trust anyone."

Did that include my client? I suspected I was about to find out. To my knowledge, Ethan hadn't been arrested, only brought in for questioning. How long would they keep him? Until they were done, however long that was.

If the cops did file charges, I was sure Hilda would post bail. I was taking a chance but felt it likely I'd find Hilda Bauer at home. With her moved firmly into the questionable column, I wanted to avoid forewarning her that I was coming. The guard might be a problem, but I crossed my fingers and hoped for the best.

I drove through the evening traffic, heading south and then east. On this visit, the guard was a disinterested man with an unbecoming five o'clock shadow. He perked up when I gave him a line about being an interior designer with an overbearing client.

"These people. They're all so high and mighty. The old bag's probably squeezing you for every dime, right?"

"Oh, yeah. A real penny pincher. I'll bet they do the same with you."

He rubbed the shadow on his chin and smirked. "You got that right. You think they'd pay better for all the protection they want."

"Amen to that," I said, trying to sound as disgruntled as Mr. Grumpy Pants looked.

"I hear you, sister. Go on in. It's fine by me."

I gave the guard a thumbs-up and drove through before he realized he hadn't even asked who I was visiting. That was excellent as far as I was concerned. I felt confident the element of surprise would work to my advantage.

Chapter 31

BY ANY MIDDLE-CLASS STANDARD, Hilda Bauer's home would be called spacious. But in this neighborhood, her home was one of the smallest. I'd heard some of the houses up here had eight bedrooms. It looked to me like Hilda was making do with three or four at the most. The poor woman was probably beside herself with house envy.

No cars were in the driveway, so I parked and went to the front door. When I rang the bell, there was no answer. I tried again. Still nothing. Frustrated that my grand plan to surprise my client had failed, I considered leaving, but the sideyard gate caught my attention. It was as though it were calling my name, just begging me to peek. What the heck? I was here. Right? Why shouldn't I see how the hoity-toity lived?

After silencing my phone to make sure it didn't go off while I was snooping, I let myself in through the gate and walked along a pathway bordered on both sides with lush and perfectly maintained roses on one side and flowering shrubs on the other. I was about to peek at the backyard when Hilda came around the corner and stopped. She gasped and put her hand to her heart.

"Oh, my God, Jade! You scared me to death. What are you doing here this late in the day?"

Her face looked white as a sheet under her floppy sunhat, and that made me feel terrible about not trusting her. Sheepishly, I said, "I came to talk to you about the case."

As Hilda's breathing settled down, I realized that she wore gardening gloves and the hand she'd put to her chest was covered in dirt. And now, so was her forest-green apron. I pointed at the dirt on her chest.

"I'm so sorry about that, Hilda."

She shook her head. "That's what it's for. I was about to put away my cart and have a glass of wine. I'm done for the day. Would you care to join me?"

So far, other than Hilda's initial shock at seeing me, she was being remarkably friendly. That seemed in stark contrast to the woman who'd hired me. Again, what the heck? "Sure. I'd love to. Wine sounds delightful."

Look at me—I even sounded like I fit in with the upper crust. Eat your heart out, grumpy guard. Hilda guided me to a spot in the backyard that was protected from the early evening sun by a vine-covered pergola. "I'll be right back, dear. I must put away my cart and wash my hands."

"Why don't you let me put the cart back for you? Where's it go?"

"That would be lovely, dear. It goes right around the corner." She pointed to the side of the house I hadn't seen yet.

I surveyed the yard as I went to get the cart, which was at the back end of the lot. The backyard was a veritable sanctuary—in a sense, a miniature botanical garden. It had sections showcasing different types of plants, some of which I'd seen in other local landscapes. In one section, butterflies fluttered around while two hummingbirds dueled over the rights to the territory.

In another section, which was a complete yet complementary contrast, towering palm trees swayed gently in the breeze, casting dappled shadows over a bed of lush ferns and colorful orchids. A trickling water feature contributed to the tranquil atmosphere.

I was still gawking at the landscaping when Hilda emerged from inside the house and set a tray with two glasses on the table. The garden cart had handles at the back, which I grabbed and used to guide it around the side of the house. I joined Hilda on the patio, settling into the Adirondack chair beside hers.

She smiled at me as I sat. "How do you like my backyard?"

"It's beautiful. It's like different worlds coexisting."

Her smile broadened under the sunhat, and her blue eyes sparkled. I hadn't seen her so lively since we'd met. "I spend most of my mornings out here. I sometimes like to come out here before dinner. It makes me feel as if I'm in touch with my father. He was an avid gardener from what I understand. Ethan helped me design this. We contracted out the hardscape and larger plantings, but I've done most of the work myself." She pointed at what I could only describe as a riot of color. "Those are all native to California. They're butterfly and hummingbird-friendly. The section for bees is at the back, so I don't bother them unless I have pruning to do."

"And that's a tropical section, right?"

"Yes. It's my little piece of paradise." Her shoulders slumped, and her smile drooped. "Sadly, I'm not sure what will happen to it when I'm gone."

"Oh, Hilda, don't talk like that."

Her laugh reminded me of wind chimes tinkling in the breeze. "That's not how I meant it, dear. I plan on being around much longer. I definitely want to see my great-grandchildren." Her deep, blue eyes smiled at me playfully.

Omigod. Now I understood why she wanted me to deal with Ethan and not her. She was making plans for the two of us. A rush of heat began low in my chest and cascaded upward. I tried to quell it by sipping on the wine but couldn't escape her encouraging gaze. Maybe she was right. It would be amazing if Ethan and I ended up together and started a family of our own. Then again, there was Gina to contend with. Why did life have to be so complicated?

Fantasies about matrimony and babies were not why I'd come here, though—it was time to steer this conversation back on course. I scanned the yard one last time, then, as my dad would say, jumped in with both feet. "Your yard is beautiful, Hilda, but that's not why I came here. I have news."

"Wonderful," she said, her blue eyes sparkling with interest.

"And questions."

'Oh? Of me? What do you need to know?"

Might as well start with the big one. If this didn't shake her, nothing would. "Who is Valkyrie?"

Hilda settled back in her chair, all evidence—or, perhaps, pretense—of friendliness now gone. "Benjamin was the one who first told me about her."

"Benji told you about Valkyrie?"

"Yes. He said she was arrogant and only willing to give up pieces she owned on her terms. He said she was the one who had the brooch but that he had figured out a way to get it from her."

Why hadn't she mentioned this before? Despite my irritation, I kept my voice level. "Did he say anything else?"

Hilda contemplated her glass, the small lines around the corners of her eyes crinkling as she thought. "Yes. He did. I told him I would buy A Mermaid's Allure from her, but he claimed this Valkyrie would never sell." Her voice grew thin, frail, like a crackling leaf. "When I asked him why, he said she was dangerous and that I shouldn't ask so many questions."

"And you believe Benji's dead because he was trying to help you."

She bit at her lower lip. Thin as it was, it practically disappeared. Tears welled in her eyes. "What have I done? A good man is dead over some jewelry."

My heart ached for Hilda. She'd had no idea what she was getting into when she'd asked Benji to retrieve her family's brooch. But the question still remained: who was Valkyrie, and why was she so dangerous?

"You couldn't have known, Hilda. That brooch belongs to your family. It never should have been taken from you in the first place. And besides, Benji's not dead because of the brooch. He's dead because of human greed. And maybe, arrogance."

Hilda pulled at the floppy brim of her sunhat, almost as though she were embarrassed. "There's something you should know about my mother's brooch, Jade. I should have told you this before. The piece has more than just monetary value, although that is significant. But it also is said that it beguiles its owner by bringing them immense wealth and prosperity."

Was that why she wanted it back so badly? Not for sentimental reasons, but because she hungered for money? "Do you believe that?"

"No," Hilda said firmly. "It has brought its owners far too much tragedy to believe it has that kind of power. However, I learned many years ago of the power of suggestion. I can see why some people would covet such a piece. Have you found it?"

Despite my desire to trust her, there were just too many red flags in this case. For now, the message had to remain a secret. "I'm still working on it. There's nothing new yet."

Hilda slumped a little further in her chair and heaved another deep sigh. "Dear, I'm getting very tired now. Ethan was supposed to come by this morning, but he never did. That's uncharacteristic of him. I'm getting very worried about him."

It surprised me that she still hadn't heard from Ethan. I knew he wouldn't want to alarm her unnecessarily, but I'd already fibbed to Hilda once. I didn't think I could pull it off a second time without consequences. "He's being questioned by the police. They consider him a murder suspect."

"Oh, my God." Hilda raised a bony hand and covered her lips. "This is not possible. You must help prove they're wrong. It does not matter how much it costs. You must prove his innocence."

"I'm already working on it," I said. "Hilda, have you heard of an attorney by the name of Isaac Johnson?"

"No. Is he somehow involved?"

I looked around. Was I just being paranoid? How much should I tell her? At this stage, as little as possible. "I'm not sure about Isaac Johnson, but have you had any workmen of any kind here at the house recently?"

"No, dear. Why do you ask?"

"Just curious. So, there's been nobody in the house except you?"

"That's correct. Why are you asking me these questions?"

Terrific. I was seeing ghosts where there were none. I was definitely getting paranoid.

Chapter 32

BEFORE I LEFT HILDA'S, I checked my phone for messages. One had come in while I was living the good life. It was from Rachel Yang, who indicated Sam had contacted her and that we should talk. Rachel said she had no plans for the evening and gave me her home address. In a case of true serendipity, I'd also received the email from Clara with the list of Benji's contacts. I checked the list and found Rachel Yang's name as well as Isaac Johnson's.

On my way out the gate, I waved to the grumpy guard. He waved back despite the scowl on his face. He seemed immune to the fact that we were having a beautiful evening. I took a moment to enjoy the warm, golden hues of the setting sun. We still had two hours to go before sunset, but a colorful blend of soft oranges, pinks, and purples already cast a gentle glow over the horizon.

I was still chuckling at the grumpy guard's attitude when I called Sam to thank her for helping me connect with Rachel.

"I'm on my way there now," I said. "I don't suppose there's any way you can meet me at her house."

"I could totally do that. I only live a mile away. I'll call her to let her know we're coming over."

"Thanks, Sam. You're a lifesaver."

"No problem. I could use a break."

As I drove to Rachel's house, I couldn't shake the feeling of being watched. Was it just my paranoia getting the better of me again? Or was someone truly following me?

Despite my paranoia, I made it to Rachel's house without incident. I still had a few of the creepy crawlies bothering me, so I parked down the street to avoid calling attention to myself.

Rachel opened the door before I even had a chance to knock. Sam stood behind her, a glass of white wine in her hand.

"Come in, come in!" Rachel said as she unlatched the screen door and pushed it open. Her dark eyes sparkled with warmth, and a radiant smile spread across her face, lighting up her entire expression. She welcomed me with a heartfelt hug, one filled with genuine joy and affection. "Hope that's okay," she said as she pulled away. "I'm a hugger."

"Everybody needs a good hug now and then," I said, even though I felt just a wee bit uncomfortable with the greeting.

Sam stepped forward and handed me a long-stemmed wine glass. "And a good glass of wine. It's after five o'clock, so I brought my other drink of choice."

"Thanks, Sam, but I really shouldn't."

"What? You don't drink wine?" Sam gasped, a mock look of horror crossing her face.

Alright, if we were going to be friends, I'd better tell the truth. I told them about my trip to see Hilda.

"No worries," Rachel said. "Dinner's almost ready."

"Dinner? You're going to feed me? I'm totally okay with that!"

Rachel led us to her dining room, where we settled in around a glass-topped rattan table and matching chairs with brightly flowered seat cushions. We chatted during dinner, which was pasta with garlic, olive oil, and chili flakes. Rachel called it aglio e olio. I just called it delicious and, about halfway through, broke down and asked for a small glass of wine.

When we'd cleared the table and finished the clean-up, Sam pulled out her laptop and began typing away while Rachel and I gave each other a brief rundown on our respective livelihoods. She thought being a private investigator was exciting; I considered her life as a professional art historian, blogger, and tour guide pretty darn cool, too.

"So Sam tells me you're trying to find the real identity of Valkyrie. Good luck."

"Thanks, but it's going to take a lot more than luck. Hilda Bauer said Benji told her Valkyrie is a woman. You identified her as a member of The Guild, but did you ever make any progress on figuring out her identity?"

"Valkyrie is an enigma you can never seem to pin down. For simplicity's sake, let's say Hilda is right. If Valkyrie is a woman, then she's the most elusive and cunning individual I've ever encountered in the art world. It would also make sense."

"Why's that?"

"Women are often underestimated and overlooked in the male-dominated art world, but that doesn't mean they aren't capable of pulling off elaborate heists. And back in the day when she started The Guild, a woman doing what she does would have been unheard of."

Desperate for some tidbit, any little piece of information that might help me, I asked, "Do you know anything else about her or The Guild?"

Rachel reiterated much of what I already knew, but then she stopped, took a sip of her wine, and tentatively added, "I think The Guild might be local."

"Excuse me?" I rested my elbows on my knees and studied Rachel's face. "Are you saying this international art theft ring might be based in Carlsbad?"

"At least a few of the main players." She smoothly pulled a piece of yellow notepaper from a folder and held it out for me to take. What she gave me reminded me of the executive team listing in a company prospectus. "Valkyrie" was at the top and designated as the CEO. "Obsidian Collections (Benji Thompson)—Acquisitions" came next. The list included one more entry—"Mystique (Michelle Wolfe)—validation."

"Wow. Seeing the names and their roles in print suddenly makes Benji's involvement seem so real."

"I told you, Jade. Rach worked on that one post for a few months."

Rachel seemed pleased with the compliment. "Oh, it's way more than that, Sam. I've been working on The Guild off-and-on for years. There's almost nothing in the news world about them. What little I have comes from word of mouth. I've pieced together information from various sources and connections. But even with all of that research, I don't have anything concrete."

"But why would they choose Carlsbad? It's a small town, not exactly a hub for international art dealers and collectors."

"I don't know. Maybe it's a cover or a way to throw off suspicion. Or maybe there's something here that we're totally missing." Rachel screwed up her face and added, "Your guess is as good as mine."

"I might have something more than a guess," I said. "Have you seen the letter of provenance for A Mermaid's Allure?"

"I've heard of the piece, but I never went looking for a letter of provenance."

Sam pulled up a copy of the letter on her computer. I had her scroll to the end. "The letter was written by Michelle Wolfe. Her business is located in Berlin. How did she get connected to the brooch and The Guild?"

"Maybe because of the estate for Lukas Müller?" Sam asked.

"I thought of that, too," I said. "But doesn't it strike you as pretty coincidental that Rachel has tied Michelle Wolfe to The Guild and Benji brokered the deal to Valkyrie? I think that's solid proof that you've got the identities right, Rachel. The part that doesn't make sense is how someone from Carlsbad connects with an art researcher halfway around the world."

"True," Rachel said. "To my knowledge, there are no help-wanted outlets for art thieves, so that probably means the connections came first."

"They must have known each other before The Guild started," I said. After explaining my reasoning, both Rachel and Sam were nodding enthusiastically.

"That would make sense. You really have to trust each other to do what these guys did, so Valkyrie probably recruited based on who knew who. Because this group is very selective about what they steal, I don't think it's a big organized network. That means it's a small, tight band." Rachel smacked her hand on the arm of her chair and let out a little whoop. "Why didn't I think of this before? They had to start somewhere."

Almost in unison, the three of us said, "So what was their first job?"

We all burst into laughter, and Sam said, "Great minds."

I didn't want to rain on anyone's parade, but we'd better be smarter than Valkyrie. Otherwise, we could end up like Benji. Which meant I needed to decide—was I willing to bring Rachel onto the team or not? The problem was that she already knew too much to be left out.

Suddenly, Rachel turned serious. "I can tell by the look on your face that you're having second thoughts about this, Jade. I'll understand if you don't want to include me right now. Heck, I had all kinds of warning bells going off when Sam told me what you were doing. But the thing is, this ring is incredibly smart and ruthless. If you want my help, I'm in. If you don't, walk away before you tell me anything else. Before you make that choice, there's something you should know about me. I grew up in a household with a deep appreciation for arts and culture. I hate the idea that these guys are getting away with this. I'd love to help you nail them. That's it. End of my pitch."

I studied Rachel's face for a few seconds and saw her passion. She obviously had commitment—she'd worked on identifying this group for years. "I've had people warning me to be careful and not trust anyone, but I don't see how I can make any progress without help. I'm out of my depth with all this talk about conspiracies and international art theft rings."

"Yeah, it's pretty heavy-duty stuff. I started out not knowing anything about The Guild. Then, four years ago, I was doing a special museum tour in San Diego about some of Vermeer's work. There was this guy on my tour who seemed very interested in one particular painting, 'The Courtyard Musicians.' It was so strange because he kept trying to take videos and photos during the tour, and that's not allowed."

Sam interrupted, her tone intense. "Jade, that painting went missing right after the exhibit."

Rachel grimaced. "I didn't learn it was missing until about a month later when I was doing another tour. The museum director was scheduled to speak with my group. When he did, he was lamenting the loss of the painting."

"That's Jonathan," Sam added, then raised her eyebrows. "And guess who the guy on the tour was?"

I shook my head. "Who?"

"Benji Thompson," Rachel said. "I couldn't shake the feeling that he'd been using my tour to do surveillance on the location, so I started asking around. I discovered that Benji traveled extensively and was a collector, too. I asked myself why a guy like that would need to go on one of my tours. Let's face it. My tours aren't for serious collectors. They're for tourists and people who have a budding interest in art."

By the time Rachel had walked me through the balance of her research, I felt compelled to trust her. Trusting, in this case, meant sharing. I told her about the message in the cryptogram and the conversation with Leo. Then, I pulled out my phone and showed her the list of Benji's contacts. "Do you recognize any of the names on that list?"

"Totally. Benji was a client of Isaac Johnson's. I know because after I published a blog about the 'disappearance' of The Courtyard Musicians, Isaac sent me a nasty letter implying that I'd slandered his client. He demanded a retraction. I told him I wouldn't take down the post, but I would remove Benji's name, and that seemed to work for him."

"So there is a connection. That's interesting because Johnson is the one who hired Jake Marlough."

"The rat," Sam muttered. "How did I not see through that man's slimy exterior?"

We both assured her that she shouldn't beat herself up over the mistake, especially because we'd all been there before. Trying to make Sam feel a little better, I asked Rachel about other names on the list.

Rachel scrunched up her nose and tugged on one ear. "Amy Kensington is the mayor. I'm not surprised Benji knew her. This one, Peter Sinclair? The name sounds familiar, but I can't place him. That's bugging me."

"He owns Sinclair's. It's a restaurant downtown. Chef Pete and Benji were friends."

"Of course." Rachel snapped her fingers. "I remember him. He took over from his father a few years ago. I've had several of my customers tell me I should go to his restaurant. From the sounds of it, I can't afford the appetizers."

I snickered. "Ethan took me there. It was not cheap. It's out of my league. But you know who else was there? The mayor. Looked like a high-power meeting of some kind."

"This is totally sounding like a tight circle of friends," Rachel said.

"And Benji crossed one of them—maybe all of them—and that's what got him killed," I mused.

"Exactly. Ladies, I think we might be onto something," Sam said.

"And since Benji told Hilda that Valkyrie was a woman, that means it's not Peter Sinclair or Isaac Johnson. It doesn't take Amy Kensington off the hook. She could be Valkyrie."

Sam nodded enthusiastically, but Rachel seemed unconvinced. "What if there's somebody else? Another person who's not even on our radar?"

"Someone we've missed? It's always possible. But I say it's time to start shaking some trees, and I know right where to start."

Chapter 33

I WAS UP EARLY WEDNESDAY morning to do some surfing, more research on A Mermaid's Allure, and see what I could dig up on Isaac Johnson. Even though the waves were flat and the research turned up almost nothing, the research and prep work for my meeting with Isaac felt like it had put me in peak form.

At ten-thirty, I marched into Isaac Johnson's office and flashed my private investigator's license at his receptionist. "Jade Cavendish. I'm here to see Mr. Johnson," I said confidently.

The woman behind the desk was a thin Latina with dark eyes and a captivating smile. Her elegance and grace left me wishing I had her charm and her ability to appear unfazed by some random PI barging into the office and demanding an audience with the boss. "Is Mr. Johnson expecting you?"

"No, but I think he'll want to see me. I'm here about the death of Benji Thompson."

"Of course," she replied, her smile never wavering. Her calm demeanor impressed me. Even when I mentioned Benji's death, not a flicker of emotion crossed her face. She remained composed and professional as if accustomed to handling sensitive or surprising information with poise. Her reaction, or lack thereof, hinted at a level of experience and control that left me wondering how much she knew or suspected about the circles she was working within.

I waited, hoping I'd be able to read Isaac Johnson's reaction to me barging in while the receptionist spoke in a measured tone on the phone. When she hung up, she graced me with a toothpaste-commercial smile. "Mr. Johnson will see you now. Follow me."

Less than a minute later, I was shaking hands with the man Sam had introduced me to at Benji's funeral. In addition to spending time with Sam, he'd flitted around from one person to the next at the reception. A somewhat imposing figure, he stood a little over six feet tall, had jet black hair, which he'd combed back neatly, and sharp, intelligent hazel eyes. His rectangular glasses sat on the edge of his straight, narrow nose.

He thanked his receptionist and gestured at one of the chairs in front of his desk. "Ms. Cavendish, how can I help you today?"

Now that we were alone, I decided to set the tone for our impromptu meeting. "Why did you plant a bug in the bouquet you sent to your girlfriend?"

His expression remained calm, though a hint of surprise flickered in his eyes. "I'm sorry, I have no idea what you're talking about."

Crossing my arms over my chest, I held my ground. "Oh, please. Don't play dumb with me. You know exactly what I'm talking about. You're interested in A Mermaid's Allure. What I can't figure out is how you knew Sam and I would be working together."

He eyed me as though I were a witness on the stand that he was about to expose as a fraud. But more important than that was the machine he had on his credenza. I'd seen photos of old cipher machines and was sure this fit the bill.

His eyes turned cold, and his voice took on a hard edge. "Ms. Cavendish, if this is some kind of joke or attempt at blackmail, let me assure you, it will not work."

"I'm not joking. And I have no interest in blackmailing anyone. But I do want answers."

Isaac seemed to realize he wasn't going to bully me. His facial expression underwent a subtle yet significant transformation. His eyes softened, shifting from a hardened stare to a more understanding and empathetic gaze, and his mouth curved slightly into a thoughtful, reassuring smile. "I understand your concern, but it's none of your business how I knew about your collaboration with Sam. What matters is that the bug was planted as a precautionary measure for her safety."

My eyebrows shot up in disbelief. "Sam's safety? From who? Valkyrie?"

He hesitated, obviously surprised by the name. "Let's just say there are people who would do anything to get their hands on that brooch—including sabotaging someone's professional relationship."

"That implies you know who Valkyrie is."

"No. I have no idea who this Valkyrie is. I've never heard the name before."

Liar, I thought. But I couldn't prove it. I had to keep pushing. "Who are these people you're so concerned about?"

Isaac's eyes narrowed, his posture shifting as he leaned in, his voice a hushed murmur that carried weight. "Ms. Cavendish, you have no idea what you're dealing with here. I suggest you drop this investigation and forget whatever you think you know. It's not worth the risk."

I felt like I'd just watched a clam snap its shell closed. His reaction might have been driven by fear, but I doubted it. No, I felt certain Isaac Johnson knew Valkyrie. Did that mean he also was part of The Guild? Without a more compelling argument, this conversation was going nowhere, so I feigned understanding. With luck, I could at least buy some time.

"You're right, Mr. Johnson. This does sound dangerous. Thank you for your advice."

He seemed taken aback by my sudden capitulation but stood when I did. He walked with me to the door, then turned to face me. "One more thing, Ms. Cavendish. You're a bad influence on Sam. Leave her alone. Good day."

I thanked him again for his concern as I left, doing my best timid-as-a-mouse impression. If I knew more about The Guild, I'd love to treat this arrogant jerk like the heavy bag at the gym. Unfortunately, at least for now, I would pretend to be intimidated by his warnings. But Isasc Johnson didn't know me. If he did, he'd know that all he'd done was fuel my determination.

I walked the two blocks back to my car, scanning the area around me. There were no white vans, no sign of Jake Marlough. Not willing to take any chances, I got in the car and checked the GPS tracker on Marlough's van. He was in Oceanside, miles away. I called Sam to tell her my suspicions. She deserved to know I didn't think her boyfriend was on the side of the good guys.

"After you found the bug, I was kind of sure that was the case. I've been mentally preparing myself ever since. I'm totally breaking up with that jerk."

"Don't do it right away, Sam. Just avoid him if you can." I did another full scan of the area, watching for some thug that Isaac might send after me. "We don't want to raise his suspicions."

She huffed, then said, "There's a problem with that. He called and said he wants to go to dinner tonight."

"When did he call?"

"Like, two minutes ago. I didn't answer, so he left a message."

"He's doing damage control," I muttered, the frustration evident in my voice. A wave of apprehension swept through me. My subconscious was telling me something, but I couldn't pin it down. "I didn't think he'd act so quickly. He must be doing whatever he can to keep you under his control."

"What do you want me to do?"

"Can you put him off? We need a day or two to get ahead of this."

"Okay. I'll text him back and say I've got a sudden project at work that my boss wants tomorrow. That's happened before."

"No, it can't be work-related. Otherwise, he'll think we're still collaborating."

"Gotcha. I can tell him I'm having dinner with my parents. He's super averse to meeting them, so that's a sure way out."

"Perfect," I replied, still surveying my surroundings as I spoke. Suddenly, I realized what had been bugging me. It was the dark sedan parked in a yellow zone on the opposite side of the street. The same car had tailed me earlier. Every instinct in my body screamed that this was not a mere coincidence. A cold shiver ran down my spine, turning my earlier frustration into a gnawing sense of danger.

"Sam, listen carefully. Somebody is watching me. I'm pretty sure it's not Marlough." I described the car, gave her the license plate number, and told her if she didn't hear from me in half an hour to call the police.

After disconnecting the call, I opened my door and started to walk. I stayed on my side of the street, but my path took me toward the sedan. The Glock hugged my lower back as I walked. My breathing quickened. Every sensation in my body was on high alert as I ducked between two cars. Whoever was in that sedan, I was ready for them.

Chapter 34

I APPROACHED THE VEHICLE WITH caution. But partway across the street, I recognized the driver. It was Val Torres. Why would a reporter want to follow me, especially one I'd known since taking over the agency? Why wouldn't she have just called me? She got out and waved as I approached.

"What's going on, Val? Why are you here?"

She sighed, then winced. "After I saw you at Benji's funeral, I was sure I was missing out on a really good story. I'm sorry if I freaked you out."

"You nearly got yourself shot," I snapped. Okay, my reaction was a little over the top, but I didn't like being tailed. "How long have you been following me?"

"Off and on since the break-in at Timeless Treasures. I heard the call on the scanner and was shocked when I checked it out and saw that you were involved. At that point, I figured you were onto something. And this morning, I decided it was the make-or-break day —I either had to get something solid or give it up. I swear, Jade, I had no clue this would upset you so much."

My heart still raced from the adrenaline rush of thinking I was walking into a dangerous situation. Now it turned out it was just a nosy reporter. "Thanks for giving me a heart attack."

Val looked genuinely apologetic. "I'm really sorry, Jade. It won't happen again."

I let out a breath and tried to calm down. Val wasn't my enemy. She was just doing her job as a journalist. And in all honesty, she might even be a good source of information.

"You know what? Maybe we can work together."

Val's face lit up. "Really? I thought you'd want to get rid of me."

"I might have a better idea, but we need to make a deal."

"What kind of deal?" she asked suspiciously.

"You help me with this case, and I'll give you exclusive access to the story."

Val's eyes widened in excitement, and I immediately regretted making the offer. "Sounds good," she said.

We shook hands to close the deal. My circle of confidantes was growing, and it was not an overwhelmingly positive feeling. "What are you doing tonight?"

She scrunched up her face and grinned in anticipation. "Meeting you for drinks?"

That was actually a good idea. If I could get everyone together, we could probably sail under The Guild's radar. The question was, where to go? Maybe the best place was the most public. It was noisy and crowded, and nobody could possibly listen in on what we were saying. "Flying Pig. Eight o'clock. I've got two others to confirm with, but I'll call you within the hour."

After confirming that both Sam and Rachel could meet us at the Flying Pig, I went to the gym, did another workout, and then went home to shower, have dinner, and get ready. At Mom and Dad's suggestion, I also invited Zoe to join us.

The Flying Pig had become a sanctuary for workers seeking a vibrant and relaxing escape after a long day, thanks to its proximity to downtown. It had become a local favorite, known for its lively atmosphere, mouth-watering food, and irresistible margaritas— especially the margaritas.

Zoe stood next to the restaurant's sign, which featured a whimsical flying pig, wings outstretched and a sombrero perched jauntily above its smiling pig snout. Strings of fairy lights overhead cast her in a warm glow, and the excitement on her face made it clear she was excited to be included in tonight's meeting.

"The place is hopping tonight," said Zoe. "I got lucky and was able to grab a table in the bar that's big enough to squeeze in the five of us." She continued rambling as we made our way to the table she'd somehow secured.

"How exactly did you get them to hold this for us?"

Zoe snickered. "Trade secret." But, as usual, keeping a secret was not in Zoe's repertoire. She went on to tell me how she and the server were in the same English class. Apparently, our server, a lanky blonde with overdone makeup and a personality that exuded enthusiasm even more than Zoe's, also had journalistic aspirations. "When I told her that Val Torres was gonna be here, Connie said she totally wanted to meet her."

"You didn't say anything about what we'd be discussing, did you?"

"No way." Zoe made a zipping motion with her fingers across her lips. "They're sealed."

I breathed a sigh of relief. As long as Connie didn't want to sit in on our conversation, everything should be fine. Rachel and Sam arrived at the same time. They looked like they'd been engaged in a lively discussion. Val arrived while we were still doing introductions, and Connie showed up about thirty seconds later with a frosty pitcher of margaritas.

We did the obligatory introduction of Val to Connie, who gushed over Val's latest exposé on a scam that had been bilking seniors out of their savings. Connie was delighted when Val shared her phone number and told her to call if she wanted to talk about the real life of a reporter.

Smiling to herself as Connie sauntered off to her next table, Val chuckled and said, "She's bubbly."

We raised our glasses in a toast, and I felt a warmth building inside. I always enjoyed getting out with friends, and now it looked like I might have some new ones. "Okay, ladies, here's the deal." I went on to recap what had happened so far. Then, with everyone up to speed, I looked at Val. "What's this story you were working on?"

Val swallowed hard and scanned the bar. She lowered her voice and leaned forward. "Benji and I were talking about a week before he died. He told me I should be looking into the mayor's campaign fund." She took a long breath, then added, "Specifically, he said I should be looking for large contributions from an organization called The Guild."

We all spent the next few seconds looking at each other. Nobody seemed sure what to say next. "The Guild isn't a legitimate organization, Val. It's an art theft ring. I doubt that they have a bank account."

"Wait, what? That would explain why I never found any contributions in their name." Val craned her neck forward, the look on her face turning skeptical. "Are you sure?"

"Positive," I said.

"That's not so crazy," Rachel said. "Amy Kensington has always had a close relationship with the police chief. What if she was using her influence to keep tabs on investigations into The Guild's activities?"

"Whoa! That's awesome thinking, Rach. And totally on point," Zoe said. "Jade, remember when I did that blog post on local crime statistics? I never told you, but Mayor K. called me and started making threats about how I was hurting the city's reputation. She backed off when I reminded her she was running for reelection, and I had solid statistics."

"It's all starting to fit together," I said. "Benji started feeling remorseful about his role in The Guild. Valkyrie must have found out about it."

"And then silenced him before he could expose the members," Rachel said.

We sat, the only quiet table in a roomful of noise. Was this about the power of corruption and how easily the truth could be covered up by those in positions of authority? Or was this about something else? "Girls, there's something not tracking here. Benji was a part of The Guild for a very long time. Why would he suddenly decide to betray them?"

"Unless he knew they were gonna kill him!" Zoe blurted.

I gaped at Zoe, who sat beside me but wasn't looking at me. She was staring at an empty space in front of her as though she was seeing something invisible to everyone except her.

"That's totally it," Sam said. "Benji had already decided to get out, and he created the cryptogram as a backup."

Val shook her head sadly. "And he contacted me as a Plan B."

"Because he knew Valkyrie would want revenge," Rachel said.

It felt like a miracle that we were all working together, but then I realized it might have been inevitable. Benji had orchestrated everything, and he'd left nothing to chance. It wasn't as if he could foresee the future, but he'd apparently been quite the chess player. He'd also known my determination.

"Jade, he must have trusted you to find all of us," Sam said.

I sipped from my frosty glass, the icy mixture of salt, sweet, and citrusy tartness a welcome relief from the dark thoughts. "I was just thinking the same thing," I said, feeling sad that Benji had felt forced to plan for his own murder.

"He had faith in you, Jade," added Val. "In all of us."

"And rightly so," I said. But as I looked around the table, I wondered how Benji had grown to trust us all so much. We had no small task ahead of us. Actually, we had three huge ones. Somehow, we had to recover a priceless brooch, unmask an art theft ring, and, yes, find a killer in the process.

I raised my glass. "To Benji's foresight!"

We clinked glasses all the way around, but through my tequila-fueled euphoria, I kept hoping that Benji's foresight really was as good as what we were toasting to.

Chapter 35

I ARRIVED AT THE OFFICE just after seven the following morning. To my surprise, Zoe was already engrossed in whatever was on her computer screen. She practically jumped out of her chair when I pushed through the door.

"Jeez! Don't do that to me, Jade!"

"What? Come to work?"

"You totally scared me to death." Zoe picked up her mug and cradled it in her hands. "So, are you gonna call Benji's nurse today?"

I dropped my bag onto my desk and plopped down into my chair. "Yes. That's on my agenda. I should have thought of it sooner because I met her at the funeral. She said Benji sometimes talked during his treatments. Unfortunately, it's too early to call her. When we met, she explained that she worked nights sometimes."

"What about Clara? Maybe she knows something about that law firm."

"She doesn't. I asked her, and she's never heard of the lawyer or the firm."

Zoe looked at me skeptically. "This is seriously messed up, Jade. You've got to get to that lawyer. You can't wait until Monday."

"What choice do I have, Zoe? The woman is off on vacation— probably in Europe or Greece or some other fancy destination." My shoulders slumped. One thing I truly, truly hated was waiting and doing nothing because of a roadblock. And right now, all forward progress seemed to be blocked by Elizabeth Carter. "I'll call. What the heck? I might as well make a pest of myself."

The same secretary answered the phone, but when I told her who I was, she said, "Oh, good. I was about to call you. Ms. Carter has asked me to see if you can come in this morning."

"I thought she was out of the office this week."

"She changed her plans to meet with you. Can you be here in an hour?"

Dumbfounded, I muttered an enthusiastic, "Yes. I'll be there."

"Excellent. I'll let Ms. Carter know."

I listened to the dead phone, then hung up. "I've got an appointment in an hour."

"Awesome! You'd better get going. Traffic's gonna be awful."

Zoe was right about the traffic. It was slow-and-go most of the way. Still, I made it to downtown San Diego with fifteen minutes to spare. I parked near the Santa Fe Depot, San Diego's iconic historic train station, and hustled along with the mix of tourists and professionals. Cars and pedestrians crowded the streets, each vying for their fifteen seconds of dominance. Horns blared when one pedestrian took too long crossing and was still in the crosswalk when the light changed.

As I approached One America Plaza, I craned my neck to follow the sleek, reflective glass facade. The building towered over others nearby. The large, automatic doors slid open as I entered a spacious and elegantly appointed lobby. This was definitely high-end, about as far on the opposite end of the architectural scale as you could get from my quaint little office.

I found the law firm listed in the directory and piled into an elevator with three other people. Within seconds, I walked off of the elevator and stood before a pair of heavy glass doors with the names Harris, Mitchell & Reynolds prominently etched into the glass. All I could think of as my shoes sunk into the plush carpet was that the grand entrance probably cost more than I'd make this year.

A receptionist smiled warmly and asked for my name. Her makeup was perfect, and her navy suit was impeccably tailored.

I gave her my name and started to tell her I had an appointment with Ms. Carter, but she instructed me to take a seat before I finished. My butt had barely hit the chair when another fashion model pushed open a glass door and looked directly at me.

"Ms. Cavendish? Please come with me. Ms. Carter will see you now."

I followed her along a wide hallway past a series of closed doors. As I walked along the hallway, I noticed the complete lack of sound. The plush carpet beneath my feet absorbed every step, even every breath, creating an eerie silence.

At the end of the hall, we came to an open door flanked by a nameplate that read, "Elizabeth Carter, Senior Partner." The secretary stepped aside so I could enter. The room was no less opulent than everything else I'd seen. What caught my eye, though, was a large photo of a sailboat with sails unfurled and leaning to one side in the wind.

A woman's voice broke the spell of silence and pulled me away from the photo. "That's one of my favorites. It was taken on our way to Catalina last year."

The voice belonged to a middle-aged woman with sharp, almond-shaped hazel eyes that reflected her keen intellect and unwavering focus. She wore her chestnut-brown hair in a sophisticated bun, further accentuating her professional demeanor.

I was immediately reminded of Isaac Johnson's passion for sailing. The boat was different from the one in the photo Sam had shown me, but I had no idea how small the sailing world might be. "Do you know an attorney named Isaac Johnson?"

Liz Carter shook her head. "No. Should I?"

"He's an attorney in Carlsbad who likes to sail."

"I see. I've never heard of the man. I sail with my husband, another partner here, and his spouse. We don't have much time to socialize in the sailing community."

I realized the secretary who'd brought me back had closed the door and disappeared. It was as though she'd melted into the walls without a sound. I grinned and stepped forward with my hand extended. "All I have is a surfboard. I'm jealous. Jade Cavendish."

"Liz Carter. Thank you for coming on such short notice. Benji was a very special client. Let's get down to business. Please, have a seat. Do you have the PIN?" This woman's high cheekbones and strong jawline gave her an air of authority and determination. I could see why Benji would have trusted her. She struck me as the type the government could trust with the keys to Fort Knox.

"Do you mean the code that was with your name?" I asked.

"Yes. It was Benji's failsafe mechanism. I'll also need to see your ID."

I pulled the paper from my pocket and read off the code. After that, I produced my PI's license and my driver's license. When Liz was satisfied I was who I said I was, she pulled a remote control from her top drawer.

"Benji hired my firm to ensure that you, and only you, see what I'm about to show you. Please, direct your attention to the screen on your left," she said, once again all business.

The flat TV screen mounted to the wall lit up. I fell into a stunned silence when Benji appeared. It was a classic head-and-shoulders shot against a white screen. The look of pain in his eyes was unmistakable. Though he had a stocky build that hinted at a historically athletic lifestyle, in this video, his silver-grey hair was in disarray, and he slumped uncharacteristically. His brown eyes seemed to hold a thousand secrets.

"Hello, Jade," Benji's voice cracked. Again, very out of character for him. I'd always known Benji as a man with a deep voice that seemed to fill the room with its sound. This version, however, sounded breathy and tentative.

He cleared his throat, took a sip from a glass of water, and then continued. "I've made many mistakes in my life that I now deeply regret."

Benji paused and looked off to the side as though he were seeking reinforcement. "Please accept my sincere apologies for burdening you with the need to correct my final error. I never wanted to involve you unless something happened to me. Obviously, I underestimated someone I once considered a friend. And, as you have no doubt learned, I was once a member of The Guild."

The video stopped, and I realized I had my hand over my heart, which broke for the anguish Benji must have gone through near the end.

"There's more," Liz Carter said. "However, at this point, he wanted me to confirm that you were aware that he was a member of this group."

"I am. At least, that was my conclusion based on what I've uncovered."

"And you're aware of what the group did?"

"Yes."

"Very well. Let's continue."

She clicked the remote, and Benji's frozen image snapped to life.

"It wasn't until I met Hilda Bauer that I realized how deeply my participation in that group hurt others. Over the past few years, I have attempted to correct my most egregious mistakes. Because you are watching this, I congratulate you on your investigative skills. I must also let you know that my efforts have been compromised by a foolish mistake I made."

Benji paused again to clear his throat. His eyes welled with tears. My heart went out to the man for the courage it must have taken to make this video when he thought he was about to die.

"I must urge you to not pursue the issue of my death. My killer will go to any extent to avoid being caught. It is also unlikely that the killer will be brought to justice. Valkyrie has far too much power. Her tentacles stretch into law enforcement. I caution you. Leave my death alone. I could not bear the thought of you also becoming a victim."

The video cut off, and my hand went to my heart again. I realized I had tears in my eyes and swiped at my cheeks. "I can't believe he had the courage to do that."

Liz Carter nodded solemnly. "Benji was a strong man. A good one, too. He was trying to atone for the mistakes he made when he was young. Sadly, his efforts were cut short. Are you okay? Do you need a minute?"

I shook my head. "No. I'll be fine. What I don't understand is how he expects me to find A Mermaid's Allure. He didn't provide me with any clues. You don't have it, do you?"

"No. I don't have the piece, but this should help you." She held up an envelope addressed to me. "In this envelope is a Durable Power of Attorney. It grants you the authority to enter safe deposit box number 1212 at Carlsbad Community Bank. Do you have the key to the box?"

"I did find a key, but I have no idea what it's for."

"May I see it?"

"Of course." I pulled out the key I'd found in Timeless Treasures and handed it across the desk.

"That's it," she said as she returned it. "According to Benji's instructions, you will find the brooch in that safe deposit box."

I took the envelope, a mixture of pride and sorrow rising inside me. A man was dead, his life cut short prematurely. And, he'd entrusted me with his final wish to right an old wrong. "Thank you," I whispered as I took the envelope.

Before letting go, Liz Carter locked her gaze onto mine. "Ms. Cavendish, I cannot stress enough the gravity of what you're being asked to do."

"Don't worry, I'll return A Mermaid's Allure to Mrs. Bauer."

"I'm not talking about the brooch. I'm referring to Benji's death. The last thing he told me was, 'Do not let her cross swords with Valkyrie. She will lose. I have also made arrangements to deal with her.'"

When Liz Carter released the envelope, it was like in the movies when the hero is suddenly tasked with taking an impossible journey. In this case, that journey meant letting someone get away with murder.

Was that something I could even bring myself to do? At this moment, I didn't know the answer to that question.

Chapter 36

ALL THE WAY BACK TO Carlsbad, I kept thinking about Benji begging me not to investigate his death. Part of me, the crusader, wanted to hunt down Valkyrie and make her pay. The other part, the pragmatist, reminded me that Detective Des was a good cop and would find Valkyrie sooner or later.

I still didn't know what I was going to do when I pulled into the parking lot at Carlsbad Community Bank. Somehow, though, the pragmatist was slowly winning me over. It wasn't my job to find a killer. In fact, Benji had explicitly requested that I not investigate. And Clara had only hired me to look into her husband's business dealings. The idea of walking away left a bad taste in my mouth. I entered the bank, the debate still raging in my head.

The cool air inside the bank was a welcome contrast to the late afternoon heat outside. The interior was a blend of modernity and tradition; polished marble floors extended towards the elegant wooden counters where tellers busied themselves with a steady stream of patrons. Glass walls offered a clear view of the conference rooms and managers' offices, giving a sense of transparency and openness to the bustling, professional atmosphere.

I strode to the reception desk, where a young woman, no older than twenty-five, greeted me with a polite smile. The nameplate on her desk read "Emily." She had wavy chestnut hair pulled back into a precise ponytail and wore a crisp, navy-blue blouse that complemented her bright eyes. "Good afternoon, how may I assist you today?" she asked, her voice carrying a hint of genuine interest that put me at ease.

"I'm here to access safe deposit box 1212," I said, presenting my identification, the power of attorney Liz Carter had given me, and the key I'd found in Benji's desk. Emily's eyes flickered over the documents, then briefly to the key. A cloud of uncertainty crossed her face, but she nodded curtly and stood.

"Of course, Ms. Cavendish. Please follow me." She stepped from behind the desk, and I followed her down a corridor adorned with framed photos of Carlsbad's historical milestones. Emily's professionalism was evident in her confident stride and attentive nature. In the vault, she quickly found box 1212 and inserted her key.

After doing the same with my key, she opened the box and gestured to a small, secure room where I could privately examine the contents. "If you need any further assistance, please don't hesitate to ask," she said, her eyes briefly meeting mine with a reassuring look before she gently closed the door behind her. The gravity of the mission ahead weighed heavily on me, but for now, my focus was on what lay inside box 1212.

The box contained only three items. A small, handwritten note to me, a #10 business envelope addressed to Detective Des Martini, and a small, square jewelry box from Timeless Treasures. Unable to contain my curiosity, I opened the box first.

My breath caught when I saw A Mermaid's Allure. Even though I'd seen the photo of it before, I wasn't prepared for the emotional rush I felt when I saw how the black opals and diamonds sparkled under the overhead lighting. The fluid lines of the setting curved around the jewels, mimicking the delicate features of a mermaid's face and the way her hair might flow in the ocean current. The piece had certainly been aptly named. It was as if I were actually looking at a miniature, real-life version of a mermaid.

Closing the case, I slipped it into my bag and turned my attention to the note.

Jade - As Ms. Carter told you, I do not want you investigating my death. Instead, my final request is for you to hand deliver this envelope directly to Detective Des Martini at the Carlsbad Police Department. Do not give it to anyone else. Let her be the one to investigate my death. Benji.

I fingered the envelope, tempted to open it. Turning it over, my hopes of snooping were dashed when I saw the elegant wax seal with the Timeless Treasures logo that had been applied over it. No matter what I did to this envelope, I knew it would be damaged. Either the seal would be broken, or the wax would leave a residue. There was no doubt the seal was designed as a safety precaution. Benji wanted to make sure I did as he'd asked. Apparently, the man knew me better than I thought.

I placed the envelope in my bag next to the brooch's case, then returned the safe deposit box to its slot in the wall and locked it with my key. On my way out, I thanked Emily and told her I was done. An odd sense of foreboding came over me when I pushed through the glass doors and saw an old blue Crown Victoria, the kind the cops used for years, parked in the spot next to mine. There were other open spaces. Why was that driver crowding me?

My self-defense training kicked into high gear when two men exited the Crown Vic. The scruffier of the two stood at the passenger door chatting with the driver, who went to the rear of the car. I told

Scruffy he was blocking access to my door. He grunted and moved past me.

I turned sideways so I could keep an eye on Scruffy. My every nerve tingled with an adrenaline rush I couldn't deny. This was a no-win situation. I had to get in my car as soon as possible.

When I stuck my key in the lock, Scruffy charged me head-on. I twisted my stance to a standard fighting position, raised my knee, and snapped my foot forward. The precisely timed kick connected perfectly. Scruffy barely had time to react before my foot landed in his groin with a sickening thud. He doubled over in pain, clutching himself as he staggered backward and crumpled to the ground.

Before I could turn to face the driver, a hiss filled the air, followed by a fine mist that enveloped my face. At first, I noticed a peculiar, almost sweet scent, barely noticeable but enough to make me pause. Within seconds, a strange warmth spread from my nostrils and mouth, radiating down my throat and into my lungs. The warmth quickly turned into a tingling sensation, as if tiny, invisible needles were pricking my skin from the inside.

My vision blurred at the edges, colors smearing together in a disorienting swirl as someone's arms enveloped me. The world seemed to pulse, each heartbeat echoing loudly in my ears. A heavy, almost oppressive drowsiness settled over me. I couldn't resist the unseen force pressing down on my eyelids, urging them to close.

I tried to escape the arms, but my limbs wouldn't move. It was like I was swimming through a vat of thick maple syrup. My thoughts fragmented as I landed on a hard surface. I curled up in a ball as pieces of reality slipped away. Confusion clouded my mind. The numbing haze deepened, pulling me inexorably towards unconsciousness. The next thing I knew, I was lying on a metal floor, trying to escape the haze that clouded my thoughts.

By the time I could focus, I realized I must be inside a shipping container. The air was stifling, thick with an oppressive heat that seemed to press down from all sides. The metal walls looked like they'd been coated with a primer that radiated an intense, almost unbearable warmth. Each breath came with tremendous effort. It was as if I were inhaling through a hot, damp cloth in a room with metallic-tasting air.

I shuffled around the container, my running shoes making a soft, rhythmic whisper against the solid steel floor that echoed like a distant heartbeat in the quiet. My mouth felt like I'd been in the desert for a week without water. Pale rays of light poked through a few spots. I found two airflow grates and put my face close, hoping the fresh air might help me think more clearly. It wasn't worth the effort.

As I waited, the haze clouding my thoughts lifted. I should have been happy that my thoughts were clearer, but it only made things worse. I was trapped with no way out. I'd lost the brooch. My gun. My phone.

The thought that someone from the bank had betrayed me hit hard, and with it came a disheartening certainty that Valkyrie had outmaneuvered me just as she had Benji.

Chapter 37

I SAT, MY BACK PLANTED against a steel wall, watching cracks of sunlight poke through the two ventilation grates. The changing angle and intensity of the light became my only sense of time. I had plenty of time to think—and drift off into another drug-induced stupor. At those times when my thoughts cleared even for a few seconds, I cursed my naive trust in the bank's receptionist and hoped someone would find me before I died from dehydration.

As the light waned, so did my hopes of escape or rescue. I had no tools. No way to communicate. Unless you count pounding on the walls of the container with my fist. Apparently, I'd tried that at some point while I was still half-drugged because my hand ached, and I couldn't remember how it had happened.

I curled forward and rested my elbows on my knees. Had I been left here to die? Everything was getting hazy again. The heat and lack of water had to be making me hallucinate because I was now hearing someone call my name.

"I'm here," I croaked, my shoulders shaking as the tears I thought had dried out streamed down my cheeks. "I'm here," I whimpered.

Again, a faint voice called out, "Jade!"

Then, another. "Cavendish!"

Was it real or a figment of my imagination? I couldn't tell anymore. I tried to call back, but my voice came out as nothing more than a hoarse whisper. Shaking my head, I stood and went to the air grate. The voices were clearer here. There were two of them. Men.

I tried to swallow, but my throat was too dry. Taking another breath, I pounded the metal siding. My hand felt like it would explode from the pain, so I stepped back and delivered a kick. The container rumbled with a sound like distant thunder. I kicked again. And again.

The voices suddenly grew louder. Whoever was calling my name was close now. I kicked again. And then, Jake Marlough's voice came through the airflow grate.

"Hey, Cavendish. First rule of being a PI? Don't let yourself get put in shipping containers."

"We'll have you out in a minute."

The second voice sounded like Ethan's. What was he doing here? How had he known I'd been kidnapped? How had Marlough known?

I stumbled to the doors and listened as metal scraped on metal. When the door opened, I tried to step out, but my knees buckled. I fell forward into Jake's arms.

"Nice to see you, too, Cavendish. Glad you're still alive."

"Drink." Ethan shoved a bottle of water in my hand. His voice had an edge to it.

What did he have to be angry about? I'm the one who'd been trapped in an oversized hothouse. I shielded my eyes and squinted at the blinding, wonderful sight on the horizon. The sun. It had almost set. How long had I been trapped in there? Four? Five hours?

I took the bottle and started to gulp down water, but Ethan pulled it away. "Not too much at once. Drink slowly. I…I thought I'd lost you."

"What do you mean?" I croaked—my voice sounding like a robot with a dying battery.

"The reason I went to Sam's office that morning was because I felt terrible about how things ended after dinner. I wanted to apologize and tell you I was wrong in questioning your judgment or your methods. I'm sorry, Jade."

Despite how lousy I felt, a warm feeling spread throughout my chest. Sam was right, I'd been clueless. Before I could tell Ethan how stupid I felt for losing faith in him, Jake cleared his throat.

"Enough, you two. Is this the part where I hand out tissues?"

Ethan shot Jake a nasty sideways look, but then grasped the gravity of the situation. "Jake's right. We can deal with this later. How did they get you in there?"

"There were two of them. I took out the first guy, but the second sprayed me with some sort of mist. I remember hearing a hiss, but that's all." My voice sounded as if I had sand in my throat, which is about how it felt. I took the bottle back and sipped slowly.

Jake nodded as he scrutinized my face. "They probably hit you with scopolamine."

My knees wobbled at the thought of those last few seconds before the world faded, but at least I was able to stand on my own. "How'd you find me?" I asked, eager to change the subject. My voice was stronger, but it still sounded like it belonged to an injured cat.

"Well, Zoe called the bar, trying to track you down. She hadn't heard from you after your trip to San Diego and was getting worried. I called Jake to see if you'd called him."

Ewww. Why would I do that? I looked around, trying to figure out where I was. "What I meant was, how'd you find me?" I gestured at the shipping and storage containers around us. "From the looks of it, this is a private storage facility."

Jake's lips curled into a grin that seemed to shimmer and fade like a mirage, leaving behind a sense of playful unpredictability. It drove me nuts that he could push my buttons so easily. He said, "Remember that homeless guy who bumped into you at lunch with your dad?"

"What?" I blinked back the haze, but I vaguely recalled the image of a homeless man pawing me. And then, the image became crystal clear. "Oh, my God. No way. That was you?"

"Cool disguise, eh, Cavendish? You never even knew I dropped a GPS tracker into your purse."

I closed my eyes and started counting as my anger grew. I didn't know if I was more angry with myself or with Jake. I should have recognized him when he bumped into me. The homeless were everywhere these days, but it was rare for them to make any kind of physical contact. My face screwed up at the memory of how grimy I'd felt after that encounter.

Jake grinned at me. "It seemed only fair. You did put one on my van."

"After you bugged Sam's office!" Taking a long breath, I swallowed my anger. I didn't like that I'd been outwitted, but Jake's tracker had probably saved my life. "You put it in my bag?"

"Yup."

"Do you have it?"

"Your bag? Nope."

I gritted my teeth. This man was infuriating. Couldn't he answer in anything other than monosyllables? I took a swig of water and snapped, "Then where is it?"

"Isaac Johnson's office...at least, it was."

"What do you mean, was?"

"It's moved on."

What was this? Freaking kindergarten? Couldn't he answer the question? I closed my eyes and pulled in a breath between my teeth. After letting it out, I hissed, "So where is it, exactly, Marlough?"

Jake's face lit up with another smile. "There she is! She's back!"

"Jake said that according to the tracker, it's in Escondido," Ethan said. He, too, looked like he was tired of Jake's juvenile behavior.

My initial reaction was to deck Isaac Johnson. After that, I'd deal with the guy who'd drugged me. "Johnson's the one who kidnapped me? Take me there!"

"Not so fast, Supergirl," Jake said. "First off, his office closed about two hours ago. Second, we need to use him, not tick him off. If you go charging in, he'll just have his thugs come back and finish you off for good. Instead, we need to come at this from the bottom up. Divide and conquer."

As much as I hated to admit it, Jake was right. Planting my fist in Isaac Johnson's face or giving him a good roundhouse kick might be satisfying, but it would only land me in jail for assault. Besides, the longer I stood here, the more I realized I was in no condition to deliver any roundhouse kicks. The problem was that I'd lost the brooch. "But A Mermaid's Allure is in my bag. Along with my phone. And I don't know where my gun is."

"Or what it will be used for." Jake rubbed his lips and jaw with his fingers. He took a long breath, then turned to Ethan. "When the guys who kidnapped Cavendish reported back to Johnson, he probably told them he only wanted the brooch. He would have wanted them to get rid of the evidence. Instead, they probably tossed her gun in her purse and still have it. I don't think they'd throw away something so valuable."

Ethan screwed up his face and looked at Jake. "How much does a gun cost? A few hundred bucks?"

"More like five," I countered. "But the real value lies in what it could be used for."

Ethan's eyes widened, and his lips parted. "Oh. So you think your gun could become a murder weapon?"

"If my line of work involved intimidation and murder, that's exactly what I'd do." Jake stroked the stubble on his chin and added, "You could use it whenever you wanted, and it always traces back to her." He looked at me and grimaced. "Didn't mean to talk about you in the third person, Cavendish, but you get the idea."

"I totally get it. I become a suspect whenever anything happens."

"Even if you report it, there's always that question of, was it really stolen or is she just a criminal mastermind?"

I glared at Jake, irritated that my muddled brain couldn't keep up. "Look, ever since I talked to Isaac, I've been wondering if he was involved in The Guild. Now, I'm sure of it. You said my purse is in Escondido. That means they've got the brooch."

"First off, they probably gave the brooch to Isaac. As for everything else, they would have taken your ID and credit cards someplace where they could divvy up the spoils."

I groaned and took another sip of water. "Oh, man. I was so focused on the brooch that I never even thought about my IDs and credit cards. I've got to get all my stuff back—especially my gun. Otherwise, who knows what will happen?"

"Which is why we need to neutralize those guys first."

Ethan craned his neck and eyed Jake. "You don't mean kill them, do you? Jake, we can't do that."

"Relax, buddy. Nothing so final. I'm thinking that since these guys provided us with such comfy accommodations, we should let them experience the luxury of the Container Chateau firsthand. That gives us plenty of time to deal with Isaac."

"And work our way up the chain," I said, admiration replacing the dryness in my voice. "That's brilliant. But how are we going to get them here?"

"Shouldn't be too hard. But it will take all three of us."

"I'm so in," I said.

Ethan crossed his arms over his chest. He eyed me first, then Jake. "Couldn't we just report them to the cops and avoid this whole kidnapping thing? Even if we're not asking for a ransom, it's still kidnapping, right?"

"They'll be out of custody in an hour," Jake said. "And Cavendish will be watching over her shoulder until someone puts a slug in her or runs her down."

"Okay! Okay!" Ethan raised his hands. "I get it."

"You don't have to do this, Ethan. I'll understand," I said.

"No. I do have to do it. I got you into this mess. And if we're going to win against The Guild, we have to play by their rules."

A warm flush grew in my chest. These two men were about to do something that could land all of us in prison for a long time. And there was nothing in this for either of them other than the satisfaction of helping me see the bad guys lose. That, in my book, was true friendship.

"Okay, Marlough, you seem to have this all figured out. What's the plan?"

"The first thing is, we need a Trojan horse. Know any good pizza places?"

"Oh, yeah," I said. "Do I ever."

Chapter 38

THE DILAPIDATED HOME LOOMING IN the darkness of this rundown Escondido neighborhood brought back memories of the stakeout my dad had taken me on. The difference was that he'd taken me to a very safe neighborhood. But tonight, this whole situation had me spooked to the max. It's strange how situations like this bring with them a sense of foreboding, even when you're the one supposedly in control. On the other hand, our plan could go sideways in the blink of an eye.

Jake sat beside me, his face partially illuminated by the soft glow of the dashboard lights, while Ethan crouched in the back of Jake's van, his eyes trained on the house.

"Are you sure this is it?" I asked, gripping the pizza box tight with one hand, Jake's Glock 19 in the other. Ordinarily, the smell of mozzarella and pepperoni would have set off my hunger alarm. But tonight, no matter how much water I drank to flush out the scopolamine, it only made me slightly nauseous.

Jake nodded, never taking his eyes off the house. "This is it. They're inside. Or, at least, your purse is."

Ethan leaned forward, his voice hushed. "It's not too late to back out, Jade. This is dangerous."

"I'm not letting these guys get away with what they did. I owe them. Besides, I'm just a delivery girl. With a gun."

I opened the door and stepped into the cool night air. Jake and Ethan did the same. The asphalt beneath my feet was cracked, and the streetlights cast long, eerie shadows. I climbed the stairs to the front door, every creak of the wooden steps under my feet making my heart pound faster. The plan was simple—the pizza was a Trojan horse. I'd use it to get the door open and lure whoever answered outside. Jake would slip in to disarm anyone else in the house. Ethan was to be in charge of prisoners. Hopefully, only the two guys who had kidnapped me would be inside.

What I couldn't figure out was, if the plan was so simple, why was my stomach churning? I told myself it was the scopolamine, not fear. But right now, I couldn't tell.

I reached the front door, knocked, and called out that I was delivering a pizza. My right hand supported the pizza box, but in that hand I also held Jake's Glock. He stood to the right of the door, his Sig Sauer handgun at the ready. Given today's events, I might just have to follow his lead and buy myself a backup.

The seconds stretched into what felt like hours before I heard footsteps approaching from the other side. Showtime.

"Pizza delivery!" I repeated in the clearest voice I could muster.

"I didn't order no pizza," a gruff voice replied.

"It's already paid for!"

I heard the door unlock. My fingers tightened around the Glock's textured grip. Jake gave me a slow nod. In the short time I'd known him, I'd never seen this side of him—intense, focused, and maybe dangerous.

It was Scruffy who opened the door—the same man I'd taken down this afternoon. When he saw me, he frowned as though he was trying to place me. The second I pointed the gun at his face, and he was staring down the barrel, he recognized me.

"Don't say a word and step outside," I said.

He swallowed hard and did as he'd been told.

"Hands behind your back."

"Thank you," Jake said quietly as he slipped behind Scruffy and secured his hands with zip ties. He turned Scruffy around, took one look at him, and shoved him to one side. Ethan grabbed Scruffy's wrists and guided him toward the van. I set the pizza box down and exchanged a nod with Jake. He made a circular motion above his head with one finger and started to enter, but I stopped him with a hand on his shoulder.

He gestured as if to say, "Ladies first."

We entered into a small foyer, not making a sound. To my surprise, the living room was empty. From there, we had two options—the kitchen to our right and a hallway to our left. I indicated that I'd take the kitchen. Jake nodded and counted on his fingers. One. Two.

On three, we made our move. The kitchen was empty, as was the attached laundry room. The house smelled of some kind of broiled fish, but to my surprise, Scruffy apparently not only cooked but also cleaned up after himself. Another door led off to a garage. The lights were out, but when I turned them on, I saw two vehicles, the blue Crown Vic and my Prius. I rushed back into the kitchen, then headed for the hallway, where I ran into Jake.

"Clear," he said.

"So is the kitchen and the garage. My car's out there, too."

"That's good. Saves you from having to buy a new one. But unfortunately, our guys must not live together. I did find this, however." Jake held up my leather bag and handed it to me.

The first thing I did was check to see if the brooch was inside. It wasn't. Neither was my wallet. Thankfully, I did find my gun. I texted Ethan to tell him we'd be less than five minutes. He responded that everything was under control out front.

"The brooch isn't here," I said.

Jake grimaced, then motioned toward the back of the house. "I'm not surprised. I'd bet a week's pay that's the reason they went to Isaac Johnson's first. However, you're going to want to see this."

The room Jake led me to was a production center for identity thieves. My IDs had been laid out on the desktop next to a scanner. There were credit card blanks and materials to make fake identification cards, everything from a driver's license to medical cards.

My insides churned at the sight of my cards and the open computer application on the screen. "Looks like we interrupted him in the middle of things. Any idea who he is?"

"The house belongs to a Joey Patel. I've seen the name before. He's a small-time hood who's got his fingers in several different pies."

I shook my head. "What are you? A walking Yellow Pages for criminals?"

Jake chuckled and nodded to himself. "I like that, Cavendish. Anyway, he also acts as the muscle for clients who don't want to get their hands dirty."

"Like Isaac Johnson."

"Exactly. Apparently, Joey is branching out into identity theft. Your show, Cavendish. What's your preference?" Jake asked. "Leave this for the cops? Or make the evidence disappear? It looks like he was just getting ready to scan you in."

"Tough call, but I don't like the idea of leaving my stuff. I say we grab and go."

"Sounds like a plan, Cavendish."

"But how do we find his partner?"

"I've seen Joey's type before—wannabe bigshot, but he just doesn't have the chops to be truly bad. I'll bet if we explain how things will go better for him if he cooperates with us, he'll get with the program."

"That works for me. By the way, you can call me Jade."

"That's okay. It's more fun to irritate you." Jake winked and gave me a crooked smile. "Let's go check on Ethan before he freaks out."

"Fine, Marlough." I jabbed him in the ribs before picking up my IDs and putting them in my bag. "I'm also taking my car."

"Works for me. Hey, I'm surprised you didn't destroy my tracker," he said as we entered the garage.

"Given that I'll probably have a target on my back by morning, I think I'll hang onto it for a little longer."

Jake flashed me another thumbs-up. "I don't think Joey's gonna give us much trouble with his hands secured. But I'll keep an eye on him anyway."

I backed my Prius out of the garage. Jake rode in the passenger's seat of my car, the pizza box on his lap. We stuffed Joey into the back seat. Apparently a quick learner, Joey gave up his partner, Ivan, with only a little coaxing.

Ethan followed in Jake's van. I was happy for him. At least one of us was spared Joey's incessant blathering. He kept trying to convince me what he and Ivan had done was nothing personal. He apologized for Ivan having sprayed me with scopolamine. He even tried to rationalize it all by saying 'it was just business.' But when he said that he had a certain admiration for a 'girl who could kick like a mule' with such accuracy, I assured him I was about ready to do the same thing again if he didn't shut up. At that point, the drive became much quieter.

Jake opened the box and eyed the pizza, which was now starting to look like a chaotic mix of toppings, cheese, and crust all jumbled together. "Hey, Cavendish, you mind if I…?"

I slapped the box shut with one hand and smacked his shoulder. "Touch that pizza, Marlough, and you'll wind up in the back with him."

He looked over his shoulder at Joey, shaking his head and letting out a heavy sigh. "You're right about her, Joey. She's stubborn as a mule, too."

The two of them laughed, but Joey stifled his when he caught me glaring at him in the rearview mirror. The street where we parked was another old neighborhood. The homes were a mishmash of original 80s architecture with some having been modernized. The landscaping was much the same, running the gamut from well-manicured lawns to overgrown weed patches.

Joey squirmed in the backseat. I turned, pointed the gun at his face, and told him to sit quietly. He got the message and stopped his nonsense. With that accomplished, we all exited the car and turned Joey over to Ethan.

"Let's go, Pizza Girl. Same drill."

I grabbed the box from Jake. It was now cold to the touch, which made me think about how the once flat and round pizza was bent and folded over on itself and how the toppings were either falling off or barely hanging on by strings of cheese. Some prop this was. I went to the door and knocked. When I saw Ivan's face, I was tempted to simply shoot him. After spraying me with scopolamine, tossing me in his trunk, and then leaving me in a storage container, I felt like he deserved it.

"Surprise, Ivan. I'm back."

He stood looking down the barrel of the Glock, but when I motioned for him to come outside, he bolted to his right. I swore and charged after him with Jake hot on my heels. Ivan bent over to pick up a handgun from the nearest side table. Instinctively, I threw the pizza box like a frisbee. The box hit his hand. His fingers brushed the gun, sending it skittering onto the floor.

"Freeze!" I yelled.

"If she doesn't get you, I will," Jake said as he drifted away from me.

The man turned to face us and realized he had no hope. His gun was several feet away, and there were two very irritated-looking people with guns pointed at him. For him, this was a no-win situation. "Come on. Can't we work this out?" he said.

"We've already got it worked out, Ivan. You're going on a little vacation. Best of all, you don't need to pack a thing," Jake said.

It was after ten when we locked Joey and Ivan in the storage container. With the door to the container secured, I surveyed the facility for the first time. It reminded me of a desolate, forgotten wasteland on the outskirts of town. Towering above the cracked asphalt and sparse weeds were the hulking beasts of old shipping containers. Rust streaked down the sides of some, giving them an even more menacing appearance under the harsh overhead lights. Each one loomed ominously like silent sentinels guarding secrets better left undiscovered. The air was thick with neglect, and the eerie silence stood as a reminder that this was a place where time didn't exist.

As the adrenaline washed out of my system, I also realized I was physically and emotionally drained. I needed sleep. And the best place to do that was where I felt safe and secure. Home.

Chapter 39

I AWOKE FRIDAY MORNING, STILL feeling the effects of the scopolamine. My head was pounding, and my body felt like I had run a marathon. It didn't matter. I had work to do, so I forced myself to sit up and assess the situation.

We had successfully taken Joey and Ivan out of action, but now we needed to figure out our next move. I reached for my phone to check the time—10 a.m. Seriously? I'd wasted half the day recovering from last night's events.

I quickly dressed and headed downstairs, where Mom and Dad were talking in hushed tones. When they saw me, Mom's hand went to her heart, and my dad frowned as though he knew what I was going through.

"Morning," I greeted both of them with a tired smile.

"Are you okay, honey?" Mom asked.

The problem with sharing yesterday's events with Mom and Dad was that they would freak out. They both knew the dangers of the business, Dad better than Mom because he'd hidden some secrets over the years. I was itching to ask him if he'd ever been kidnapped, but didn't dare for fear he'd put me on lockdown in my room.

"I'm fine, thanks to some friends."

Mom faked a smile. "That's good."

Dad nodded, serious now. "We need to talk about what you want me to do. Do you need help?"

I filled a mug with coffee and sat, bracing myself for whatever they had in mind. My dad was always one step ahead, and I was sure he already had a plan.

"No, Dad. I've got this under control. I got a bit of a surprise yesterday, but I'm on top of it now. Another PI, one who's a friend of Ethan's, is helping me."

"What's his name?"

"Jake Marlough."

Dad let out a long breath. "Watch out for him, honey. I'm not sure how much you can trust him."

Based on what he'd done for me yesterday, I totally disagreed. The man had most likely saved my life. True, he seemed to have a few too many tricks up his sleeve to be one hundred percent on the up-and-up. But he was good at his job, and for now, he was helping me. "I will," I promised.

After reassuring my parents that I was okay, I grabbed a quick breakfast and headed to the office, where it looked like a town meeting was taking place. My first thought was that Valkyrie had come for me, and then I recognized the faces. Zoe, followed by Sam, Val, and Rachel, swarmed me like bees on honey. Jake and Ethan seemed content to let the girls hover and hung out at my desk to watch the spectacle.

Zoe peppered me with questions faster than I could answer. Are you okay? Were you scared? Did you get hurt yesterday?

I finally held up my hands to stop her barrage. "I'm fine, Zoe. Thanks for asking."

Sam's expression was grim, and her voice was determined. "Zoe called and told us what happened. I totally want to make Isaac pay for what he did to you."

Rachel and Val were equally angry about yesterday's events, but I was able to assure all of them that I had a plan. Once the swarm parted, I went to Jake and Ethan. "Thank you both for what you did yesterday. You saved my life. If there's anything either of you ever need, just say the word."

Ethan, who had a look of genuine concern in his eyes, said, "I'm just glad you're okay."

Jake, on the other hand, was, well, Jake. He waved away my offer with that irritating smirk of his. "About time you came to work, Cavendish. You slept away half the day."

My chest warmed at his flip response. Couldn't the guy ever be serious? Was it his cavalier attitude that irritated me? Or was he challenging me to break through my...what? Tenseness? I couldn't tell. I cleared my throat. "Okay, everyone. Thank you all for being here, but as I found out yesterday, this case is more dangerous than I thought. I'm convinced someone at the bank betrayed me, and that's how those two goons found me."

"I'm totally sure the manager is the one who sold you out," Zoe said. "I checked, and he was involved in a nasty divorce last year. Guess who his attorney was."

"Isaac Johnson?" I asked.

"Bingo."

"The other problem is that The Guild now has Hilda's family heirloom. I don't know if Johnson still has it or if he's passed it on to Valkyrie."

"Maybe we need to force the play," Jake said.

Ethan had a wary look in his eyes. "What are you planning on doing? We already kidnapped those two guys last night. We can't just go around grabbing people because we think they're part of some international art theft ring. And what are we going to do about those two? We can't just leave them there."

"Chill, buddy. No kidnapping required."

"You're thinking we make it look like Isaac has betrayed Valkyrie to draw her out?"

"Great minds, Cavendish."

Val rolled her eyes and shook her head. "You've got another problem. Ethan's right. What are you going to do about those guys you kidnapped last night?"

"Yeah, aren't those guys going to talk?" Rachel asked.

"How can they without confessing to kidnapping, assault, and a host of other felonies?" I said. "Besides, I can't imagine that admitting you were kidnapped by the woman you were supposed to keep locked up is going to be good for their professional reputations."

Val chuckled. "Alright, you've got a point. Maybe they won't talk, but what if they want revenge?"

"That's not too hard," I said. "All we have to do is make them realize they've got a vested interest in making sure no harm comes to us. If we make a video of when we release them from the container, we can use it for insurance. That's where you and Rachel come in. Rachel, you've got video equipment, right?"

"For sure. I'll need to go home to grab it, though."

"No problem. We can't let those two out until after we deal with Isaac. Val, you can get photos and let them know that if something happens to me or Jake, you'll be covering their story. The paper will make sure they're the first ones the cops go looking for."

"I can interview them from the container," Val said. "My work gets backed up to the cloud, and if something happens to me, there are several other reporters who will jump on the story."

"Sweet," Jake grinned. "We like redundancy."

"I'll go grab my equipment," Rachel said. "If I can get a directional microphone within a few feet of them, I should be able to get everything."

"If you're willing to share the video with me, I can just hold the mic," Val said.

The two of them exchanged a high-five. It sounded like we might actually pull this off. I gave both a thumbs up.

"Perfect. Now, about Isaac. Sam, can you lure him away from the office? Maybe suggest meeting up for coffee?"

She swallowed hard but also nodded her agreement. "Okay. Anyplace special you want me to do this?"

"Joe's Coffee House. Zoe knows the place. She'll be your backup until I get there. If anything goes haywire before Jake and I arrive, call the cops."

"Got it. What are you doing?"

"We're going to visit Isaac's office and see if the brooch is there."

"Pretty sure that's a problem," Jake said. "Isaac has a safe."

I groaned, and my shoulders slumped. Could anything be easy about this case? "Unless you know how to crack a safe, we're screwed, then."

Jake, an unusually thoughtful expression on his face, stroked his chin. His fingers brushed against the rough stubble that had grown over the past three days. "Not necessarily. We just change the plan a little. You go to Joe's with Sam. Isaac will freak out when he finds out you're not locked up. While he's rattled, tell him you invited him to coffee to lure him out of the office and that I've got the combination to his safe. If I know the guy, he'll hightail it back to the office to check."

It sounded like a good plan up to a point. "What if the brooch isn't there? What if he took it home? Or already gave it to Valkyrie?"

"He wouldn't take it home," Sam said. "Isaac's super focused on keeping work and his personal life separate."

"It's not that I don't believe you, Sam. But there's a lot riding on this."

"I think we've got to go for it, Cavendish. You rattle Isaac's cage. He rushes back to check his stash. We nab him. Simple."

Once again, my insides churned over that last word. It was just like last night. While that had worked out, sometimes, simple just wasn't good enough.

Chapter 40

I STOOD ON THE BOARDWALK gazing out at the ocean. Lazy waves drifted in, lapping weakly at the shore. Overhead, a few wispy clouds dotted the deep blue sky. The outside world felt calm—a stark contrast to the chaos that swirled inside me. Everyone was in place. Val and Rachel were setting up at the shipping container, Jake was at Isaac's office with Zoe serving as his backup, and Sam and I were waiting for Isaac.

Gripping my cup of Joe's coffee tightly, I raised it to my lips. Was this it? Would Isaac crumble? I hoped so. We'd know in just a few minutes. He parked in the lot and swaggered toward Joe's, looking self-assured. I hoped to change that very soon. Turning in Sam's direction, our eyes seemed to connect even though we were a hundred feet apart. I nodded to indicate that Isaac was on his way.

When Isaac reached Sam's table, Sam didn't rise to greet him. He seemed to sense a change in their relationship. He pointed toward the counter and went to order. Less than a minute later, he returned with one of Joe's cups in his hand. He sat on the opposite side of the table from Sam, which is exactly what we'd wanted. His back was to me, so I could move without being seen.

Jake had complete confidence in his plan. He was sure that Isaac had put the brooch in his safe. But what kept nagging at me was why an attorney would take the chance of keeping stolen property in his office. Safe or not, the cops could show up with a warrant, and he'd be hard-pressed to explain that one. The problem was that there were plenty of places he could hide it where the cops wouldn't think to search.

I hurried to the table where Sam and Isaac sat. As soon as I was within earshot, I could sense the tension in the conversation. Sam did a great job of focusing on Isaac, which set me up to surprise him. Then, she dropped the bomb.

"Why did you bug my office? You told Jade you did it to protect me. I don't believe that for a second. I want to know why, Isaac."

"It's true, Sam. I don't want you getting hurt. There are some dangerous people after that brooch."

"How do you know that?" Sam demanded.

"You just have to trust me."

"I don't think so."

I stepped into Isaac's field of view. "Neither do I."

Isaac's jaw dropped. "What? What are you doing…? How did you get here?"

"You'll find your henchmen in the storage container where they left me. And if you don't cooperate with us, you might wind up there yourself."

"So this was a trap." Isaac stood. "We're done here." He turned to Sam, the ice in his tone making his words unnecessary. "And we're done, too."

"For the record, we were done the minute you planted that bug," Sam countered.

I stepped in front of Isaac to block his exit. "I know you've got the brooch. We've got someone retrieving it right now. Once we have it,

I'll report everything to the police. There's easily enough evidence to take you down."

Isaac scoffed. "You have nothing. You'll never find the brooch. Besides, the cops won't believe a small-time PI like you. I can guarantee it."

How could he do that? Unless he had someone inside the police department high enough up to ensure he was protected. "I know all about Valkyrie and her reach. And I think once she knows you've been exposed as a member of The Guild, she won't have any use for you anymore."

Isaac's jaw tensed. I recognized the cornered animal look in his eyes. But that only lasted for a second. "You have no idea who you're dealing with."

"Oh, I think I do."

He leaned closer and lowered his voice to a whisper. "Watch your back, little girl. Yesterday was just a warning. If Valkyrie wants to get rid of you, all she has to do is snap her fingers."

He tossed his cup in the trash and walked away. Sam started to rise, but I shook my head. I waited until Isaac was out of sight to check the trash. I was in luck. They'd just emptied the trash, and his cup was the only thing in the container. I picked out the cup, making sure not to smudge his fingerprints, and set it on the table.

"I'll be right back. Don't touch that. Looks like your ex just made his first mistake. I'm going to the counter to get a baggie. Sit tight for a sec."

After bagging the cup and the lid, I called Jake to let him know Isaac should be on his way. I then asked Sam if she was okay.

She gripped her sides and made a face. "You know, I hoped things would work out with Isaac, but when I look back on the times we were together, it seems so…I don't know. Flat? You know what I mean?"

"Yeah, I do. Sometimes, we see what we want to see instead of the reality of a situation."

Sam nodded understandingly. "So what's going to happen now?"

"First off, I'm saving this cup as a backup. What I'm really hoping is that Jake catches Isaac red-handed. If that really does happen, he'll be brought to justice for his involvement in my kidnapping and theft." I reached across the table and took Sam's hand. "And maybe you'll find someone who appreciates and values you."

She smiled weakly. "Thanks, I hope so, too."

"Are you ready to see what kind of hornet's nest we've kicked over?"

"Totally. I can't wait to see his face when he realizes he got tricked into giving it up."

"Let's hope that's what happens."

It only took us five minutes to drive to Isaac's office. When we got there, Jake looked at me and raised his hands to his sides. "What happened? Where is he?"

"He left Joe's about ten minutes ago. I guess he wasn't coming here," I said. "Let's find out where he's going."

"What did you do, put a tracker on his car?"

"Nope. I didn't want to take a chance on something like that with a lawyer." I dialed Ethan's number. "Where are you?"

"On the way to San Diego. You were right. He wasn't going to his office. The problem is that traffic's heavy, and this guy drives like a crazy man. I'm trying to follow, but—no!"

I heard a loud thud, then something like a steady drone. "Ethan!" I called his name again, but he didn't answer.

"What happened?" Sam asked.

"I think he dropped the phone." No sooner had I said that than Ethan came back on the line.

"Sorry about that. Traffic came to a standstill. Isaac's a few cars ahead of me. He just changed lanes, and I'm blocked in. I've got to go if I'm going to keep him in sight."

I cursed myself for not planting a tracker on Isaac's car when I had the opportunity. "I think we're screwed. Traffic's heavy, and Ethan's worried he may not be able to stay with him."

Jake and I both had plenty of self-recriminations about not planning better for this contingency, but we agreed that we needed to know where Isaac was headed. "Jake, I think it's time we let Joey and Ivan out. Maybe they know where Isaac is going."

"Good idea. I can't wait to see their faces when they find out they're the subjects of a mini-documentary."

I snickered. "Somehow, I don't think this is a documentary they'll want to be in."

We'd taken a huge risk by kidnapping those two. On the other hand, we'd also stopped them from cloning my identity and using my gun to commit a crime. I called Val to see if she and Rachel were in place. I was relieved to learn they'd arrived and were ready whenever we were.

Jake and I took two cars in case we needed to split up. Sam rode with me and stayed in the car at the storage facility, I was amazed at how much different it looked in full daylight. What had looked like hulking beasts last night now looked completely innocent. This wasn't an active shipping yard like the port. It was actually some kind of sales yard for new and used containers. As we entered the lot, I also realized that security was practically nonexistent, which meant this was an ideal place to make things, or people, disappear.

Val joined us while we were parking our cars out of sight of the container. She looked nervously over her shoulder. "They're pretty quiet in there."

"Let's hope they're still alive," I said. "Where's Rachel?"

She pointed at the top of a nearby container, where Rachel was lying down with a fancy-looking video camera pointed our way. Rachel waved.

"How'd she get up there?" I asked.

"Easy," Jake chuckled. "Girl's part monkey."

Val rolled her eyes. "He's not far off. Come on, let's get this show on the road. It's hot out here."

Jake and I pulled our guns and went to the container. After putting two bottles of water on the asphalt between us, Jake went to the door. Neither of us knew what we'd find inside. I only hoped the two men weren't dead.

Chapter 41

WHEN JAKE PULLED THE DOOR open, I had a flashback of my time inside the container. It gave me shivers despite the heat of the sun. And when I saw Ivan sitting with his back against the container and looking like he'd passed out, I shuddered.

Joey stood just inside the door, shielding his eyes against the sunlight. "You!" he bellowed when he saw me.

"Smile, Joey. You and Ivan are on camera." I pointed over my shoulder at Rachel.

Val held up the microphone and aimed it at Joey. "And audio. Anything incriminating you'd like to say?" She paused for a second, pressed her hand to her ear and nodded. "Oh, and my girl Rachel tells me the audio's coming through perfectly and that this is being uploaded to the cloud as we speak."

Jake stepped forward and raised his gun. "You're screwed, Joey. Tell you what. What say we let bygones be bygones? Val will take your story. You can tell her how you were abused as a child or whatever excuse you come up with for being a lowlife. We'll be happy to add it to our little documentary. You should be thrilled. You and Ivan are gonna be the stars. That ought to be worth something, huh?"

"I don't want to be in no documentary! What are you trying to pull?"

"Joey, here me and Cavendish thought you'd appreciate being rescued. If you'd rather, we can put you back inside and come back. I've got some time, say, a week from Tuesday. That work for you?"

"No! That don't work for me. You gotta get us out of here now. Ivan's not doing good."

He was right; Ivan looked terrible. He was slumped against the side of the container, sweating profusely, and his skin was splotchy. "Neither was I after you two drugged me and left me in there for dead."

"No way, lady. We were only supposed to keep you out of touch for twenty-four hours."

"Why twenty-four hours?" I shot back.

"I don't know. That's how long we were told to keep you here."

Jake raised a finger and cleared his throat. "Uh, Joey. This is kind of like a point-of-order thing. You wanna be aware that you just confessed to kidnapping Cavendish on camera. Soooo…lest I sound a little repetitious, you're screwed. How about that bygones thing, huh?"

"I aint saying nothing else, man."

"Don't be like that, Joey. Think of Ivan. He's looking like he's gonna throw up all over your shoes. So, here's the deal. Unless you'd rather go through the hottest part of the day in that sweatbox, I suggest you answer two questions. First question. Who were you working for?"

"Tell 'em, Joey," Ivan croaked. "I don't feel so good."

Joey looked at his partner, then swore to himself. "We ain't got no loyalty to him. He was supposed to pay us when we turned over that brooch thing, but when we gave it to him, he said we'd get paid after the twenty-four hours. I got a feeling he's leaving the country, anyway. It's Isaac Johnson."

That was good news. Joey wasn't lying to us. Exactly what Jake and I had hoped for.

"Sign of good faith, Joey. Here." Jake picked up a bottle and tossed it. "Now, second question. Where's he headed?"

"I dunno, man. All I know is that he said he was gonna disappear before somebody named Valkyrie got him. That's it. I swear."

My entire body tensed at the mention of Valkyrie's name. I narrowed my gaze at Joey and then Ivan, whose brow was a river of sweat cascading down his face and neck. His shirt reminded me of a wet dishtowel.

"No way you want to go down for kidnapping. Do you, Joey?" Jake asked.

"No, man."

Jake shrugged one shoulder and looked at me. "Then let's call things square. Right, Cavendish? Unless you'd rather just lock them up and forget about them."

"I'm good with calling it even," I said. "And Joey, just so you know, the first place all that video will go if something happens to any of us is Detective Des Martini."

"Who's she?" Joey asked.

"A tough-as-nails homicide detective. Let's just say Detective Des makes Columbo look like a friendly barista. You don't even want to mess with her. Are we good?"

Joey exchanged a look with Ivan, and the two men agreed that as long as we let them go, they'd keep the entire incident quiet. Call it an uneasy truce, but once Val and Rachel documented everything, Joey and Ivan would probably never want to see us again.

Jake picked up the second bottle of water and tossed it to Joey. We stepped back so we could talk without being overheard but kept an eye on the two men. I was relieved that Ivan started looking better as he drank.

Jake suggested he stay behind with Val and Rachel while I went after Isaac. I still couldn't figure out why Valkyrie had been eliminating members of The Guild, but I'd bet anything that if we dug deep enough, we'd find out the death of Peter Sinclair's father hadn't been accidental at all. We'd probably find the same thing if it were possible to dig into Michelle Wolfe's accident. And now, Benji was dead. Would Isaac be next? Or would we get to him first?

When I got to my car, I found Sam pacing. I said, "You look like something's bothering you. What's up?"

"You're right. I couldn't figure out what it was until just a second ago. I know where Isaac is going."

"Where?"

"His boat. It all makes sense. He took I-5 south because he's going to the marina. He always said he wanted to live someplace where it was warm all year round. The day he took that photo you saw in my office? He specifically mentioned Vanuatu."

"Hang on." I called Jake and told him what Sam had said.

"Smart guy. He's going there, not because of the weather, but because that's one of the countries in the Pacific with no extradition treaty with the US. Leave it to a lawyer to figure that one out."

A lawyer, maybe, but why did Jake know that? This was no time to ask. "Jake, I think Sam and I should drive to the marina. Ethan can't stop Isaac on his own."

"You're right, Cavendish. You and Sam need to go after him. We got this. Go."

I felt terrible leaving Jake, Val, and Rachel alone with two criminals, but the alternative was to let Isaac escape. Sam and I were just getting on the road when my cell rang with a call from Ethan. I put him on speaker.

"Jade, I've lost him. I've been trying to catch up, but I think he jumped off the freeway somewhere."

"Are you sure you know where he's going, Sam?" I asked.

"One hundred percent," Sam said confidently. "Ethan, he's headed for the Kona Kai Marina. It's where he keeps his sailboat."

"I just passed the exit. I'll have to double back."

"No! I don't want you confronting him." As much as I wanted to stop Isaac, I wasn't willing to risk Ethan's safety. "We're on our way. We'll meet up when we get there. Just call me back and tell me where you're parked, okay?"

Because Sam and I could use the carpool lane, we made up some of the time Ethan and Isaac had lost in traffic. It still took us nearly thirty minutes, but Ethan flagged us down as we approached the entrance. He'd parked on the street not far from the marina, so I pulled into a parking spot near his.

"It's restricted access," Ethan said frantically. "Are you sure he's going to be here?"

"It's our best guess," I said. "Hop in. Sam's still got the gate key card Isaac gave her from when she was sailing with him."

"Awesome."

After Ethan hopped in the back seat, we went through the parking lot gate. I followed Sam's directions to the section of the marina nearest Isaac's boat and parked. Fortunately, Sam remembered the combination to the dock security gate. She then led the way to Isaac's slip. My heart leaped when I saw that the boat was still there. I broke into a run but stopped just short of the slip.

A man floated in the water face down. I recognized the clothing. Sam stood next to me, gripping my arm as though it were a lifeline. Her eyes glistened, and when she spoke, her words were barely audible. "He's dead?"

"Yes, Sam, he is. I don't know how she did it, but Valkyrie got here first."

Chapter 42

I PULLED OUT MY PHONE, grimacing at the thought of what was to come. With Isaac now a face-down drifter, we'd probably be stuck here for an eternity answering questions from who knows how many agencies. Nothing in my DNA would let me walk away without reporting this, so I told Sam and Ethan what I was doing as I dialed 9-1-1.

"Where do you think Valkyrie is now?" Ethan asked after I hung up.

"Great question. For all we know, she's around here watching." Seeing Sam's reaction, what looked like a shiver down her spine, I quickly added, "But more likely she's long gone. I don't think she'd want to stick around the scene of the crime."

It didn't take long for us to be swarmed by the authorities. Between the marina's security, the police, the Harbor Patrol, and a representative from the marina's office, it felt like we were the guests of honor at a bureaucratic jamboree.

I answered as many questions as possible while also trying to comfort Sam, who was in anguish. I soon realized that even though Sam had claimed to be over Isaac, the shock of finding his body had brought up feelings she thought she didn't have. It was heartbreaking to witness, and all I could do was be there for her.

After what felt like hours, the authorities finally finished their initial investigation, and we were allowed to leave. We all piled into my car and dropped Ethan off before returning to Carlsbad. It was a somber drive, with Sam sobbing quietly to herself while I fumed over having been outmaneuvered by Valkyrie.

After Sam assured me she was okay to drive, I left her in her car and turned my attention to Detective Des. San Diego Police would contact her, but she deserved a heads-up about Isaac's murder before that call. I picked up the phone and called the business line. The officer I spoke to would only say the detective was unavailable. Crossing my fingers that I wasn't committing the ultimate faux pas, I resorted to using her cell number.

To my surprise, she answered immediately. "Ms. Cavendish, I wondered how long it would take to hear from you."

Uh oh. SDPD must have called already. "Does that mean you've heard about Isaac Johnson?"

"I have a message that three individuals from this area were involved in a homicide. One of those individuals was described as a spunky PI. I figured it was you."

She thought I was spunky? Wow. That was actually kind of awesome. "I was hoping to get to you before you heard about it through official channels, but I guess they didn't waste any time."

"A good homicide detective seldom does," she countered.

Ignoring the jab, I remained cool. "I also think Isaac Johnson's death is related to Benji Thompson's."

"Are you saying you know who the killer is?"

"Kind of, but not exactly."

"Ms. Cavendish, you either do or you don't."

"Right. Well then, I guess I'd have to say I don't. But does the name Valkyrie mean anything to you?"

I'd seldom heard Detective Des pause for much of anything. In addition to looking like she'd just walked off the cover of Vogue, she was lightning-fast at picking up clues and handling a conversation. From what I'd seen, she intimidated more than a few of her male colleagues, and I assumed she might one day run her own police department.

I heard a long breath before she said, "We need to talk. Off the record—for now."

That did not sound good. "Where?" I managed.

"Joe's. I could use a break. Fifteen minutes?"

"I'll be there."

I checked the mirror. I looked like I hadn't slept in days. My hair was a mess. My clothes had that lived-in look. But worst of all, my stomach was growling like a lion in heat. Great. Just what a girl loved to do—make a good impression.

In addition to great coffee, Joe's also made a dynamite sandwich. It didn't surprise me that a cop would know that, but the fact that Detective Des wanted to meet there had caught me off guard. I seldom ate at Joe's because I always felt like I was betraying Charlie. And, to be truthful, I also got free food at Charlie's. Be that as it may, if Detective Des wanted to eat at Joe's, I could rationalize the trade-off.

Twenty minutes later, we'd both ordered and had our food. Detective Des looked exactly the way I'd expected her to—perfect makeup, impeccably tailored suit, and awesome shoes. We looked like the odd couple, new millennium style.

"I'm surprised you wanted to meet here," I said when we were both seated.

"This is one of my favorite hangouts. I typically come here on my days off."

I blinked, never having thought about the fact that this woman might not work every day of the year. "Wow. Next thing you'll be telling me you surf."

"Of course I do. How do you think I paid for my classes at UCSD? I had surfing scholarships almost all the way through."

Not knowing what else to say, I went with the noncommital, "That's awesome." The fact was, once again, I was jealous of Detective Des Martini. While I'd worked crappy part-time jobs to pay for my schooling, she'd been surfing.

Rather than setting myself up for more depressing comparisons between our lives, I went through the entire explanation of what had happened in San Diego and how we'd gotten there, being sure to leave out the part about kidnapping Isaac's henchmen. When I was done, Detective Des nodded thoughtfully. Gone were the razor-sharp retorts and barbs when she replied. For once, she was just a person with a problem.

"I'm being pressured to close out the case by the higher-ups. But my gut is telling me there was nothing accidental about Benji Thompson's death. The problem is there's really no physical evidence and no witnesses. I can see plenty of parties with an apparent motive, but I have no suspects other than some ghost called Valkyrie."

"And you can't bring in a ghost."

"Exactly."

"What do you need me to do?" I couldn't believe I was asking, but maybe, just maybe, if I pulled this off, I might get some points.

"Jade, you know who Valkyrie is."

I shook my head, trying to reconcile two huge contradictions with reality. First, I still didn't know who Valkyrie was. Second, Detective Des had just called me by my first name. Stunned, I ignored the second because I didn't think this sudden friendship would last. As for the first, I decided the truth was the best option. "That's the problem. I don't know who she is."

"Actually, you just think you don't. I've seen how your mind works, and I know you'll eventually put the pieces together. It's why Benji trusted you with that cryptogram. It's why I'm confident we'll solve this case."

"We?"

"Yes, Jade. We. You are going to help me solve Benji Thompson's murder."

You know that feeling you get when someone drops a bombshell on you, and you're suddenly flailing around in space, trying to understand how life works? That was me when Des informed me she needed my help. And to top it off, she was being nice to me? What kind of alternate reality was this?

I contemplated my sandwich, doing everything I could to keep a silly grin off my face. It wasn't the first time I'd helped Des, but last time, everything happened through an intermediary. She wanted to work with me? As in, together? Total mind freeze frenzy alert. The words popped out before I could stop them. "You want my help? Again? So we're, like, besties?"

Detective Des raised one eyebrow and skewered me with one of her classic ice-queen stares. She made a move like she would stand, and I knew I'd be lucky if she didn't walk away and exile me forever.

"Sorry," I said. "I totally went too far."

The ice melted just a smidge, and she sat back down. "Well, Jade, it seems that our paths keep crossing. As much as I dislike relying on a civilian, I have no other options at this time. Besides, I do kind of like you."

Okay, so there were at least three caveats in that sentence. The first was that our paths kept crossing. Call it serendipity or fate, the fact was that we were, again, bumping up against each other. Number two was the 'at this time' phrase. That probably meant she'd cut me loose at the first available opportunity. But number three gave me hope—she kind of liked me. I'd take it. It was the first time she'd admitted it, so maybe there was hope for us yet.

It turned out Detective Des wanted me to follow up with Benji's nurse, Nora O'Sullivan. I was supposed to have done that yesterday, but had gone to see Liz Carter instead. If it hadn't been for Joey and Ivan, I might have been able to catch up with Nora. In any case, now was a great time to call her. At the funeral, she'd said that Benji wasn't a well man. She'd also told Detective Des that Benji had confided in her, but she couldn't elaborate, citing a need to maintain her client's confidentiality.

Detective Des was also certain that a subpoena would be difficult because she couldn't prove she was doing anything other than fishing for information. That's where I came in. She wanted me to take a run at Nora because, as she put it, 'the woman wants to talk.'

What the heck? I still wanted to follow up with Nora about the argument my dad had documented in his investigation of Benji. So, this was a big win. It was way better than being banished from my hometown.

Chapter 43

I CAUGHT NORA AT HOME. She had a shift later that night but said if I could be at her condo in less than half an hour, she'd talk to me. I agreed to be there in fifteen minutes.

Nora lived in a condo in Bressi Ranch. I'd seen those buildings go up a few years ago. Very boxy. Modern. And definitely not cheap. On the other hand, they were within walking distance of three markets, a drug store, coffee shops, restaurants, and more. Overall, I had visions of moving to this kind of neighborhood, ditching my car, and hoofing it everywhere.

With streets the size of pencils, parking was limited to designated spots only. At this time of day, those spots were filling up. I parked a couple of blocks away and walked toward Nora's place, thinking about how, if I ever made enough money at the agency to move out on my own, this might be the kind of place I'd like to live.

Nora greeted me at the door. She'd pulled her auburn hair back into a ponytail and wore a green tank top. Her piercing green eyes remained impassive as she leaned against the doorjamb, her hands cupping it in a relaxed stretch. "What's this about you investigating Benji's death, Jade?"

"We think Benji's death was not an accident." I went on to explain how the police were zeroing in on a connection to The Guild.

"That's probably what that detective was trying to ask me about. That woman needs to learn how to relax."

I smiled and nodded, doing my best to establish rapport with Nora. "Detective Des is definitely intense."

Nora's weary smile made it appear that she hadn't slept in days. "That's putting it mildly."

She tilted her head but maintained direct eye contact. I took that to be my cue to ask away. "At the funeral, you told me Benji had come to peace with his past. I never did find out what you meant by that."

"Benji never shared specifics. But sometimes, when he'd get into a relaxed state, he'd say things that led me to believe he'd been involved in something illegal when he was younger. He said he'd been righting some old wrongs. He never gave me specifics—and I didn't ask. I try not to pry with my patients. However, he made a comment recently that I took to mean he expected trouble—something very serious."

"And so when I told you the police were at the funeral, that's why you assumed Benji had been murdered."

"Exactly." Nora's thin brows knitted together. She took a long breath. "Are they any closer to finding the killer?"

Detective Des and I had agreed that we wouldn't tell anyone we had no clue who Valkyrie was. It might be the only way we'd flush her out. So, I gave Nora the standard we're-making-progress answer. She seemed satisfied, and I didn't allow her time to think. "Did you and Benji ever talk about anything else?"

"Oh, sure. Benji loved food. He always said one of his favorite places was Sinclair's." Nora stopped and put her hand to her mouth. Her eyes misted over, and she smiled weakly. "We got into a number of arguments over food. I always encouraged him to eat more fruits and vegetables, and he'd say there was no point."

"Did you ever go into the store to talk to him?"

Nora did a double take. "That's an odd question. But, yes, back when I first took him on as a patient. Why do you ask?"

"I thought I remembered seeing you in the store once when I was walking by." The lie seemed to satisfy Nora. It also satisfied my curiosity about my dad's observation. But best of all, I'd pulled it off without revealing my real reason for asking. "You said Benji liked Sinclair's a lot," I asked innocently.

"Absolutely. He was a huge fan. When I told him I could never afford a place like that, he offered to take me there. I told him I didn't think that would be appropriate, so he got me a gift certificate for a complete dinner for two, along with wine, appetizers, and dessert."

The thought of my dinner with Ethan—and how everything had gone sideways after that—came rushing back to me. No. What was done was done. I had to stay focused on the here and now. "Wow. That could be a couple hundred bucks."

"Easily." Nora sighed and made a face, her long, slender nose wrinkling in the process. "I never had anyone to share it with, so I never went. I still have the gift certificate around here somewhere."

"The chef at Sinclair's told me Benji was a regular."

"Right. He said he went there all the time with friends."

"Do you know who these friends were?"

"No clue. But I'm sure if you went there and asked, they could tell you. If he was a regular, they'll probably know. You should ask them."

I'd definitely circle back to Sinclair's and ask that question. "Is there anything else you can tell me that might help with the investigation?"

"Benji was terminal. He didn't have much time left, but he never shared that with anyone, so whoever killed him probably didn't know about his illness. Not to be crass, but they did him a favor."

More likely, they wanted to stop him from righting more of those wrongs. Benji had gone to extraordinary lengths to hide what he was doing, and it hadn't been enough. Now, with Isaac's death, it was almost certain that Valkyrie was eliminating the last members of The Guild.

I thanked Nora for her time and drove straight to Sinclair's. I was hoping to beat the dinner rush and have time to talk with Chef Pete and maybe even his staff before things got hectic. Since the restaurant was only two blocks from the office, I parked in my usual spot and reveled in the evening breeze on my walk to Sinclair's.

Jessica greeted me with raised eyebrows and a friendly smile. "You're back! Will Ethan be joining you?"

The girl's enthusiasm reminded me of a puppy wagging its tail, eager to please. "Not today, just me. And I'm not here for dinner. I just have a few questions."

"Oh, for sure. What do you want to know?"

"It's about Benji Thompson."

Jessica's lips tightened into a thin line, the corners of her mouth turning downward. Her eyes glistened, and her eyebrows came together in a pained expression. "He was such a wonderful customer. Always generous and treated the staff well."

It sounded like a well-practiced, politically correct way to tell me she didn't want to talk about it. "How often was he in? Did he always come with the same people?" I threw a little lilt at the end of my sentence, hoping Jessica got the point that I was asking a question and expecting an answer.

"He came in a lot. He was usually with the same group of people, but sometimes, he brought in others. He and his wife had started coming in for dinner, too."

"When you say he was here with the same group, how many people are we talking about?"

Jessica started to say something, then stopped. Her eyes flickered with uncertainty, and she shifted her weight from one foot to the other. "Why all the questions?"

"It's part of an investigation."

Her eyes widened. "Are you with the police?"

"In a manner of speaking."

"Oh. Maybe you should be talking to Chef Pete. He knows—knew—all of them."

"I will, but who were they?" I pressed, adding just a hint of authority to my voice.

Jessica swallowed and let out a hard breath. "I don't want to get in trouble."

"I'll make sure your boss understands you didn't have a choice."

"Fine," she huffed. "Mayor Amy, Isaac Johnson—he's an attorney here in town—and Luna Martinez. She's some kind of big art collector."

My mind reeled with questions, none of which Jessica could answer. I knew Luna well, or so I thought. I'd taken her case when her home had been 'burglarized.' It turned out the burglar was her niece, who needed extra spending money and had gotten very resourceful in finding ways to get it. Was it possible, though, that Luna was a member of The Guild? What about the mayor? Or both of them?

"How long have they been coming here, Jessica?"

The girl screwed up her face, and her confident persona gave way to that of an insecure teenager. "I don't know. I've only worked here for a few months. Chef Pete's the one you need to be asking these questions."

"Would you get him for me?"

Jessica nodded hastily and was gone before I could say thanks. I had pushed her pretty hard, but if she was going to law school and wanted to become an attorney, she needed to toughen up.

A couple arrived looking hungry and impatient; another stood a few feet behind them. I turned to them, smiled, and said, "She'll be right back. Great girl. She's doing me a favor."

They inched away, which made me realize how I probably looked. It had been a long day, and unlike Detective Des, who maintained her fashionista vibe until the end, my wear and tear was showing in spades. A few seconds later, Jessica reappeared with Chef Pete trailing two steps behind her. He gave the new arrivals a pleasant greeting, and with obvious irritation, his eyes narrowed. "Come with me."

He stopped short of grabbing my arm and pulling me away, but the emotion was clear. I'd ticked off someone else. Great. I'd already irritated my source, and I hadn't even asked my first question.

Chapter 44

GIVEN HOW CHEF PETE HAD called me to his office, I anticipated his private space would be a shrine to his own ego. I'd heard that successful chefs didn't take criticism well. That they could be self-centered and egotistical. But as Chef Pete closed the door and asked me to sit. His expression transformed from angry to guarded.

"Ms. Cavendish," he said, perching on the edge of his desk. "I'm not sure what you're looking for here."

"I'm conducting an investigation into the death of Benji Thompson and now, of Isaac Johnson," I said bluntly.

Chef Pete's jaw dropped. "Isaac Johnson is dead? When?"

"As of this morning."

His broad shoulders slumped a bit; his eyes looked suddenly tired. "Jessica said you're with the police. Can I see your identification?"

I pulled out my PI license and showed it to him. "I'm not a police officer. As you can see, I'm a private investigator. I am, however, working with a detective who's been assigned this case. I'm sure you understand my interest in the regular meetings that both Benji and Mr. Johnson attended here."

He returned my ID and pointed at a wall of family photos. "My father and grandfather both taught me that repeat customers are essential to a restaurant's survival."

"So you aren't just following in your father's footsteps. You come from a long line of chefs."

My comment seemed to jolt him out of his thoughts. "Yes, restaurants are kind of a family tradition. At least for the last few generations. My father started Sinclair's, but he was an executive chef who traveled the world before that. He'd spent time in London, Amsterdam, and Berlin. He cooked for some very wealthy people."

My heart felt like it had just skipped a beat. Maybe several. Berlin? "Chef? How did your father die?"

He again focused on the wall. Specifically, he looked obsessed with a photo of two men in chef's standing next to each other. One looked like a younger version of Chef Pete; the other was older, but I could see a resemblance. They both flashed a thumbs-up to the camera.

"It was an accident. He closed up one night and was crossing the street." Chef Pete paused, took a breath, and added, "It was a hit-and-run. Carlsbad PD never found the car or the driver."

A cold chill ran down my spine. An accident? Or murder? I felt an overwhelming sense of foreboding—almost as though I were watching a massive ocean wave tower over me before it pulled me under. But I couldn't just ask, so was your dad an art thief? I needed a more subtle way to approach this.

"What was his first name?"

"Rolf."

"How did he become an executive chef?"

"He started out as a child in my grandparents' restaurant in LA. They started the tradition in the heart of Hollywood. After he worked there for a few years, he heard about a corporate opening, applied, and got the job. Within a couple of years, he'd gone independent. It wasn't until after he met my mom that he decided to settle down. That's when he returned to my parents' restaurant. He hated how manic everything was, so when my grandparents wanted to retire, they all agreed to sell the business."

"And that's when your father moved to Carlsbad?"

"Yes. The nice thing is that even though we get busy, we don't have an hour-long commute after putting in a long day."

"I take it you live in town?"

Chef Pete nodded, and I detected a hint of embarrassment. "Thanks to my parents. When my dad passed, we moved into my parents' place up on Hillside. It's old, but it's got plenty of room for all of us. It has a view I don't get to see often enough, but it's close by."

"I'm sorry about your dad. When did you lose him?"

"A few years back. That's when I took over full-time."

"So your dad went from working for your grandparents to traveling the world as a chef to starting his own business here and being able to buy a home in Carlsbad?"

Chef Pete hesitated, then grimaced. "That's the thing. He didn't have enough money to open Sinclair's and buy a house on his own."

I raised my eyebrows. "Chef, I understand this is pretty personal, but it could help find a killer."

"Alright. My grandparents certainly did well with the sale of the restaurant. And my dad did get a portion because my grandparents wanted to help him. He had some savings, but he had to take on some private investors. When I took over, my dad insisted on paying them off first." He paused and rubbed the back of his neck. "How is this going to help you find a killer?"

Sensing that I was getting close, I ignored his question. "Why did your dad insist on paying off the investors?"

"I don't know. They're nice enough people, but he said it wasn't good being beholden to anyone else."

The hairs on the back of my neck rose. I could see where this was leading. "Who are these investors?"

"They're all still regulars—the ones that are left, anyway. It was Benji, Isaac, Luna, and Amy. They were the original investors. My dad said he knew them from his days as an executive chef."

And now, there were only two left. I closed my eyes, trying to envision the group that had been here with the mayor. But, other than the encounter with Mayor Amy and the fact that I'd recognized Luna, I had no idea who the others were. When I looked at Chef Pete, there were tears in his eyes. His hand covered his mouth, and I could tell he'd come to the same conclusion I had.

"You think either Luna or Amy is a killer." His voice cracked and drifted off.

"Possibly. When your father was traveling all over the world, did he ever collect valuable artwork?"

"What does my dad's art collection have to do with anything?"

Empathy made me want to assure him my question meant nothing, but I'd seen the recognition on his face. The widening of his eyes. The quick intake of breath. How many of those pieces belonged to people like Hilda? Was there another way, a less painful way, to handle this? Perhaps something less direct that would achieve the same result but not poison my relationship with him? "All of those investors are—or were—collectors of fine art. All I'm saying is that your father may have gotten the bug and picked up a few pieces during his travels."

Chef Pete again seemed to drift off to another world—perhaps a place without questions or insinuations about his family. He might have stayed there, but the pinging of a message on my phone broke the silence. "Do you need to get that?" he asked.

I shook my head. Whoever it was, they could wait.

He ran his hand down his face and throat, his anguish obvious. "What exactly are you saying?"

Giving people bad news was the hardest part of being a PI. And I took no pleasure in saying what I needed to. "Chef Pete, it's possible those pieces were stolen."

"This would kill my mother, but I've wondered about some of the pieces my father gave her. He always said they were very expensive, and I wondered how he could put aside enough money to pay for them. What would happen if I had them appraised and it turned out that you're right?"

"You might wind up having to return them. If I'm right, your father may have been a member of what is called The Guild."

Chef Pete's jaw dropped. "What did you say?"

"He might have been a member—wait, have you heard of The Guild before?"

"It's what my father used to say when they showed up. He called that group The Guild."

I didn't know whether to be excited or terrified. But as the emotions rushed through me, I realized the secrets were just beginning to unravel. If Chef Pete's father had been part of The Guild, his death had most likely been part of Valkyrie's clean-up operation. The question was not only why she had started it but which of the remaining two was Valkyrie.

"Chef, you've already guessed this, but one member of The Guild may be eliminating the others. I have no idea why, but four members have died. That includes Benji, Isaac Johnson, and a woman in Berlin named Michelle Wolfe."

"You said four members. Are you saying my father was the fourth?"

"I don't know for sure, but it's possible his death wasn't an accident. What I do know is that the leader's code name is Valkyrie. I'm almost positive either Luna Martinez or Mayor Amy is Valkyrie. Can you tell me anything—anything at all—that you think might help?"

Chef Pete ran his fingers over the stubble on his chin. His dark eyes now looked distant, as if he wanted to be somewhere else, far away.

"Please," I insisted. "Anything. I don't care how small or unimportant you think it might be."

"No," he said as he took a long breath. "I can't think of anything."

Another dead end. But at least this time, I was down to two suspects. Which one was Valkyrie? And what would happen if I was wrong?

Chapter 45

THE MESSAGE THAT HAD INTERRUPTED my conversation with Chef Pete was from Gina. She insisted I call her ASAP, and she finished off the message with three exclamation points. With Gina, everything could be an emergency, but three exclamation points were a lot—even for her. It had to be at least moderately important.

"Hey, what's up?" I asked when she answered.

"We need to talk. In person. ASAP!"

"Gina, I'm in the middle of a case. I really don't have time to do this."

"I'm at your office. Where are you?"

Wow. She really had a bee under her bonnet. "I'm only a couple of blocks away. I'll be there in a few minutes."

Gina and her drama could be draining. But she was a friend, and I could use all the friends I could get right now. Besides, on a professional level, Gina had access to the upper echelon of the San Diego elite—those with money. The kinds of people who could easily hire someone like me.

By the time I arrived at my office, I'd convinced myself that putting up with a little drama was a small price to pay for having Gina as a friend, both on a personal and professional level. Zoe was at her desk, and Gina sat opposite her when I walked through the door.

"You're here! Finally!" Gina popped up, brushed her hair back with her hands, and headed straight for me. She had the look of a woman on a mission, so I wasn't surprised by her abrupt tone of voice. "We have to talk!"

"You said that on the phone. What's up?"

Zoe made a horror-movie face and started packing up her stuff. "Jake called. He said he found something at Isaac Johnson's house."

I threw up my hands. "What is he doing there? I thought he'd be heading back to LA after he got rid of Joey and Ivan."

"Jake? Joey? Ivan? Who are they?" Gina pressed.

"Irrelevant. That's what they are. Don't worry about it."

Zoe rolled her eyes and finished off the drama routine by slanting her eyes towards Gina. "Gotta run, Jade. I have a class tonight."

Liar, liar, I thought. She was bailing on me.

"I had lunch with Amy today," Gina snapped. "You have no idea how upset she is. She said Isaac Johnson was murdered right on his boat! She's convinced your investigation got him killed. You have to stop this!"

"Whoa, Gina, slow down. Stop what? And how did she even know about the murder?"

Gina blinked. "What? You don't know? It's all over the news!"

So, what did our illustrious mayor do? Sit around all day waiting for a hot news story? Or maybe she'd known sooner? "Gina, I'm sorry, but this case is very sensitive."

"You're darn right it's sensitive, Jade. You've upset a good friend of mine. She said that if you don't stop, she'll have your license pulled."

I'd had about enough of Gina's drama. "Private citizens can't do that, Gina. My license is issued by the state."

Gina straightened up and locked her arms over her chest. "Well, Amy has plenty of friends at the state level."

"Ask yourself this, Gina. Why would our mayor not want me to return Hilda Bauer's family brooch to her? Why would she want to let whoever killed two of her constituents get away with it?"

For once, Gina looked stumped. She brushed away the strands of long, blonde hair that hung over her shoulders. Her lower lip moved as if she were going to say something but couldn't get the words out.

"Why would she not want to see justice done?" I insisted, then leaned closer. "And why is she taking such a personal interest by sending you to do her dirty work?"

"I don't know. You'd have to ask her."

"Good idea. I think I'll do that right now. If you'll excuse me, I'm going to go ask Madame Mayor those questions. Do you know where I can find her?"

"She'll be at Kensington Art Institute. They're open until eight because of a special exhibit." Gina stopped and put her hand over her heart. "You don't think she's involved, do you?"

"Up to her neck," I said curtly. When Gina pushed out her lower lip, I realized I'd been too abrupt. "Sorry. Gina, I have two suspects, and right now, our mayor is the frontrunner. She's told me to my face that my investigation is a mistake. And now she's sent you as her emissary. Am I right?"

"Well, she did call me. And she did go on a rant. When I said I could talk to you, she thought that was a good idea."

"In other words, she guilted you into coming here." Softening my voice, I tried to sound like I was consoling her, not being critical. "Gina, you've been vulnerable since Bert's death. I think your friend knows that and figured she could make you feel like you had to help her."

Gina's eyes glistened. Her lower lip trembled. "I've messed everything up. Haven't I? Are you mad at me?"

I took her hands in mine and gave them a gentle squeeze. "No, Gina, I'm not mad at you. You're my friend, and friends put up with their friends' foibles. They even call them on it sometimes."

A tear dribbled down Gina's cheek, and she swiped it away. "You're the best friend I could ever have." She stepped forward and wrapped her arms around me. We hugged for a few seconds, then she backed away. "I should go with you. I want to tell Amy she shouldn't have manipulated me like that."

"I don't know, Gina. This could turn into a confrontation, and you don't want any part of that."

She giggled. "Jade, one thing you should realize. People who run charities don't like to upset people with money. If Amy wants my support to continue, she'll stop trying to manipulate me."

Gina had a point. If Amy Kensington was Valkyrie, I was pretty sure she wouldn't do anything with Gina in the room. Plus, having a witness when conducting a conversation with a murderer was always a good idea. "Okay, Gina. You can go with me, but you need to know something first. This could be dangerous. It's possible that Amy Kensington is part of an art theft ring. She may be responsible for Benji's and Isaac Johnson's murders. Are you sure you still want to go with me?"

Gina hesitated, her brow furrowing as she seemed to finally absorb what I was saying. To my surprise, she said, "I'm totally with you, Jade. I don't want to believe Amy did all of that, but I trust your instincts. You believed in me when nobody else would, so I'm with you. One hundred percent."

I thought about calling Detective Des and letting her know what I was doing, but when I considered the possible repercussions for her, decided it was better if she didn't know. If this went sideways, at least her job should be safe.

"Let's go then. But you have to let me do the talking."

The drive to Kensington Art Institute only took about fifteen minutes. Nestled between the Carlsbad Flower Fields and Legoland, with an amazing view of the Pacific Ocean, it was a spectacular location for any business. The address alone indicated how much money the institute handled in a year.

The institute was housed in a modern commercial building with a sleek contemporary design consisting of equal parts glass, steel, and concrete. Large windows and glass panels dominated the facade, and the landscaping featured native plants and carefully arranged greenery that complemented the structure's modern design.

Gina commented on how few cars were in the lot as I parked. "A few hours ago, this lot was almost full of people here for a presentation Amy was doing about Van Gogh." Apparently forgetting the reason we were here, she prattled on about Amy's presentation skills and how she'd done these types of things all over the world. Carlsbad was lucky to have her. But I wasn't listening. I was thinking about how easy it would have been for someone with that background to gain access to valuable art all over the globe.

I felt the reassuring press of my Glock against my lower back as we pushed through the heavy glass doors. Inside, the open architecture felt welcoming. A sign pointed right toward the "Virtual Van Gogh Exhibit" in the Exhibit Hall.

An elderly woman with gray hair and a friendly smile sat behind an oversized curving desk. She looked small and insignificant sitting there, almost as if she were a miniature person. At a wave from Gina, the woman smiled and went back to watching her computer monitor.

"Dora's such a sweetheart," Gina whispered as she took my arm.

She turned me sideways so I could look into the Exhibit Hall. A couple held hands as they stood before the image of a painting with dynamic, vibrant blues and yellows. Even from this distance, the artist's talent was obvious. He'd captured the night sky's tumultuous and dreamlike essence on canvas, except that the 'canvas' wasn't real. It was a projected image.

"Those two are on their honeymoon," Dora said. "They're the nicest people. They've been married for five days."

Gina pointed at the hall and said, "You really have to come back before this exhibit ends. It's amazing. It's the best."

Who knew people would pay to see virtual art? What would they think of next? I was intrigued, but right now, I had more important things to do. "Gina, I'll think about it. But I'm not here for the art. I'm here to see Amy Kensington."

A stern voice from the hallway behind where Dora sat said, "That would be me. Ms. Cavendish, I've had it with your so-called investigation. All you've done is cause trouble. If you don't leave this very minute, I'll call the police."

Dora gasped, apparently not used to patrons receiving such harsh treatment. I, on the other hand, was used to it. I wasn't concerned with what our mayor wanted. I was focused instead on the woman hiding behind her. From the woman's posture to the way she held her arm, I was almost positive she had a gun pointed at Amy's back.

It was too late to pull mine. Too late for many things. If only I'd put the pieces together sooner. "So, you must be Valkyrie."

All I got in return was a nod and a wave of the pistol. At least I was no longer dealing with a ghost.

Chapter 46

DORA SEEMED TO BE DOING her best to ignore the conversation. She sat with her back facing the hallway where her boss stood and had her gaze fixed on her computer monitor. Obviously, she had no idea Luna Martinez stood behind Mayor Amy with a gun pointed at her back. Poor Dora was oblivious to the potential danger, but Gina understood. She was next to me, her complexion a splotchy mess. From the looks of it, she was in full panic mode.

There was no way Amy could miss the fact that she would be Luna's shield in a gun battle. My skin tingled with the burning question—how in the world was I going to get out of this? Luna could easily get off three shots in the time it would take me to pull the Glock, aim, and fire. Wait, I told myself. Don't rush this.

"Why'd you come here, Luna?" I asked.

"I did what you asked. Let me go," Amy whimpered.

Amy's pleading only seemed to irritate Luna. She smirked, jabbed the gun into Amy's back, and pushed her forward into the main lobby. "Not a chance, Madame Mayor. You're my ticket out of here. Take the gun out and put it down, Jade."

At the word 'gun,' Dora's gaze jerked up from her monitor. She turned, saw what was happening, and her back went rigid.

"I'm not armed," I said, desperate to keep Luna's attention on me rather than any of the others. A chill ran down my spine. How many people were in the building? I knew about the one couple in the Exhibit Hall. Four more right here, including Amy, Dora, Gina, and myself. How many others were there? If a gunfight broke out, innocent people would get hurt.

Luna seemed to read my thoughts. "I suggest you do as I say," she growled. "If you don't, I'll shoot one of them." Her eyes flickered towards Dora, then Gina.

"Fine," I said, reaching behind my back to pull the Glock from its holster. My heart raced as I bent down and placed it at my feet. "Why'd you do it?"

"Kick it over here."

"Not until you answer my question. Why did you kill off the members of The Guild?" I was hoping desperately that breaking one of the primary rules of hostage situations—follow instructions—wouldn't get someone shot.

"They couldn't be trusted anymore. Now kick it over here."

Focusing all my energy on my breathing to steady my nerves, I spoke calmly. "I get it. Benji was trying to change his life, and you couldn't tolerate that kind of betrayal. I understand why you killed him, but why the others? Why Michelle Wolfe? Why Rolf Sinclair? Isaac Johnson?"

Luna smirked and nodded. "I give you credit. You've done your homework. I knew when I hired you to find out who was burglarizing my house that you were smart. But you're not as smart as you think. You're the one who exposed Benji."

"It wasn't Benji who stole your jewelry. It was your niece."

"Ashley? You're almost correct."

Hearing Ashley's name nearly knocked me over as the pieces fell into place. Ashley was the midnight caller that Clara told me about. Benji brokered the purchase of the brooch to Luna, aka Valkyrie Collections. I felt foolish for not connecting those dots sooner, but how would I have known? "You used the excuse of someone breaking into your house as a ruse so I'd find out who put your niece up to taking A Mermaid's Allure. You never told me it had been stolen when you hired me."

"I didn't think it was something you needed to know."

Deep inside, I scoffed at the absurdity of the lie. But for everyone else's sake, I kept my tone level. "Oh, please, Luna, don't lie to me. You didn't care about the other thefts—those were petty. What you cared about was the brooch. And I'm guessing you suspected Benji all along."

"Very well. If you insist, I didn't suspect Ashley until you discovered she was the thief. At that point, I realized everything Ashley stole, with one exception, was just a smokescreen. All the thefts were a ruse to disguise the real one."

I felt like I was caught in a duh tsunami—how could I have missed the obvious? I should have figured this out the moment Clara mentioned the midnight calls between Benji and a woman named Ashley. "How did you know?"

"I found the burner phone Benji had given her. It was all his fault she turned against me. He came up with the plan. She confessed everything when I confronted her. She even told me about how he intended to return the brooch to that woman."

"So you killed Benji," I countered. "And what about Michelle and the others?"

"They were all involved in some way or another. Michelle screwed up the letter of provenance. Her mistake exposed me to risk. Rolf Sinclair decided he was tired of roaming the globe and wanted to open his own restaurant. His propensity for loose talk was a danger I couldn't tolerate."

"So you silenced them permanently."

"Exactly," Luna said with a cold smile.

I couldn't believe what I was hearing. Her former partners-in-crime were disposable to her, just pawns in her twisted game.

"What about your niece? Are you going to kill her, too, for stealing from you?"

"Enough. I'm tired of this game. Kick the gun over here, or someone dies."

A piercing scream came from the Exhibit Hall. Luna pivoted, holding her gun with a practiced two-hand stance.

"Luna! Don't!" I yelled.

As quickly as she spun on the couple emerging from the Exhibit Hall, she aimed her pistol at me. I held up my hands. "They're just innocent bystanders. Let them go."

She made a flicking motion with the gun. "You two, get over there with them. You, too, Dora."

The couple from the Exhibit Hall scurried towards me and Gina. All the while, the man consoled his new wife and did his best to keep her from having a total meltdown. Dora joined us without a word.

"Is that everyone in the building?" Luna asked.

"Yes," Dora said.

"Good. Now, Jade, I have had it with you and your stalling tactics. I doubt that any of these people are innocent. You either hand over your gun by the count of three, or one of these so-called innocent bystanders dies."

If I could get within six feet of her—if she got distracted—if nobody did anything stupid. There were too many ifs. I needed a better plan.

"Here's the gun." I reached down slowly to pick it up by the barrel. "I'm going to put it on the desk. It'll be right there for you. Okay?"

The crow's feet around Luna's eyes crinkled.

"I could kick it across the room if you'd rather, but then you've got to look down. I'm just trying to keep things simple." I took two slow steps, all the while maintaining eye contact with Luna. "Why don't you let the others go? You've got me."

"Not a chance, Jade. You're too smart for your own good."

I set my Glock on top of the curved desk and pulled my hand back. "There. Okay?"

Suddenly, Luna grunted out a huff. "So that's your game. You have a backup. Hand it over. And be quick about it."

"I don't have a backup," I said. "I don't even usually carry a gun."

"If you're lying to me, I will kill you right here. Right now."

Shaking my head, I turned and rested my palms on the desktop, making sure to keep them well away from the Glock. "Go ahead and search me. I don't carry a second gun."

Luna stepped behind me and pressed the barrel against the back of my neck while she patted me down, starting near my shoulders.

She'd gotten to my waist when a man wearing a loud Hawaiian shirt pushed open the front door. Good God, it was Jake, and he was drunk.

"You guys open?" Jake bellowed.

Luna jerked toward the entrance. I reacted instantly, grabbing her wrist and twisting it hard toward the desk. The gun fired, Luna screamed in pain, and the weapon clattered to the floor. She lashed out at my face with her free hand, but I deflected her blow with a quick block. A swift palm strike to her shoulder threw her off balance. She staggered back. I seized her wrist and applied a joint lock, forcing her to the ground.

I looked up to see Jake standing next to me with his gun drawn and pointing it at Luna. I rolled my eyes and shook my head. "Really?"

"Hey, Cavendish. Just thought you might need a little help. That's all." Jake shrugged, then cast a hurt puppy look in my direction.

"You don't need to shoot her. Just get me something to secure her wrists."

Jake flipped his thumb toward the front door as two Carlsbad police officers burst through. "Already handled, Cavendish. Already handled."

The cops had guns drawn and started shouting orders. Oh, brother, talk about the testosterone levels in the room being off the charts. Without letting go of Luna, I identified myself, told them what had happened, and asked them to call Detective Des Martini.

The two cops lowered their guns but stayed alert. While one approached me, handcuffed Luna, and read her her rights, the other used his radio to inform Detective Des of the situation. She told him to take statements and said she was on her way.

She walked in minutes after two more police cars and an EMT unit arrived. The cops began securing the scene while the EMTs checked over everyone in the lobby. The whole thing turned into a zoo with cops and EMTs running around and Amy Kensington, the woman I'd once thought might be a cold-blooded killer, having an emotional meltdown in Dora's chair. Dora stood next to her, rubbing her boss's shoulders while she shook her head and assured her boss that all was going to be fine.

The biggest shock came while I was giving a statement to one of the officers. I was in the middle of reiterating Luna's confession when the Ice Queen walked by. She looked me in the eye, flashed me a quick smile, and winked. Faster than you could say, "What just happened?" she was again barking orders.

Chapter 47

I TOOK THE NEXT FEW days off to decompress and wrap up the loose ends from the case. That included a final meeting with Clara Thompson, a strategy session with Detective Des, and some time to surf.

Val, of course, published her story and gave me far more credit than I thought I deserved for solving Benji's murder and finding A Mermaid's Allure. During her investigation, she also uncovered Luna's illegal campaign contributions to Mayor Amy's campaign. In exchange for the money, the mayor kept Luna informed and tried to subtly influence the investigation into Benji's death.

The day after the story broke, the agency phone started ringing. Zoe threatened to quit if I didn't raise my rates and give us both a bump in pay. And that same afternoon, Gina showed up looking as contrite as I'd ever seen her.

"What's up Gina? You look upset about something," I said.

"I betrayed you, Jade. I stopped in to see you when you were down in San Diego."

I cut her off with a sharp, "How did you…oh, my gawd. Did Zoe tell you where I was?"

"Yes. All she said was that it had something to do with a case you were working on."

"And who did you tell?"

"Amy. And Luna. We had a meeting that morning at the institute about the exhibit. I never suspected either of them could do something like this. If I hadn't had such a big mouth, Isaac Johnson might still be alive."

"And be well on his way to the South Pacific," I countered.

"Maybe, but I didn't take your case seriously enough. I nearly got you killed."

"Gina, don't worry about it. You meant well, and that's all that matters."

"No, Jade. I was being selfish and immature. I'm stepping back from things so I can find myself again. I'll be leaving tomorrow morning and going to Honolulu. I'll be there for a while."

Even though I was totally jealous of Gina's way to 'find herself' and wondered what it would be like to have that kind of money, I wished her well before I returned to the business of wrapping up.

Hilda was so elated over the news that the police would eventually return the brooch to her that she hosted a party in her backyard for everyone who had helped. She asked me to extend the invitations but assured me she'd handle everything else. Little did I know she meant she'd have the party catered by one of Carlsbad's top caterers. Thankfully, it wasn't Peter Sinclair. That might have been just a little too awkward.

Detective Des declined the invitation, telling me she was working that day. After explaining that to Hilda, she waved away the excuse. "That detective is just a stick-in-the-mud. There's no reason she couldn't be here. Nevertheless, it's her loss. Now, introduce me to some of your team."

Sam, Rachel Yang, and Val Torres were standing in the California native plants section. They stepped apart when they saw us coming so we could join them. After doing introductions, Hilda said, "I want to personally thank you all for your help. You especially, Samantha. I understand you were the one who helped Jade initially."

"It was my pleasure, Mrs. Bauer. Thanks to Jade, I learned that my boyfriend was not who I thought he was. Jade, will Luna be charged with Isaac's murder?"

"When I talked to Detective Des, she said they have a strong case, and the DA wants to try for the maximum."

"The police believe Luna is also the one who killed Benjamin?" Hilda asked.

"Yes, and she'll face those charges, too. They got a warrant to search her home and found files on the old jobs The Guild had done. They also found dossiers on each of the members. It's basically a diary, but for the cops, it's a roadmap to a conviction on multiple counts of murder. What about you, Sam? When I talked to Detective Des, she asked if you might be interested in consulting as an art historian for a couple of other cases."

"They called and talked to my boss. He wants me to finish my current job and start consulting with them on Monday. He seems to think this will be good for business."

Rachel snickered. "Don't get your hopes up, Sam. I doubt that the Carlsbad PD has much need for an art historian."

"I've covered City Council stories before, Sam," Val said. "There's so much red tape that your boss will eventually throw up his hands and surrender. You should be back at your office soon enough."

Sam laughed and clapped her hands together. "Wonderful. As long as I have my coffeemaker, I'd much rather work out of my office!"

We all laughed, and when Hilda looked confused, I explained to her about Sam's super-special coffeemaker. Ethan and Jake came over to ask what was so funny, so I went through the explanation again.

"Hey, Cavendish, I think you owe me a fancy coffee. Seeing as I'm the one who saved your bacon from Old Lady Lunatoons."

I felt a little heat burning in my chest. How was it that this man could push my buttons so easily? I shot back playfully, hoping that would be the end of it. "No way. I had everything under control. You almost blew my whole plan."

"Uh huh, sure. That's why I was the one holding the gun on her instead of you."

"I didn't need a gun," I snapped. The heat was coming on full blast now, and the more Jake grinned at me, the angrier I got.

"Alright, alright, Cavendish. No need to get snippy about it. I agree you were pretty quick with the old karate chop there."

He made a couple of quick chopping motions in the air. It was more than I could handle. "There was no karate chop, Marlough! I used a joint lock to bring her to the ground."

"That's after you smacked her in the face."

I realized that Jake and I had become the center of attention. Everyone, and I mean everyone, was watching us banter.

Zoe was smiling at me like she'd just won the lottery. "Look at those sparks fly!"

Oh, gawd. That was never happening. Not with Jake Marlough. I was no fashion icon, but given his bad taste in clothing—no way.

After taking in a long, slow breath and mentally counting to ten, I spoke in the calmest, most adult voice I could muster. "Jake, you're baiting me. It was a shoulder strike, and I'm not playing your little game anymore."

Jake staggered backward and clutched his heart. "Oh, Cavendish, you wound me deeply!"

Rolling his eyes, Ethan took Jake's arm. "Come on, Shakespeare. I'll buy you a drink at my grandmother's bar." Ethan then led the way to where the hired bartender waited patiently.

I gritted my teeth and growled. "That man!"

"I know," Zoe said as she watched Jake and Ethan saunter away. "Isn't he awesome?"

I looked around the circle of women. The only one who wasn't nodding enthusiastically was Hilda. "I think he's disgusting."

"I agree," I said.

"Liar, liar," Zoe, Rachel, and Sam chanted in unison.

I gave them a nasty look and grabbed Hilda's arm. "Come on, Hilda. Let's enjoy the zen of your fountain. There's too many meddlers here."

We walked away, but I kept glancing back at the two men. The second time it happened, my heart nearly stopped. I hated to admit it, but I wasn't looking for Ethan. I was missing Jake.

www.ingramcontent.com/pod-product-compliance
Lightning Source LLC
Chambersburg PA
CBHW051955240626
47153CB00005B/1770